Wishmaster, Book1.5

FINDING THE Way

Astrid V.J.

Finding the Way
©2021 Astrid Vogel

First edition December 2022
Editing by Joy Sephton
Cover design by Emily's World of Design

ISBN (ebook) 978-91-987063-8-3
ISBN (paperback) 978-91-987996-2-0

Published by New Wings Press
Vedelsfridsgatan 13C, Malmo, Sweden

This is a work of fiction. It is the combined product of the collective
subconscious as transmitted by the students of human potential and
transformation, including but not limited to, Viktor Frankl, Mary Morrissey,
Henry David Thoreau, the Greek Philosophers and Napoleon Hill and the
imagination of the author. Any similarities to the real world are either a
product of the human experience—we are humans with shared human
emotions, experiences and responses—or entirely coincidental. Now, leave
this boring real-world stuff and enter a new realm where shifters and
Intergalactic spaceships, thankfully, do exist.

To
Renato
Because I believe you, too,
can achieve anything you put your mind to.

No temas, ¿No estoy yo aquí que soy tu Madre?

DO NOT BE AFRAID. AM I NOT HERE, I WHO AM YOUR MOTHER?

— VIRGIN OF GUADALUPE

Contents

PART I
DREAMS AND DEEDS

Chapter One

Things are moving too quickly for Viola, and as she absorbs the rocking swells of the mighty river she's being paddled over in a rickety dugout, she considers the hurtling meteorite that's change in her life. Glancing back at the cluster of buildings on the river's edge, she takes in that beacon of rainbow splashes against the deep green background of trees. Morning cool is quickly transforming into heavy tropical air. Her uncovered arms relish the wind's tickle and the soothing swish of waves issuing from the boat's prow.

For the first time in months, she feels alone. What will she do now that she's abandoned her apprentice? *I have not deserted him,* she reprimands herself. *Our paths have diverged. This is nothing to feel guilty about.* But if that were true, why does she feel the creep of guilt in her heart?

The brown liquid expanse separating her from the bank she left behind nudges her memory with an image of a sandy desert dotted with hardy shrubs holding onto life in the face of impossible odds. What strange twists led her to meet a boy, some thirteen summers old, in that inhospitable place? And what improbabilities have brought her here, to the heart of a strange wilderness on a planet so utterly different?

Viola looks back to the shore again, but she can't see Jo anymore. The loss of his presence strikes her. She's spent such a long time alone, and this reaction comes as a surprise —particularly that she misses his incessant talking. Viola stares out over the brown water and allows the ache in her heart to swell. How many times has she walked away from people she cares about and not given herself the opportunity to grieve?

Too many.

She considers this unexpected turn of events. *I have been travelling on my own for decades, but now I do not relish the solitude as I once did. What has come over me? What did that confounded boy do to me?*

She chuckles, a dry sound even to her own ears.

The man at the oars looks up, his gaze briefly meeting Viola's. Then he shifts and looks in the direction the boat is headed; his arms flex and extend in time to the swish of wood meeting water. Viola looks ahead. Brown water is separated from the azure sky by a tiny strip of dark green. They still have a long way to go.

The cluster of colourful houses on the river bank behind them has shrunk to a blurry impression, too far distant for Viola to make out any of the structures, least of all the boy she left behind on that embankment.

Her heart is heavy. The ache increases while she ponders the manner of their goodbye: stiff and unfeeling, so common for her. *I am not good at farewells*, she admits. Every single farewell in her long life has been one disaster after another. Considering the recording she left her apprentice, Viola acknowledges it's the first time she's made an attempt to do better. *Not the first time*, her memory corrects with an image fresh as still-drying paint, not dulled by the years that have passed.

Her mother, shimmering obsidian hair twisted into an elaborate updo, water lily pins glinting mother-of-pearl against that dark background, eyes ablaze with anger. *If you choose this path, you are no longer my daughter.* That voice, laced with disappointment and the fierceness of one who believes only they understand the world.

The stubborn, youthful response echoes in Viola's mind: *Then I go forth to be reborn, child of the universe, daughter of Haldria. I must follow my path, and neither you nor anyone else will stop me.*

A life lost, an existence gained. Once more, Viola finds herself standing upon the cliff. Change is coming. She can feel it. Memories converge. The distant past overlays the more recent, and she begins to see things she never noted before. The determination and zeal of her youth mirror what she's just re-learned from her apprentice. Jo. The boy who showed her she didn't have to go back on the empire's terms but could choose how things played out.

I have been on the run for most of my life. All the dodging and slipping through the cracks has left a toll on her, but Viola feels that question again; what fuelled her decision to leave home in the first place? The only thing the boy has done is remind her of what she's always known. The thought is sobering.

A life wasted.

Viola considers that. *Is it really?* She's learnt many things on her travels, seen the Haldrian Empire in all its glory, and also the less favourable outcomes of the imperial undertaking. She's experienced her fair share of suffering—and seen so much worse. Still, all that hardship hasn't extinguished the ember of hope. It has remained muted and hidden throughout her adult life, to be rekindled by a little boy, whose blazing determination and deep-seated conviction that anything is possible, has made her see the truth she's forgotten.

We come full circle. The teaching of the ancients that life is cyclical resonates more strongly than ever with Viola. Over the years, she convinced herself she didn't believe in anything, that higher powers and ancient wisdoms were fables for children. And here she finds herself confronted with just that, the truth within the teachings.

Maybe Jo is right. His words echo in her mind, bringing back to her senses the dust hanging in the air, the heat of two blazing suns shrivelling skin and parched lips. *We live in a bountiful, abundant universe. The greater powers always want to help us so that something good can come out of the darkness. Wherever I look, I see opportunities. I know we humans are more powerful than you give us credit for, and I know we can all be agents for good.*

Viola can acknowledge there appears to be some truth to what he said so many months ago. Perhaps everything she's been through does have a purpose. Her thoughts rebel. *There is nothing out there. It is just wishful thinking. Fate and gods are the province of those who do not know better, who cling to something to take away the fear of obliteration. Everything is meaningless.*

A splash draws Viola's attention to the present. Ripples grow in rings from a point a short way to her right. A shadow rises under the muddied waters, and then a sleek grey creature rises into the air, white foam churning off its sides to reveal a shimmering tail. The animal arches through the air, letting forth a nattering call reminiscent of laughter. *Splash*, and the being is gone, swallowed by the murky liquid of its home.

"Lumba-lumba," the man whispers from behind Viola. He pauses, clears his throat, and corrects himself, "Ah, *delfin* in Haldrian."

Viola looks out over the water. Her heart is beating with

excitement and wonder. She's never seen a creature like this before. Of course she's heard of them, but to witness the sleek fish-like body with its dorsal fin pointed into the air—that's spellbinding.

A third splash draws Viola's attention, and she witnesses another tail just before it disappears under the water. More and more bodies appear at the surface, their heaving dance rocking the boat with scudding waves. Rounded snouts reach for the sky. Laughter fills the air. Sunlight glints off smooth bodies and shimmers on ripples of water. There's a music to the rhythmic splashes and chuckles of joy—the ecstasy of animalistic freedom.

Beauty.

There's something to this moment. Her heart expands, and goosebumps prickle upon her arms. This spectacle is for her.

As if to reiterate the thought, the boatman says, "I've only seen them twice before, and I ferry people over the river almost every day." Emotion constricts his voice, and he returns his gaze to the animals chuckling and splashing beside the boat, his oars forgotten, motionless wings sticking from the vessel's dragonfly body.

Passing through here a little sooner or later, I would have missed them. And what made them choose this spot and not another on this wide, impossibly long river? In answer to Viola's thoughts, Jo's words from a conversation on Mshrali resurface in her mind. It was a lifetime away when he'd stopped a mob of blight-stricken meerkats through will alone and didn't wonder at such a gift but begged for forgiveness for killing those creatures that hadn't survived. *What of all the interconnections that make things happen? What of circumstance? We live in a bountiful, abundant universe.*

Viola ponders his words and everything she experienced with him on their journey through Mshrali, and after, on the

Startraveller's Hope. It has been an eventful time filled with new ideas, and she wryly chastises herself for rejecting Jo's ideas out of hand. How much could she have learned if she'd only listened?

I was not ready, she admits, as she observes the deep greens of the rainforest growing larger on the horizon ahead. *But now I am, and I will do better. There is truth to his words, I know it.* Thinking about him, she regrets how they parted ways. She should have taken him to Cerddor, left Jo at the right door, and not continued on her journey until he was in safe harbour. In front of her, the dense green wall looms large, while behind, the smallest sliver of green separates the brown waters from the blue above. Going back isn't an option. Viola faces forwards, thinking about the task ahead, about where she's going. *Friendships, both old and new, are precious. I have been truly blessed with my friends.*

With her excitement growing, Viola turns her thoughts to the future and its possibilities.

Chapter Two

Wood grinds against sand, and the boat comes to a standstill on the beach. The boatman swings his body over the side, landing with a splash and sending droplets to cool Viola's bare arms. As the boat is pushed up onto the beach, Viola spies a dirt road cutting straight into the viridian thicket. A boarded-up stall stands nearby; its dilapidated walls lean together like balanced cards, ready to topple at the slightest breath of wind and held together only by a few rusty nails.

"How far to the nearest hamlet?" She presses some coins into the man's hand. Thankfully, the imperial system means the coins she received in Mshrali can also be used here on Téarman.

The boatman stares down the path, which disappears into the gloom a few feet from the beach. "On foot? Three miles." He pauses, considering for a heartbeat before continuing, "About one Haldrian league."

Viola nods; the sun will be halfway to its zenith by then, and chances are the mosquitoes will be out. She also can't change the fact that the boatman has figured out she's not a local—or not even from Téarman. Shrugging, she thanks him and steps onto the sand. Her bare feet embrace the cool abrasiveness, and she acknowledges this is a problem she must deal with as soon as possible. The man by the boat might see her as dressed in sturdy clothes and boots, but that's far from the truth.

She can't maintain this illusion forever. Already it's sapping her strength, and she knows it will leave a magical trail for the imperial hunters to follow should they decide to use their magic-reading devices. It's possible the recent events outside Baile will throw them off the scent for a while, but she can't count on it being a definitive solution.

I need clothes and provisions. A new backpack would not go amiss, either. She sighs. The lost rucksack is the least of her worries, and Viola brushes away the next thought. What happened in the forest outside Baile is something she does not want to think about. That backpack may have contained everything of her twenty-eight years of life on the run, but at least she is still alive, even if that is left behind now, too.

Viola considers the tattered white outfit she's wearing, and her thoughts turn to the events of the past few days. She's bombarded with a blend of memories: sneaking out of the ambassador's palace in Baile and her escape over the wall with the help of a palm tree; getting caught in a downpour moments later and being rescued by Jo and the Imperial Guard accompanying him, only to be tricked by those very same guards.

The next memory threatens to sweep up her mind in a mute storm whirling around her encounter with death. No. She does not want to think about how the monster whipped through the rainforest's massive trees on scaled coils too big for any conceivable creature, accompanied by shrieks, her pursuers cut down, their lives snuffed out— The stench of blood—

Viola clenches her knees to stop them from buckling under the pounding assault of her thoughts. She fills her lungs with air and murmurs, "I am lucky to be alive."

Self-conscious, she turns back towards the boatman, ready to explain herself, but he's already pushed his vessel into the stream and rows against the current. With a shrug, Viola begins her trudge into the woods. Birds sing. Crickets chirp. Little animals flit and dart up the tree trunks. The movement provides hints of bright colours, and steam visibly rises off leaves as wide as alfil ears.

The veritable cacophony surges relief through Viola's system. This living forest is so very different from the heart of death she traversed with Jo a few days ago outside Baile. It brings into stark focus her mood from before setting foot on Téarman. She'd had those melodramatic moments when she contemplated ending it all. Jo's words from one such occasion ring in her memory, resonating with the newfound joy of life she feels: *What would happen to everything you've done so far? Your experiences, everything you've ever done, what you've suffered and what you achieved despite the suffering—it will all be lost, and you, Viola Alerion, Master of Words, greatest storyteller to grace this empire, you will be forgotten. What possible good could come of such loss?*

He is right, she admits. *I am grateful now to be alive, and by some miracle, I also find myself free of the hounds who have been after me since the very beginning.* A creature of habit, Viola goes through the motion of hitching her backpack into a more comfortable position on her shoulders, only to realise she doesn't have a pack anymore. She misses the sturdy straps of her old and worn rucksack. It accompanied her for such a long time, and now its absence weighs heavy. Taking stock of her situation, Viola realises she's pouring sweat. Her right hand slips into her trouser pocket and comes up empty. She tries the other side—also nothing. Where could her handkerchief be?

She grumbles. She doesn't even have a hankie with her when she used to own several. *What a pain.* She wipes the sweat from her face using a tattered sleeve and gives off a huff.

There's nothing for it now. The pack is gone, and Viola must find a replacement for it, no matter how irritating that is. At least she still has her bamboo staff and quartz crystal amplifier. Together with the pouch of coins, that will have to be enough to get her through this part of her—

She pauses to ponder this thought as her eyes rove over the tall trees reaching into the heavens.

Adventure?

Can she really consider her life an adventure? *Maybe it is one big misadventure if I am completely honest with myself.*

Viola's knees ache, the right one in particular. Movement will probably help to work through the discomfort, although more likely than not, the joint will need medical attention. *You have to hold out for a little while longer*, she thinks, and puts her weight onto the bamboo staff. At least she can use it as a cane in the meanwhile.

The sun is close to its zenith when the trees begin to thin, and Viola sees the first signs of buildings. A shiny slanted roof peeks out above the lower vegetation, and a few steps later, she can make out a reed building next to it.

Her attention is drawn away from the signs of civilisation when a pale streak whizzes towards her. It's moving so fast she can't make out what it is, but it's large and heading straight for her. With her heart rate spiking, Viola stops and holds her breath, bracing against the upcoming onslaught.

Woof.

The creature comes to a mud-spitting halt right in front of

her, tongue lolling from a long muzzle. It's a tall dog—all bones —standing higher than Viola's waist. Its fur is matted, muddy tangles marring what looks like long cream-coloured hair. She blinks at the unexpected sight.

She tries to step around the mutt that's planted its rear in the path she's been walking. Tail wagging, the animal leaps up, snuffling at her leg.

Viola swats at it, trying to stay clear of its muddy foot pads. "Shoo!"

The dog huffs goodnaturedly, prancing backwards a step and dancing forwards, pink tongue contrasting against the otherwise dull look of the creature. Ongoing, deep, throaty barks ring in Viola's ears.

"No, really. Go away!"

Waving hands do nothing to deter the animal, which weaves around her, snuffling at her leg before gambolling out of reach when she spins to face it.

"Go!" Viola commands.

The dog instinctively sits back on its haunches, but it's still smiling at her as if it knows a good joke she's missed. As soon as Viola takes a step towards the houses beckoning her with the promise of a cold shower and some food, the animal races forwards once more, blocking her path.

Stopping again, Viola folds her arms and scrutinises her harasser. The dog grins at her.

She's about to take another step when a shift in her vision occurs. Viola finds herself looking at a mirage of her most deep-seated dream. Her own words echo, reinforcing the image before her.

A little cottage with a small garden to tend. A warm climate and taking care of myself. The opportunity to share my stories and a dog resting beside my desk. Taking walks and maybe getting to know my neighbours.

Her eyes hop between the real, live, and undernourished dog sitting in the path in front of her and the slender, well-brushed white dog with long legs trotting beside her in the vision.

Blink.

The image is gone, but the dog still sits in front of Viola, beaming at her as if it knows she's just understood.

"No." She waves her hands at the stray again. "It is not happening."

Whine.

"No way! It is not an option. I am not taking you with me."

Large brown eyes stare up at her, brows twitching into pleading triangles.

"No!" Viola steps around the dog and strides purposefully along the path, rounding a stand of palm trees after a few paces and coming out among buildings as dense as the trees had been in the forest. Wood, iron, reeds, and palm leaves vie for dominance in the human jungle, where houses, large and small, jumble together in a maze. Children play a ball game with something that distinctly looks like a bunch of rags bound together with string. Their laughter and shouts remind Viola of her loneliness. Their language, different from her own, is a whisper of wind on the leaves. It bubbles like a brook, dances to the cadences of unusual music.

There's a snuffle behind Viola, and she looks over her shoulder to see the dog, head low in submission, standing less than a foot away from her. She shakes her head.

"No."

The animal's brows twitch, giving it that pleading look again.

"No is no is no is *no!*"

Huff.

Now I am having a conversation with a dog. What next?

Viola turns away from the creature, ignoring it once more as she stomps up the alley she's come into. A few adults in clothes that are worn—some even torn and dirty—hurry about their business, their heads to the ground. One or two notice her and stop to stare. Realising her sophisticated clothes and different complexion are what's drawing their attention, anxiety sparks in her chest. Clenching and unclenching her hands, she continues with renewed purpose. She doesn't want people to notice her. She needs to stay unobtrusive.

But that was before. The imperial trackers probably think I am dead and will call off the hunt.

Considering this possibility, Viola sucks air back into her lungs, but she can't quite shake the need to be inconspicuous. She's also feeling tired. The power needed to maintain the illusion is sapping her, and she also needs proper equipment for her journey as soon as possible.

As she progresses through the winding alley, Viola notices the buildings become solid and less dilapidated. More people jostle along the dried-mud street, which widens somewhat. Viola feels an increasing number of stares, so she speeds up. With her heart thumping in her throat, she wonders if it's curiosity or hostility they're exhibiting. Her knee is acting up, and she knows she can't keep up the pace she's set, but she grits her teeth and keeps going.

On high alert, she follows the trajectory of peoples' scrutiny and realises they're not looking at her but just behind her. Glancing over her shoulder, she catches sight of the starving dog again. It trots along at exactly two paces behind her, as if this were the most ordinary thing.

Frustration bubbling, Viola faces the creature again, bringing it to an abrupt stop. The dog responds to the flare of emotion within her and squats down, tummy to the ground, brown eyes glued to hers. The twitch of its brows indicates confusion, perhaps insecurity.

Whine.

The altercation draws a crowd. Exasperation slips into fear. What now? How can she get out of this mess caused by a stray dog?

People are pointing, some laughing. Others from further afield sense the commotion and join the gathering throng. For the time being, Viola can see only curiosity in their eyes, but she knows from experience: the shift to outrage and violence doesn't take much.

Resigning herself to the fact that she's already made a scene, she calls out, "Whose dog is this? It has been following me since I arrived on the outskirts of town."

Silence greets Viola's question. She considers rewording her query when movement on one side of the crowd draws her attention. A woman pushes through the throng. She's short and round. Grey streaks her dark hair, and wrinkles line her face. Her brown trousers and green blouse are much like what all the other women are wearing, although the way the others step aside to let her pass, Viola considers this some form of spokesperson.

The old woman's voice is rich, and she carries her frame with confidence. "The animal jus' show up—" She waves with her hands. "A few—uh—weeks ago. Jus' walks and steal' food. No bother us."

Viola sighs. "Is there anyone who could look after it? I cannot take it with me."

Muttering flares up in the gathered crowd. People are shaking their heads, and even though Viola doesn't need the confirmation, the spokeswoman says, "No."

Shrugging, Viola decides she'll worry about the dog later.

Now that she's drawn attention to herself, she'd like to get her bearings in this town. "Is there a market here?"

The other woman shakes her head. "Market in Abhainn." She gestures in the direction from which Viola has come. "Other side river."

With a sigh, Viola considers her options. "Is there any transport to Bryniau from here?"

The woman tilts her head as if struggling to understand Viola's meaning. After a moment, she says, "We no have machines. Boats—that's how you move in forest."

"Is there someone who could guide me to Bryniau then? I can pay for passage on a boat."

A mumble goes up in the crowd, whispers batted back and forth. At length, the spokesperson raises her voice, shouting something and gesticulating as she speaks. Viola doesn't understand a word of it. The gathering seethes, the movement rippling from the back of the crowd to the front. Then someone steps through and bows to the older woman standing before Viola.

It's a young man built like a mop: tall, thin and topped with a cascade of long black hair that hides his face. He converses in low tones with the stout woman for a while before he nods.

The spokesperson steps towards Viola. "Lelaki take you to highway. Bryniau on other side forest. Difficult with rivers. Imperial highway fastest way."

"Thank you. I shall also need some provisions, a backpack and a change of clothes. I have Imperial Notes—"

"No," the group's spokeswoman cuts in. "We no work with money. We give you provisions. A gift."

The statement is followed by muttering, and Viola sees heads nodding in agreement. "That would be helpful." She cracks a smile, hoping it might alleviate the tension in the air. It feels like she's asked for too much, but nonetheless, the woman beckons Viola over to a wooden bench on a veranda outside one of the houses and sends a few people off with instructions in her own tongue before heading inside the building. Strings of colourful beads dance in the doorway.

Viola settles down to observe the comings and goings as the crowd gradually disperses. The bothersome dog stretches out in the dust beside her, head resting on its paws. The local woman comes out, her approach announced by the clacking of beads.

"Here," she says, holding out a wooden cup. "Drink."

"Thank you." Viola accepts the beverage and watches the woman leave again, causing the coloured strings to leap about in the doorway, clinking and rustling. She sniffs the liquid in the cup. It smells fruity but isn't something she's come across before. Having learned not to trust anything but water when in unknown territory, she glances about.

The street is mostly empty again, and Viola considers the situation while pouring the drink over the side of the veranda. It's rare to come across people who reject the empire to the extent of declining money. In the greater scheme of things, Téarman is an insignificant player in the politics of the empire, but they've been part of the planetary alliance for centuries. Imperial coinage should be common out here, and yet, when she thinks about it, it's curious that her cousin, Natesari, is stationed in this meaningless backwater as ambassador for the empire. Has something happened? Could it be some form of punishment? Did Natesari displease the empress?

A short while later, the young man she'd been introduced to earlier steps under the overhang. He carries a fibre bag, the contents bulging beneath the rough surface. Viola stands, accepts the provisions and takes a peek inside. There are fruits and a water flask, as well as some dried fish that smell rank. Three rounds of flatbread are packaged inside a covering of green leaves. Underneath it all, she can make out a rough homespun shirt and possibly a pair of trousers.

"Thank you. I also need new boots." She points to her illusion of scuffed leather with a hole in the toe.

Lelaki makes eye contact with Viola and says, "Follow," before turning and striding up the street.

With a sigh, Viola slings the bag of provisions over one shoulder. She does as she's told, noticing her guide pauses to look back as he reaches a crossroad between the closely-stacked houses. He beckons her up the left turn. As she comes around the corner, she spies the dog trotting behind her again, as if this is where it belongs.

With a sigh of forbearance, Viola continues a few paces behind Lelaki, who waves or calls out to people as they pass. He's all smiles for the people going about their daily business in the town's unpaved dirt streets. They turn right again before Lelaki stops in front of a shop. Strips of leather hang from the eaves, and it doesn't take long for Viola to come out with a new pair of riding boots. It was sheer luck the cobbler had some in her size, something about a customer not wanting the commissioned pair.

She shrugs off the coincidence. Thankfully, the cobbler accepts her coinage, so she pays for the footwear. The sound of the coins clinking onto the counter is still fresh in Viola's mind when she notices Lelaki is already out the door again. She rushes to catch up and almost trips over the dog stretched out in front of the shop's wooden step.

A short while later, Viola can see dense green foliage towering above the roofs ahead. Lelaki guides her past the last row of houses and back into the evernight of the forest.

A footpath leads into the buzzing, chirping, and trilling jungle. Trees overflow with creeper plants smothering their trunks, and the ground is covered with fresh green. As it twists and turns through the thicket, only the muddy ribbon of the path Lelaki leads Viola along breaks the overwhelming verdant monochrome.

Every now and then, Viola glances back. The dog still follows her, tongue lolling out in self-assured entitlement. Heat prickles beads of sweat into existence, and she swipes at her brow every few steps. Viola hates sweat. It's the only thing she's never been able to get used to throughout all these years of travelling. And the one thing she can think of that's worse than the heat and dust of the desert planet, Mshrali, is the oppressive, inescapable jungle-heat of Téarman.

Why am I even here?

All the question does is remind her of her life on the run. Viola's been everywhere simply to outrun her pursuers, but now she finds herself in a unique position: there's a distinct possibility she may have escaped them all. She thinks back on her time spent evading her pursuers, and those occasions she thought she might have given the hunters the slip, only to find Haldrian forces swarming whatever inn she was staying at. Having to escape through a back door, or once even hiding in a latrine.

Even if I have lost them again, it will not be for long. Viola knows they won't give up. She has twenty-eight years of proof that they won't do so. She reiterates the realisation she shared with her apprentice a few weeks ago. *I have spent annums avoiding my duty and running away from the truth I have known in my heart. If I am to move forwards, I must take the reins back into my hands.*

Lelaki trudges ahead of her, his footfalls light on the soft loam. In comparison, Viola, using her fighting staff as a walking stick, feels like a puffing engine, one of those ancient ones she saw in the Haldrian Grand Exhibition when she was a child. Old and ungainly, that's what she's become.

Behind her, a good-natured snort draws Viola's attention to the dog. She turns to face it, looking at it sternly. The canine sits back on its haunches, tail sweeping the ground behind it. Expectation glints in its eyes.

Viola points her finger the way they've come. "Go back."

It looks at her hand, glances back at her face, and whines.

"No, really. You are not coming with me. Go."

Huff.

"Argh!"

Viola turns away and stomps up the path. Out of the corner of her eye, she sees Lelaki grin at her just before he continues on his way. Frowning in response to the young man's amusement, she keeps walking. *Stupid, stubborn dog,* she thinks.

Her mind shifts, tugging into her awareness a memory from less than an Imperial annum ago. A boy followed her then, wouldn't take no for an answer—

He insisted on accompanying her and becoming her apprentice— And taking him with her, giving in to that tug on her heartstrings, had been the best decision she could ever have made. Her life was changing before her very eyes because she'd listened and given in then.

What if—

Viola shakes her head. She doesn't want to take this mangy dog with her. Continuing up the path, she tries to ignore the mutt and focuses on the tangled roots creating a web beneath her feet, mirrored by the green canopy above. Her own words from a few weeks ago toy with her: *a dog resting beside my desk—*

She glances back, observing the animal trotting in her wake. It is a sturdy breed, and clearly, it knows how to take care of itself. This animal might be thin, but it looks strong. There's no sign of illness, and it hasn't scratched for fleas since crossing her path.

Clenching her jaw and rolling her eyes heavenwards, Viola

sighs. "Oh, all right then," she mutters, more to herself than anyone else. Her lips twitch. *That boy really is something.* The knowledge is solid rock, immovable and unbreakable. This dog is a gift from him in some unfathomable twist of circumstance, but Viola realises she has to believe it—is compelled to accept it.

A veil has been lifted from her mind, and for the first time in her life, she sees a glimpse of truth. The motion of Viola's legs is strong. She feels energy coursing through her, senses the cool tingle of air on her face and arms. She's grateful for the trees. They're a blessing against the oppressive power of sun and heat.

Glancing back again, she catches sight of the dog still following. Its head bobs along as it pads forward, its tongue lols to one side, pink—bright in contrast to the off-white coat. Again she remembers the boy following her back in Mshrali. *I still do not know his real name.* The thought brings her back to the dog.

"Well, doggo. You will need a name, will you not? I refuse to call you 'dog' for the rest of our time together."

The animal trots up beside her, responding to the friendlier tone.

After some time spent in thought, Viola nods. "Mokoto. Yes, that is a good name for you. I shall call you Mokoto."

Chapter Three

Lelaki stops, and where he stands, Viola notices the treeline ends. She comes to a halt beside him and is greeted by a brown scar cutting through the expanse of natural pillars so tall they seem to brush the sky. The road is identical to the one she travelled with her apprentice a few days ago, miles away on the other side of the giant river.

"Bryniau that way." Lelaki points up the Imperial Highway to the right. "Half—" he pauses, stumbling over his thoughts, "Segment. It's one *half segment* walking."

Viola nods. "Thank you for your help."

The young man shrugs, slipping past Viola to head back the way they've come. Sighing, Viola considers calling him back and insisting on paying him, but she shakes her head. From experience, she knows there are times such persistence won't work, and this is one of them. She lets the heavy satchel fall to the ground at her feet and stretches out the taut muscles in her shoulder.

Be grateful, she chides herself. Here she is, in the middle of nowhere, on a planet she visited a very long time ago, and things seem to have changed tremendously. Last time, paying her way with Imperial Notes had been easy, and no one had raised an eyebrow. They'd been friendly then too, but she couldn't shake the sensation that her experience today was different. *It is as if they could not get rid of me fast enough.*

Allowing her shoulders to sink against a tree trunk on the side of the road, Viola considers that. Weariness drags at her senses. The moss-covered bark is spongy, cushioning her brittle frame from the hardness of the tree. She looks back and catches a glimpse of Lelaki hurrying through the pillars of the forest. His head bobs into view one last time, and then he vanishes from sight. The dog sits beside her, interested eyes peering into the forest after Lelaki. As soon as Viola turns her sights on the road, the dog hops up and scoots into the open area.

Not knowing what is going on is the worst. Viola abhors it. Her stomach clenches, and her fingers curl and release several times. She racks her brain for any news of Téarman from her time spent on the Startraveller's Hope, but she'd been distracted on that journey. She'd had no intention of disembarking on Téarman, so she hadn't listened to any gossip on the subject.

Once again, Viola finds herself unprepared for what lies ahead. Too many plans have been tossed about in the vicious autumn gale of her life. The last few months were no different. She has to pick up the pieces and keep going.

I will get it together. The thought is countercurrent to all the uncertainty and anxiety multiplying with each gust of life's wind. She's done the unthinkable already: escaped the ambassador's residence in Báile and survived the Leviathan. Walking through the rainforest on a well-tended road for ten days shouldn't be too difficult. *I have been through much worse*, she chides herself.

But first things first: change of clothes.

The new outfit will take some getting used to, but it's better than the tattered remains of the white trousers and top her cousin had made her wear back in Baile. At least now she's dressed like people from around here. The boots chafe against her toes, but she knew it was a risk and breaking in a pair of shoes is the least of her worries. She'll need to watch her rations and be sure to stock up at every opportunity. Hopefully, there will be some hamlets along the highway.

A trickle of sweat plunges down between her eyebrows and inches its way towards the tip of her nose. With a long-suffering sigh, Viola tears what remains of her old blouse into several squares, stashes three of them into the satchel, and dabs her face with the last.

She pushes herself upright and steps out into the brown swath that cleaves the sea of trees. Her staff is strong, and although her knee twinges, it seems to be settling back into the routine of walking. Viola supposes she'll get used to it. A shuffle from behind draws her attention to the dog, which wags its tail.

"Come along then, Motoko. If you insist on accompanying me, I do not mind." She turns her feet in the direction Lelaki has pointed her and rearranges the satchel over her shoulder and across her chest. All that does is make her acutely aware of the accumulated sweat on her back. She pushes aside the thought of dirt and her wish for a bath.

Staff in hand, Viola proceeds, hoping this journey will be uneventful and she won't need the crystal that's safely stashed in the pocket of her new trousers.

The sun is high in the sky, and the heat unbearable when Viola seeks shelter under the trees. The mugginess, combined with her fatigue from holding the illusion for most of the day, have combined into a soporific of the highest degree.

A few steps into the cool of the forest and she collapses against the trunk of a mighty tree. With the last of her strength, she wriggles her feet out of the new boots and breathes a sigh. She'll look at the damage later.

Viola is woken by a monstrous growl that tears from the heavens. She looks up into a roiling sea of grey, barely visible above the green canopy overhead. The air isn't quite as sticky as it was earlier. Remembering her encounter with the tropical rain during her escape from Baile, she looks around her.

It's dark in the cavern of the forest, and the silent hush in anticipation of the coming rain is palpable. She knows the leaves above her will provide little shelter from the downpour about to unleash its fury. Silkiness nudges Viola's hand, and she looks over at Motoko. The dog brushes past, nose to the ground. She doesn't follow, her mind preoccupied with the need to find cover from the elements. Her eyes dart around the gloomy underbrush.

Whine.

Viola strains her eyes against the darkness, making out a pale patch in the undergrowth. Not seeing anywhere nearby to hide, she is spurred on by another ominous rumble. She grabs her boots and follows, her aching feet complaining with each step. Motoko sits beside a bunch of ferns that crowd around the base of a tree. It's a veritable giant, its roots creating buttresses taller than she is.

The dog wriggles into the ferns, and Viola hunkers down to see where it's going. A limb has fallen across two of the tree's massive roots, creating as good a shelter as she's going to find. She groans as she shifts onto all fours, the weight of her satchel tugging at her weary shoulder. As she begins to shuffle her way towards the wooden overhang, a third bout of thunder assaults her ears, and the first ice-cold water-bomb careens into her arm.

Viola crawls; the need to reach that spot of safety beside Motoko takes over her mind. With every movement, the bag of provisions knocks against her midriff, but Viola ignores the awkwardness of it and focuses all her attention on reaching the haven beside the dog.

Water pounds onto the ground, bringing with it a symphony of rustles and splashes. Viola scuttles into the small space just as the aerial onslaught bombards the forest, filling the air with the fresh smell of rain-soaked earth. After struggling out of the satchel's cross-wise strap, she props up the bag beside her and folds herself further into the cranny.

The pattering of raindrops lulls her into the in-between. It's that magical place where she can taste the sparkle of life and feel it humming through her. The storm washes away the worries and memories, leaving her with this moment, sitting in the protective embrace of a mother-tree.

A snuffle brings her out of the trance. Motoko is running in circles, buffeting Viola every once in a while, damp fur tickling her arms. The flurry of activity comes to an end when the dog lowers its long legs to the ground. The action reminds her of hours spent perfecting the art of paper folding—a pastime from so long ago it feels like a different life.

Petting the animal's head, she admits, "I am glad you are here, Motoko. Thank you for finding us this wonderful spot."

Many days pass in the stretching and contracting of time. Viola wonders at the complete desertion of the road. No one has passed her. Nothing moves apart from her and Motoko. The few signs of habitation she's encountered have all been abandoned. Wells she's found aplenty, but little to no sign of human life apart from the clear path she's travelling.

How does the empire keep the road clear of undergrowth if there's no one to tend it? *Perhaps they have used some treatment to make the soil barren?* A long time ago, she heard of such practices in Daria. *They have probably propagated the method everywhere they can.* Viola shudders at the thought of the damage being done to the environment on most of the planets encompassing the empire. She shakes her head and focuses instead on trudging. *There is no use thinking about such things now. I need to get to Bryniau.*

The walking blends into moments huddled under rocks or trees while the skies vent their anger upon the forest. Nights of thick air ring with the song of cicadas and merge with time spent in the semi-dark beneath the mighty trees.

Once again, it's mid-afternoon, and the clouds are preparing their lines for battle. Viola and Motoko have begun their search for a place to keep dry. The dog has run ahead, as usual, nose to the ground and tail in the air, while Viola trudges after at a more leisurely pace, her mind absorbed in worry over her dwindling supplies. Even after having eaten but one meal a day for the past two days, she only has enough left for a single small repast.

Something tingles in her midriff. It is a crawling sensation that brings a shiver to her spine. Viola glances around. There's nothing she can see or hear to provoke this sensation. The forest is still, but there's a tension to it. Where normally the quiet before the afternoon shower is the gentle breath of sleep, now the forest holds its breath in preparation for some calamity.

Woof.

The unexpected sound slices through the mute forest, cuts into Viola's brain, and makes her jump. She looks over at the dog, who stands rigid, his eyes intent on something inside a cluster of ferns at the base of a cathedral-sized tree.

A doggy growl echoes the more ominous rumbles coming from the sky as Motoko crouches down, nose still pointing into the thicket. Approaching with her intestines squirming, Viola's eyes and ears strain into the gathering gloom of the forest. Her fingers grasp the staff resting in her palm. The worn surface is familiar to her touch, and she clings to it now as apprehension curdles her insides.

"What is it?"

They've seen birds and the odd squirrel but nothing else, and Viola wonders what other creatures reside in this forest. Predatory cats would live in this type of jungle. At least, that's according to her old school books, which she's learned to question a time or two.

The dog growls again, and Viola becomes aware of a buzzing sound coming from inside the tree. Her gut clenches, and she takes a step backwards, but too late.

Even as the first raindrops begin their attack on the region, something small and orange streaks out of a crevice in the tree and hurtles towards her. She side-steps and turns, watching whatever the glowing thing is arc at high speed and hurtle back, colliding with Motoko's rear. In the instant before impact, Viola's brain categorises the glowing orange speck as an insect.

The dog howls and a vicious buzzing erupts from the tree trunk. She turns back in time to see a swarm of the vibrant bugs blasting in her direction. Motoko takes one look at the undulating mass and gives another terrified howl. The sound cuts over the angry hum of the insects until it ends on a whine. Motoko tucks his tail between his legs and flees into the darkness under the onslaught of the rain.

Viola is soaked. She can't run. The ache in her knee won't allow it. Her bamboo staff is in her hand, but the crucial magical amplifier rests in her satchel, tucked away in safety. She knows she needs the piece of quartz if she's to use her magic to its fullest potential, but there's no time to get it out of its hiding place.

The swarm is upon her, each insect about thumb-length, with beady black eyes and aglow in the fiery intensity of their lower abdomens, which smoulder and give off orange sparks. The cloud of glimmering insects descends upon her. Viola shifts her stance and slips into the in-between, where she finds the source of her power as easily as she steadies her breath. Raising the staff, she twirls it until it blurs in her vision.

In quick succession, small, vulnerable bodies bounce off the barricade of the whirling stick and tumble to the ground, silver wing membranes crushed from the impact. The buzz increases and takes over Viola's brain. There is no room for anything else.

An insect slips through Viola's defences and charges at her. It throws its gleaming body against her, and the brand imprints on her left forearm, sizzling flesh. A shriek tears from Viola's throat even as the scent of roasted skin assaults her nose. Through the pain, she catches sight of a second assailant making straight for her face. She ducks and swats it aside with her injured arm. The staff flounders in its spinning motions as another stab of pain courses through her, where she came into contact with the insect.

Dratted fireflies.

Viola steels herself. She grits her teeth as a third insect careens through her faltering defences. She focuses all her attention on gripping the staff in both hands and whirling it in front of her, despite the searing agony of that third firefly burning along her neck. She wants to swat at it, but that would break the flow of her staff again and let even more of the beasts through.

Battered insects litter the ground at Viola's feet, crunching underfoot as she steadies her stance. The downpour bursts into her senses. Cool water alleviates some of the pain in her arm and neck, the *pitter-patter* of plum-sized drops whispers through the intense green canopy, the smell of damp loam hits her nostrils.

The buzzing of the fireflies subsides, and Viola watches a few stragglers fight their way through the assault from the heavens and back towards their home in the massive tree trunk a few feet away. The last orange glimmer extinguishes, leaving Viola in the dark, drenched to the bone and shivering —standing upon a graveyard of fireflies.

She casts about her in the hope she might find some form of shelter, but there isn't anything easily visible. Vaguely, she wonders what might have become of Motoko, but her trembling frame tells her she doesn't have time to worry about the dog. Loneliness washes over her. Once again, she's alone. Can she rely on no one but herself? With a shudder, she shuffles towards a tree trunk away from the fireflies' hive and drops the almost empty satchel at her feet. She huddles against the rough pillar, pressing herself against its support.

Viola's head swims. Exhaustion leaks the last of her strength out of her, washing it away as surely as the water pounding around her soothes the sting from her burns. She glances down at her arm; a black oval comes into view. It takes great effort to remember what happened. She got burned. Fireflies. The magic she used to keep them at bay. But this fogginess, the struggle to think, that can't be from overusing magic, can it? Fireflies. Something tugs at the back of her memory. What does she know about Téarmanian fireflies? She ought to remember. But it's gone, blotted out by the clouds of dizziness.

A droning whirr breaks through the fog in her mind. Looking towards the sound, through the streaking rain she can make out an orange glow. Something about the hum and the smouldering light sends warning bells clanging in Viola's mind. She needs to protect herself. *Why?* It escapes her. She crumples to her knees. There's a bag at her feet. She must get—

What?

The buzzing increases, slicing through the incessant pounding of water on leaves and earth. Fear pulsates through Viola, and she fumbles with the rough fabric of her satchel. It pops open, and a hand-sized pink crystal falls onto the ground. It glints dully in the forest-induced dark.

Out of the corner of her eye, Viola catches sight of an undulating mass of luminous orange charging through the rain. With a gasp, she lets her fear give her enough of a boost to grab onto the stone, jagged edges pressing comfortingly into the palm of her hand. She no longer has the dexterity to affix the crystal to her staff where it can become a potent weapon. There's no time to think.

She looks up into the approaching glow, a swarm of lights. Her head is filled with the buzzing from the fireflies, and the burns on her arm and neck seem to pulsate in time to that symphony.

It's all rather beautiful, and Viola can't quite place why she was flustered a moment ago. A lethargy is coming over her. It creeps into her frozen bones, slows everything to a sluggish mire of disjointed ideas with no connection to any movement.

There's something in her hand. A light pink rock. It, too, is beautiful.

The charging, undulating serpent of sparks bears down on her. Viola looks at the little glimmers, each unique light a pinprick that spans all the universe in beauty and glory.

What about the light? What about beauty? What of all the interconnections that make things happen? What of circumstance? We live in a bountiful, abundant universe. The greater powers always want to help us so that something good can come out of the darkness. Wherever I look, I see opportunities.

The words seem to come out of nowhere. The onslaught of blazing fireflies slows; they're pulled into whatever lethargy tugs at Viola's mind. But those words are important. She remembers them. They were spoken with vehemence. The memory of them tingles urgency and lights a glimmer of fire in Viola's heart. They were words of life, spoken in the face of death.

An idea pulsates through Viola's mind as she takes in the oncoming lights. It's half-formed, inelegant, but it's powerful. Those incandescent globules hurtling towards her spell death. No matter how beautiful they are, no matter how they lift her spirits, she knows she must guard herself against them. Her response is brutal in its decisiveness. In her mind, she forms a protective wall, and the stone in her hand warms to the touch.

In the blink of an eye, a cocoon of bright, pulsating light wraps itself around Viola. It shields her from the oncoming fireflies. In her half-conscious state, she's aware of the insects that pummel into the barrier. Wings are crushed, bodies implode. The patter of raindrops is joined with the harmonies of tiny bodies that fall to the ground, stick legs bristle in the air, and glowing abdomens extinguish forever. Viola sees it all with clarity as the image of the rain-drenched forest littered with the bodies of thousands of dead insects sears itself into her brain.

Guilt tears through her. This is wrong. So much death should not be. Strong and decisive in the way only conviction can confer, a voice says, *We committed sacrilege against the Great Parent. Care for all living things. That's the teaching I was raised on. I can't rejoice in this loss.*

Viola's mind supplies an answer. It's distant, coming from somewhere else entirely, and yet connected to that first statement in her mind by some unremembered thread. *How is he not moved by what he did? Does he not understand the significance of it? Instead of marvelling in wonder, he spouts gibberish about the sanctity of life and begs forgiveness from gods. How can he be so innocent that he does not know this is a kill-or-be-killed world?*

The disjointedness of the two voices pouring over each other in her mind is overwhelming. Who are these people? Something about the voices seems familiar to Viola, but she can't place it. Why is everything so hard? Life has always been like fighting through quicksand with weights tied to her feet. Kill-or-be-killed. That's a truth she can remember, but why does even that have to be difficult. Couldn't it—something—anything—just be easy for once?

Exhaustion makes itself manifest once more, and Viola considers closing her eyes. Yes, that would be easy. Sleep—the warmth of darkness—is most welcoming, but something holds her back.

Sanctity of life, a voice in her head supplies. Where did that come from? It's a familiar thought, and yet there's a senselessness to it. Her mind offers yet another piece of useless information. *Warring Lions*. It's as if those words hold some meaning, but she can't place it. It slips through her fingers.

Viola stares at her surroundings. Where is she? The sky is green. It's strange and yet beautiful. That's a word she's had in her mind a lot lately. Into her head pops a memory of delfins arcing out of the water, droplets spraying around their lithe grey bodies. She's glad she had the good fortune to see such loveliness. It's a special thing she treasures.

Another voice comes to mind. This one is older, or to be more precise, it comes from a more distant time, so very, very long ago it's barely remembered. *There are peoples on several planets within the empire who believe delfins are the bearers of souls, that they announce death and carry the spirit to whatever place lies beyond the physical realm.*

Viola blinks. Her vision shifts away from the memory of playing delfins and returns to the darkness around her. She's alone. Cold is a vague companion; it gnaws at her fingers and feet. Could this be it? Has her time come? She shudders, but fighting has become a distant thought; it isn't tangible.

Her perception tunnels, darkness closes in. It threatens to swallow everything in its wide-open maw. There's no fear, though. If this is the end, Viola finds herself uncharacteristically calm. How long did she rail against everything she faced? How much energy did she spend fighting and pushing and refusing all that is? And yet, here she finds herself at a crossroads, where letting go becomes the easiest thing.

She can rest now. She can relinquish all she's spent her years clinging to. She is. That is all.

And as if in reward for this acceptance and Viola's decision to finally let it all go, a gentle voice, both unknown and immeasurably familiar, whispers over her. *Live, and do better another day. That is all.*

Chapter Four

Viola walked along a wooded alley. As she came around a bend in the path, a grey brick cottage came into view. Green tendrils of ivy trailed over one wall, trained to arch around the dark wooden doorway. A pair of dormer windows glinted in the late afternoon sunlight, smiling in welcome. Although she'd never seen this place in her life, it felt familiar.

She stepped forwards and walked up two steps to the entrance door. A large brass bell shone beside the entrance, but instead of ringing, Viola pushed the door open. She was welcomed by a bark. A tall, thin dog with luxurious white fur and a long friendly face bounded towards her. It was huge, by all accounts. The animal reached above her middle, and even as she thought about the strange familiarity of knowing and yet not knowing this creature, Viola reached out and scratched it behind an ear. Silky fur ran through her fingers.

Motoko.

The name came to her even though the dog before her looked nothing like the mangy stray she'd picked up in Téarman's jungle. Nevertheless, through the disbelief, certainty thumped in time with her heart. The whole unknown place felt like home. She might never have set foot in it in her life, but still, it was her *dwelling*.

To Viola's left was a staircase, and in the nook it created against the wall, there stood a desk. She knew it was the place where she worked furiously on the incredible project she'd been given. Although she didn't have the faintest idea what that work might be, the thought of it made her blood sizzle with excitement.

She made her way to the kitchen, where a pot of her favourite beverage brewed. The dog curled up on a mat in one corner. There was a large wooden table in the centre of the kitchen, and Viola found herself seated there, ladling delicious stew into her mouth. The flavour reminded her of a time she'd eaten stew in the company of a person important to her. Who it was, she couldn't quite place, but their absence was a void inside her. Unbearable in its weight and unfathomable for her inability to remember why this person was so important or even who they were.

Viola felt her brows draw together. "This has to be a dream," she muttered to herself. There was no way it could be anything else. How could she know things she'd never seen before and yet feel so lost at the same time?

Shaking herself, she tried to wake from the vision. She didn't have time for dreams. She'd been busy with something very important. The notion took hold and wouldn't let her go. But the dream refused to dissipate. It felt so real.

The doorbell rang. Viola jumped to her feet, marvelling that her leg didn't twinge at all with the speed she rushed down the hall. Another sign of this being a dream. She almost frowned at herself for the uncharacteristic bounce in her step and the fast hammering of her heart. Her whole being seemed to expect whoever was at the door while her brain remained perplexed.

The door swung open to reveal a shadowy figure Viola didn't recognise at all. Her heart was happy to see the person, and she invited them in right away, even as her mind screamed at her this could be a trap and never to trust anyone. Frantically, she tried to make herself *shut the door and stop whoever the other person was from entering the house.*

With a start, Viola wakes, but her eyes stay shut. She's tucked up in a bed. The room feels unfamiliar. There's something in the way the air tastes that tells her she's never been here before. Her awareness of herself filters to the surface: her body aches all over, and she's lying on a bed much like the one she remembers from her childhood. Light filters into the room and she tries to open her eyes, but the lids are heavy. She struggles to pry them open.

The dream lingers; however, Viola knows something dreadful has happened. What was it?

She strains her mind. She'd been on a spaceship and was forced to disembark because of an order from the imperial units who hunted her. She remembers being taken in by her cousin, who was in ridiculous Baile dress—so inelegant and nothing like the style of The Capital where they'd both grown up. Something else happened, and Viola found a chance to escape her luxurious prison at the imperial ambassador's home. Apprentice. Now she remembers. Jo helped her by causing a diversion. Thanks to him, she was able to escape not only the ambassador's compound but also the city of Baile, despite being caught unprepared in a tropical downpour.

In the next heartbeat, Viola's memory latches onto the Leviathan. Rippling death whipped between trees and left her pursuers in dismembered pieces. A shudder convulses through her, and she follows the train of thought to her desperate bid to save herself and Jo, that dear boy who'd become her apprentice by stubbornness alone. She'd overexerted herself and used much too much magical power in a go, but they managed to reach one of the Haldrian forces' hover cars and made good their getaway before she collapsed from exhaustion.

Viola's heart squeezes at the next recollection—of leaving Jo to his new life as apprentice to the famed musician, Cerddor. She wonders how her one-time apprentice fares with the talented virtuoso. Guilt still plagues her for not bidding Jo goodbye properly, not to mention the string of other disastrous farewells or lack thereof that she's been party to throughout the past twenty-eight years. But her mind refuses to linger on such negativity. She remembers sleek water creatures who crossed her path, jumping and splashing, as she was ferried over the river.

Ah, yes. Now Viola recalls. She had been on her way to Bryniau to visit with Maitri and begin to mend the bridges she'd broken when she severed all ties to her past. As if the returning remembrances are a sign she's ready now, she opens her eyes with ease.

"Well then," a woman's voice says, cracked and thin. "You're awake."

Viola turns her head. Beside the doorway to the room sits a hunched old woman. She looks frail; her light, flower-print kaftan hangs from thin shoulders, and the woman's tightly coiled hair is almost white with but a few streaks of ebony hinting at the strands' former glory. A pair of dark brown eyes meet Viola's gaze and wash away all thought of age—there's so much power in those cocoa gems.

It isn't just the liveliness and potent energy radiating from the woman that dissolves all thought, confining Viola's words to the tip of her tongue. In that instant, eyes locked, she is sucked into another memory, long distant, almost forgotten, considering how long it's been buried within her psyche. She remembers those eyes and the scolding tone, softened now by age. Once, it had been lacerating. She stares, struck dumb, cataloguing the deep wrinkles on a face she remembers as smooth and distinguished. The high cheekbones and prominent nose with flaring nostrils are still the same, as are the woman's full lips, but everything else around those once proud features has sagged under the ravages of time.

Viola snaps her mouth shut. *How is such a coincidence possible? I was looking for Maitri, and here I am, in her home!*

The woman pulls herself to her feet. Her voice is what has changed most, and Viola laments the loss of the smooth tones her mind calls forth, overlaying the memory onto the woman's words.

"Whatever gods favour you have finally decided to spit you back out this side of the veil."

Viola's hackles rise at the talk of gods. It was thanks to this woman's relentless teachings that she decided to set aside all faith and believe in herself. The spark of her reaction is hot and comes fast; it drags her back into the attitudes of her youth. Before she can even think about the situation and what response would be called for under the circumstances, she allows the roiling sharpness free rein over her voice, which is back as if it had never been stuck at all.

"Of all the people in this confounded empire, you should know I set no store by gods, Maitri. I thought you knew me better."

The woman blinks, her thin eyebrows arching high as she levels a hard stare at Viola. "Do I know you? When and how did we meet? For I've absolutely no recollection of ever having met you before." She gestures with a wizened hand. "A day ago, a commotion out in the streets drew me from my studies. In the streets of Bryniau, the townspeople were chasing after a mangy dog who behaved erratically and utterly incomprehensibly. It grabbed people and tugged them towards the forest, whining and yapping. The folk of this town pelted it with stones, but the creature would run to the outskirts and stop on the road to Abhainn. No one was willing to follow it down that route. The path is seen to be cursed. Well—it used to be. We now know otherwise."

Folding her arms, the woman leans back in her chair. "To cut this short, as the cur kept insisting someone follow, I eventually brought together a group brave enough to venture after it, and we found you collapsed among the ruins of a hive of fireflies with an illegal magic staff by your side. How you survived the poison, I can't begin to imagine, but at least you've helped us see why people kept vanishing on that road. We've had no communication via the imperial highway in several years, simply because anyone using it would have succumbed to the fireflies' venom."

Viola pushes herself into a sitting position. "Where is Motoko?" A wave of vertigo hits her, and she reels, blinking away the black spots encroaching on her vision. The other woman leaps to her feet and crosses the room.

"You were at death's gate. You'd best give your body time to rest. The dog, if that's who you're worried about, is outside this door." She gestures towards the opening. "It's well and no worse for wear. The fireflies' poison never came into contact with the animal's skin. His fur stopped it from penetrating so far."

Viola relaxes into the pillows. At least the dog is alive and safe.

Maitri seems satisfied and steps away, saying, "Now, who are you, and why do you believe we know each other?"

Chuckling, Viola looks into Maitri's dark brown eyes. She's taken back to a time when this woman's hair was as black as coals, and she wore pearls to mark her status as the court tutor. "Think back thirty years, Maitri. I cannot believe you would forget me so easily, although I know much has changed in my appearance since my days at court."

An eyebrow arches into the woman's forehead, and her mouth forms an 'o'. She leans forwards, and her eyes narrow for a heartbeat before she whispers, "Isperia, is that really you?"

Viola shrugs. "*That* name and everything it signifies is not who I am anymore. I go by Viola Alerion these days. "

Maitri settles onto the edge of the bed. The movement brings Viola's attention to her own body. Every muscle groans, and her arms feel tight. Without lifting her head, she angles her eyes and sees white bandages wrapped around her forearms. Her thoughts are drawn back to Maitri when her former teacher speaks.

"You do know things don't work that way? Haven't I taught you anything, Isperia? Every experience you've had informs who you are. You can't go around cutting out parts of yourself. That will only come back to haunt you."

"Which it has." Viola meets her teacher's gaze. "It is also the reason I have come here before going back to face my mother. There are answers I need, and I think you are the only one who can provide them without politics getting in the way."

"Officially, you've been labelled mad, and I was under the impression you'd been placed in an institution. I can hardly believe it's really you." She places a hand on the cover over Viola's leg. There's a ring on her index finger, and one large red gemstone glints in the sunlight. The golden setting around it is almost claw-like, and runes etch the sides.

Viola barks a laugh, but it dissipates quickly. The physical contact is strange. When she thinks about it, she realises she hasn't touched a fellow human being or been touched in a very long time.

"Well, I suppose Mother would consider my desire to see

the world and master the art of storytelling a form of madness. And making up a story that suits her image is definitely something she would do. She cannot bear to lose control. I suppose that is why she sent her hunters after me while making everyone else believe all is well."

Maitri looks sharply at Viola. The expression sends the former student back to her childhood and the moments when this look of disapproval featured on her teacher's face almost daily. The older woman's voice drops when she asks, "Are you bringing trouble to Bryniau? If you're being pursued by imperial hunters and you cause more unrest than there already is here, I promise you—"

"Maitri," Viola cuts in. "That is part of the reason I have come to you. Outside Baile, something happened. I will not be followed anymore. They will think I am dead, along with everyone else. We encountered a—" She shudders. Her head fills with the screams of the dying, and the memory of blood hits her nose with its iron tang. She takes a deep breath and notices Maitri's narrowed eyes. Viola shakes off the memories and tries again.

"Strange things are happening all over the empire. Not just here on Téarman but everywhere." Viola's fingers twist in the sheets as her mind takes her back to the moment a horde of blight-struck meerkats launched themselves at her. "All the lands are sick."

She glances up from looking at her bandaged arms. "Even the fireflies I encountered did not behave as they are said to do. They were aggressive. I was not so close to their hive that the whole thing should have emptied and attacked me, and yet, I fear every last one of those insects perished."

Maitri nods. "Yes, the hive was extinguished. They lie decomposing on the forest floor, not two miles from here." She rises to her feet. "Well, then. Let me get you something to eat, and—after—you can tell me everything."

Viola dabs sauce from her upper lip and lets the fabric serviette drop into a crumpled heap over the empty bowl and plate stacked on a tray in her lap. Her bandaged hands make her clumsy, and the crockery voices its discontent with a loud *chink* as it slips from her grasp. Thankfully, it all comes to rest in her lap, and Maitri bounces to her feet, fussing as she lifts the tray out of the way.

"Thank you, Maitri," Viola says while her former teacher heads through the doorway. "That was very tasty. I have missed flatbread with alpukat spread."

Maitri grins as she steps back into the room. "Clearly, I raised you well, Isperia." Viola frowns but chooses not to correct Maitri, who continues, "There's nothing better. The food is one of the main reasons I never settled permanently in the capital after my parents passed away."

"I am so sorry, Maitri. When was that?"

The older woman shoos away the condolences. "Not long after I lost my most promising student." She scowls at Viola. "So, no more deflecting. What brings you to me? You said you have questions."

Viola can't help but smile. This is the no-nonsense teacher she's always admired. She pauses and considers where to start her tale. Her mind fills with memories of her young apprentice with a brightness to his eyes so uncommon and captivating. She sighs. "When I was travelling the planet Mshrali, in the Fásach region commonly called the Dust Bowl, I met a young boy who eventually became my apprentice."

She shifts and pulls the blanket up to her waist. Settling

back into the cushions behind her, Viola meets Maitri's gaze. "He is different. There is so much about him that is otherworldly; I am not quite sure where to start."

She pauses. Lint on the fabric covering her thighs draws her eye, and her fingers follow. As she begins picking away the little balls of fuzz, Viola continues, "I suppose what struck me first is the strangeness of his beliefs. He comes from some outlying community in the Dust Bowl, but he had very little knowledge of the empire or its structure. Then again, he knows things thirteen-year-old boys from a backwater in Mshrali simply should not know."

Her mind wanders to that moment he warned her about a drone circling overhead in search of her. The way he'd said the word 'drone', somehow as if he were testing a new word. And yet there hadn't been anyone to teach him that; he'd known it all on his own, just like in the forest of Téarman outside Baile when the—

Viola swallows. The contents of her stomach threaten to leap right back out again. She clenches her eyes shut and takes a deep breath. Her hands tremble, and it's the first thing she notices when she opens her eyes.

Maitri clears her throat, and Viola snaps her attention to the older woman. A groove has materialised in the space between Maitri's eyebrows.

"Ah, yes." Viola bobs her head and tries to shake off the lingering memories to focus on the questions as her attention returns to the lint on the coverlet. "From what I can tell, he comes from an unsanctioned religious community. The beliefs he spouted were decidedly strange. The doctrine is clearly strong with strict—um—I think he called them *ordinances*." She licks her lips and tries to gather her thoughts. Her fingers stop moving when Maitri speaks.

The older woman's tone is stern and bordering on disbelieving. "You came all this way to ask me about a cult?"

Viola shifts again and throws her head back with a sigh. "Yes, but it is not just that. I need to know more about who he is and where he comes from. There is something—I do not know—important about him." She throws up her hands. "As in world-changing. His power is—" Viola's scattered thoughts converge, and she meets Maitri's eyes. "There is a thing about that community. He claims both women and men from his home wield magic, and yet there is no sign of him having elven ancestry. He seems exclusively human. And yet he has some powerful magic I have never encountered before, not even in your classes. I need to know more about him—to understand. I—"

Maitri holds up a hand and gives Viola a calming smile. "One thing at a time, Isperia." She leans forwards. "It may not have come up in your magical training as it's now become a quite irrelevant point, but men do have magic." Viola feels her eyebrows caterpillar their way to her hairline. Maitri gives her a pointed look and continues. "In the past, any boy with magical promise was filtered into the church. In Haldria, at least, with the Dragon Sanctuary, that was the custom. As soon as a boy showed the first signs of magical ability, he was taken into the order. Once the Haldrian Empire was established, that tradition was implemented on all planets. Whatever system existed on the new planet for the training of magical ability was co-opted into the priesthood. It was the women's magical abilities that were suppressed for a very long time as 'unnatural'."

"Really?"

"Yes, there was a movement in the early days of—what was it called—the place in the mountains—in the Old World." Maitri paused, her eyes distant. "Vendale, that's it." She bobs her head and smiles. "And later adopted in Danaya as well. I think there was a time when the use of magic among women was restricted to the upper classes, but a shift happened at some point, which is when Koshki Tower was built, and that community of female magic users became so prominent. I suppose now they do exactly what the priests do for the boys. Between the two institutions, you wouldn't know there are magic users beyond the royal family. They're simply kept out of sight from the general populace."

"So you are saying this boy, who became my apprentice, should have been taken in by the priests? They missed him? Or what?"

Maitri shrugs. "There are some places the priesthood doesn't reach. I think Mshrali is one of the planets where their hold is tenuous at most."

"That is true. Apart from Ilwych, I have not seen them around much in those parts."

"Which brings us to your question about a cult. What kind of beliefs did he have that set you so on edge?"

Viola looks up and chuckles. "You always had a way of reading me—as if you know my mind." She pauses, thinking back on some of her conversations with Jo. The discussion they had after the incident with the blightstruck meerkats bubbles to the surface of her mind. "The Dust Bowl is infested with a disease they call 'the blight'. It creeps further in year after year, leaving only death in its wake. No one really knows what it is, but it spreads through all living things, corrupts them, and eventually, there remains nought but dry sand and bones."

She inhales slowly, remembering the violet tinge to the plants. "The blight affects animals most profoundly. It creeps in, and before you know it, common herbivores are flesh-eating monsters. Blight-struck humans are the worst, of course. They feast on the raw meat of anything they can get their hands on, and when the madness takes them, they become destructive in ways you cannot imagine. On our travels, my apprentice and I met with a mob of meerkats struck by the blight. The tales of what such creatures can do are quite horrific, but we were lucky. I was fending off the hoard of salivating, mad animals when that boy did something. I still have no idea what or how, but he stopped the onslaught by merely willing it so. Afterwards, he begged his god for forgiveness for the animals that died, saying he had a duty to care for all living things. The boy was utterly distraught about the deaths of a handful of beasts."

Maitri stands. "Care for all living things? As a religious ordinance?" She strides from the room and calls over her shoulder, "You know, I think I have indeed heard that somewhere before. Give me a moment."

Viola follows the sound of papers rustling and a drawer being opened. She hears some muttered oaths and things being moved around before Maitri gives a satisfied, "Here it is." Moments later, she plops back into her chair, folding her right leg over the left and propping up a flat device the likes of which Viola hasn't seen in over two decades.

"You still have your 'know-it-all' tabula from your teaching days?"

Maitri grins. She glances at the device propped against her slanted thigh and lets her fingers dance across its surface. There's a moment of silence broken by Maitri's left foot as it taps on the earthen floor. Viola takes in the incongruity of the high-tech device in the squalid little mud-brick shack with no glass in the windows. It's an apt representation of this whole empire, the lucky few able at the mere click of a button to access vast resources and information across distances spanning the galaxy, while others are reduced to squalor and lives eked out in a few acres or less. She thinks about all the abandoned villages in Mshrali and the way Jo railed against poverty and injustice. His indignation has rubbed off on Viola. It's clear she can't simply stand by and watch it any longer. It's part of what's gnawing at her.

"Ah, here we go." Maitri startles Viola from her thoughts. "The list of cults and other unsanctioned religious groupings—it's kept up to date by the priesthood themselves. So, let's see if the commandment to take care of all living things gives us any results. That would be the easiest way to find it. Do you know something more about this religion?"

"My apprentice kept pontificating about 'the Mother-Father'. It seems to be their deity and is clearly referred to as an androgynous being."

Maitri nods and continues her search.

While she waits, Viola considers more of the conversation she had with Jo that day. When she tried to tell him to harden his heart against the injustices of the world and to prepare himself to face disappointment and the evil so often wreaked by one person upon another. His response had been forceful and overflowed with conviction. *It's a poor world you see, Master. You see only death and hatefulness. What about the light? What about beauty? What of all the interconnections that make things happen? What of circumstance? We live in a bountiful, abundant universe. The greater powers always want to help us so something good can come out of the darkness. Wherever I look, I see opportunities. I know we humans are more powerful than you give us credit for, and I know we can all be agents for good.*

She wonders at the different versions of reality they experienced, for she's seen with her own eyes how this boy seems to walk through life with perfect ease—as if he's a part of a river cutting its way through rock and all he needs to do is follow that flow. Viola shakes her head. *There is more agency and delib-*

erate choice in Jo's actions and speech, she thinks. It's strange to consider how much she's changed.

"Ah, here we go. The Way, a belief system of a people scattered throughout the Haldrian Empire whose origins are unknown."

Viola's mind flits to the strange origin story Jo shared with her. "So, what does it say about them? Or their beliefs?"

"Nothing much. They're made up of small communities of up to twenty families at most. They're spread out across the empire in small enclaves—mostly in rural areas. There's only one known group of this sect located in a city, and it's based in The Capital. They call themselves simply The Custodians, but as they keep to themselves and don't interact much with outsiders, there doesn't seem to be any more about them as a people."

Maitri flicks her finger across the device, and light glints off the wine-red gemstone on her ring. "Well then, here we go." She leans forwards, her focus intent upon the screen, and she begins to read. "The Way, also known as 'to walk in the Mother-Father's smile', has twelve prescripts, which are as follows: one, be your truest self; two, be kind to yourself; three, pursue the highest meaning in your life; four, speak the truth as you know it."

Viola leans forwards. She remembers that one. As soon as Maitri speaks the words, she recalls what Jo said next, and she adds, "Listen to the Truth of others."

Maitri glances up. "Yes, precisely. And right after that is: care for all living things. Next," she turns her attention back to the list on her tabula. "Seven, do what you know to be right; eight, acknowledge your failings; nine, strive to do better; ten, you're solely responsible for your own life; eleven, learn from Life; and finally, twelve, be open to new experiences, people, and things."

"Yes." Viola pushes herself up against the pillow behind her, seeking a more comfortable position. "That sounds exactly like Jo. So, he is probably from a community of these 'Custodians'."

"Was there anything else?" Maitri looks up from the device and studies Viola's features.

Viola squirms under her former teacher's gaze and considers the other things she's wondered about the boy who became her apprentice. "He claimed the whole community was not only able to use magic but could take away the blight." She shakes her head. "It really seems far-fetched to me. Although I know you have confirmed the first part of it, Maitri, do you think it is really possible for around twenty to thirty adults— that is also the impression I had from him—to be able to remove the worst kind of disease known in the empire and cleanse everything it affected? From what I understand, science is stumped. They do not know what the blight is or how it comes about, so they do not know how to treat it. Is it really possible for a tiny sect to have the answers to this?"

She licks her lips. Tiredness is closing in. It's a weight that adds to the aches in her limbs, but she blinks it all away and continues, "And also, if they know how to remove the sickness from the plants and the animals, why are the authorities of Mshrali unaware of it? I do not understand why they do not do something to propagate whatever these Custodians are doing so the whole Dust Bowl can become what it used to be: good land to raise livestock."

Maitri shrugs. Her eyes scan the information on the device, and her finger flicks over the smooth surface several times before she shakes her head. "No, it says nothing more about them. It's pretty much the rules they follow, and that their origins are unknown, repeated in several different entries by both the priesthood and the imperial bureau, which has included these Custodians in the most recent census." She sighs and looks up. "Anything else?"

A laugh bubbles out of Viola. "Oh, a bursting shuttle full, but I think it will have to wait." She yawns.

"Yes, quite right. Take a rest."

A few days later, under the shade roof at the front of the abode, Maitri unwinds the bandages on Viola's arms. Beside Viola, tendrils of smoke rise from a fire pit, the warmth pleasant but the acrid smell a little less so. She considers the strangeness of encountering Maitri in such conditions. Even though Viola has lived this sort of life and even worse on her travels through the Haldrian Empire, the image she has of Maitri from their time in The Capital is incompatible with this life.

"Why do you live here when you could have the comforts of the empire at your fingertips?"

Maitri looks up, her dark brown eyes blazing. "I could ask you the same thing, Isperia."

Viola shakes her head. "I was young and foolish. I am definitely not relishing the thought of keeping up this kind of lifestyle in the moons and annums to come. It is one of the main reasons I am going to go back to The Capital as soon as I can. I must make amends with my mother."

Nodding, Maitri balls up the soiled bandages and tosses them into the fire pit, where they blacken before bursting into flame. She applies a salve, and the smell of some acrid plant Viola doesn't know the name of irritates her nostrils, but the ointment is cool and soothes the itchiness of her skin. The fireflies singed her arms pretty badly, but she's grateful they didn't damage her fingers.

A white snout and bristly hair nudge Viola's arm. She looks into bright brown eyes, and her heart lifts. "I have not thanked you properly for saving my life, Motoko," she says and lets her hand run over the animal's head. The dog gives a sigh and leans into her, the weight of his head sinks onto her thigh, and she lets her fingers tickle behind his ears.

Her thoughts wander to Jo and their discussions on the Startraveller's Hope when they were coming to Téarman. She'd mentioned the possibility of a dog. *A dog could be incredible,* she'd said. And here Motoko is, right by her side. Truly astonishing.

"It is almost as if he sent you so you could watch over me." Viola muses as her hands gently pull on the animal's ears. It really does seem that way. She turns to Maitri. "Do you think that is possible? Jo, my apprentice, he always seems to get whatever he wants. Do you think he could have magically brought this dog into being to accompany me? Sometimes I really believe he might be capable of such things."

Maitri's eyes widen. "You really think he's able to do something like that? Magic, as you well know, isn't about pulling things out of thin air. You have to use existing energies to create something new. It's unusual for someone to be powerful enough to manipulate the energies on behalf of others. You honestly think he created the dog?"

Viola shifts in her seat, turning so she's facing Maitri more but leaving her hand to rest on Motoko's shoulder. "I do not know. He stopped a mob of blightstruck meerkats. We should have died that day, and yet we walked away with not even a single bite mark." She thinks back on all the situations they've been through and adds, "In Ilwych, after his first performance, it was as if the people were bewitched by him. The market-place is one of the most disgusting locations I have ever been to. They butcher the animals right there, and although they clean up the blood after, grime always coats the plaza—and it smells. The sky is perpetually obscured by noxious purple clouds of industrial brew, and they drizzle a dark dust onto everything. Nevertheless, after his performance, that market-place and the streets around it had somehow been scrubbed clean so you could see the cobblestones."

Her fingers caress the soft fur behind Motoko's ears as she continued, "Both of his spontaneous open performances made him more money than I have ever achieved in such settings. In Baile, I do not know how he did it, but he managed to pull off a city-wide performance in the great square. Even Natesari attended."

Maitri raised an eyebrow. "Really? Your cousin attended a public storytelling? How unlike her."

"Yes, I know. I wonder if it was more out of a desire to see him fail and be able to rub salt into my wounds with the knowledge, but when his diversion worked, and I was able to escape the ambassador's palace, he mentioned she had even asked him to stay. It stretches my mind. But he is the most honest person I have ever met, so I have absolutely no reason to doubt him."

Leaning back, Maitri asks, "Is there anything else that makes his magic stand out?"

"Whenever he gets deep into the storytelling, it shows itself visibly. He gets this aura of shimmering rainbow light, a little like the aurora's flickering lights at the poles. It shimmers off him in undulating sheets of brilliance. I tried to contain it, but on the Startraveller's Hope, he was telling stories almost every day; it was part of the condition for his permission to travel. His power became so strong it easily broke through my containment. He was also completely oblivious to it until I pointed it out to him. It is so strange. I have never seen anything like it."

Maitri lets her head tilt backwards. Her hands rest in her lap, but the fingers of her left hand twist at the ring on the other. Viola wonders how much knowledge is stored in that woman's brain. She's always been a marvel. Whereas other people Viola knows turn to whatever device they have on hand, Maitri thinks first.

At length, the teacher stirs. "You know," she exhales softly, "the only phenomenon I can think of with that kind of power is the 'Guardians' from the old tales. The old Haldrian folk tales particularly have reference to beings that have immense magical power and can create pockets of time or magical items. But of course, those are just folk tales." She pauses again and sighs. "No, I don't think there are any documented meetings with these Guardians. In the legends, they do tend to be human, although they have incredible shape-shifting abilities, among other mind-boggling powers. I don't know. Well, it's the only thing that comes to mind."

Viola sighs. "Would your tabula be able to help? Is there some way to search for this sort of thing?"

Maitri rises. "Yes, of course, how silly of me to forget it. Let me fetch that for you."

After hours of talking and searching different topics, Viola throws up her hands. "He is an enigma! I do not think I will ever figure out what his powers are."

Maitri's laugh draws Viola's gaze to her teacher. "You were always impatient, Isperia. The answers will present themselves in time. So, tell me, what have you done with this apprentice of yours anyway? Why does he not travel with you?"

Viola shrugs. "I left him in Abhainn. He is with Cerddor, studying music. It seemed the right thing to do as trouble follows me, and he needed a place he could study in peace. I also realised on the ship—when we were travelling here to Téarman—that his magic seems to activate more powerfully with a strong rhythm to the verse. The visual manifestation was much weaker with prose."

"Do I know this Cerddor?"

Motoko whines and Viola gives another scratch, her attention on him as she answers. "I am not sure. Cerddor used to perform at The Capital a long time ago. I met him again when I was travelling out here in Téarman, back when I first escaped The Capital. He owed me a favour, and this is me cashing in on it." She shrugs again. "He is a typical artist, total recluse, but I think if Jo could do me good and bring me out of my shell, then Cerddor needs him as much as Jo needs a music teacher. They might just be good for each other."

"Cerddor—oh, I remember. The prodigy. I attended one of his early performances. Didn't he disappear?"

"Yes, exactly. He left the stage and chose to become a teacher in Abhainn. I have no idea why," Viola laughs. "That is where he is, the great musical prodigy. I think the pressures of stage life and how young he was took a big toll on him, and it seems this is what he prefers to do."

They sit and talk as the light wanes and move inside once the nyamuk and other insects come out.

Chapter Five

"Are you certain you want to go back now?" Maitri looks at Viola over the top of her cup. Their plates are pushed aside, and Viola leans back from the table to scratch Motoko's head. The dog rests beside her chair.

Maitri sets down the cup with a soft *clink*. "You've only just healed and are barely back on your feet."

"It is time, Maitri. If I stay here, I am putting it off, and I know that is going to get me stuck all over again. I need to keep the momentum going. I want things to be right—for me."

"Fair enough. I'm just protective of you, dearest student."

Viola is thrown back into the reactions of her younger years. She has consciously to stop the temptation to roll her eyes. "I will need my staff and amplifying crystal. Please tell me you kept it."

Maitri grunts. "Of course; I've taken good care of it. Let me fetch that for you." She shuffles into the hut.

When she reemerges, Viola asks, "Is there another port nearer here than Baile?"

Maitri chuckles. "You're most certainly driven. No, Baile is the only intergalactic port on Téarman. This is a remote planet, after all."

"What do you mean?" Viola cuts in, her eyebrows drawing together. "Téarman is right on the crossroads of shipping lanes. It is where every ship has to stop on the routes to the colonies."

"Yes, that is true, but the port in Baile is the only attraction this planet has. We don't have resources like Harland, Logulen and Daria, or for that matter, even Oruna with their fabrics and power crystals. No, no. Téarman is the sad backwater where life simply goes on, and imperial politics rarely reach. Why do you think I ran off to The Capital to study and spent so many years there, rising in the ranks until becoming the imperial tutor?"

"Well, I suppose I never thought of it that way. So why did you come back here?"

"I'd been caring for my parents over the years. They didn't want to leave this house, and once I achieved my position at court, it was quite easy to manage. I'm the only surviving child and wilful, so my parents always did everything they could to see me achieve my dreams. It was the least I could do to support them through their old age in a way they considered dignified."

Maitri smiles softly, and Viola considers the emotional connection her teacher had to her parents. Thinking of the situation with her own family and the damaged relationships she has, Viola wonders if death in her family would affect her so deeply. She sighs. It's another indication she must return and do her best to mend what is broken.

A thought sparks to life in her mind. She turns to Maitri, leaning forwards again. "How did you do it? Travelling back and forth. I do not remember you ever being away. Or did you start coming back here after I left?"

"Now you're asking the right questions, Isperia." Maitri chuckles. "I procured a magical item, a travelling stone."

Viola glances at the crimson gem Maitri wears on her finger. "The ring?" She gestures towards it with her head.

"Yes. This ring," Maitri pulls it from her finger. "I don't have a use for it anymore. I haven't visited The Capital since —" she pauses and waves off the thought. "Well, no matter now. My place is here, and I've no intention of leaving this town. My people need me, and I'm content here. Besides, living in The Capital made me feel complicit in all the things I don't agree with that are done in the name of the empire." She holds out the ring towards Viola. "Take it, Isperia. It's the last gift I can give you, and it will bring you to The Capital on Haldria in the space of a few hours, as opposed to the months it would take you by ship."

"But that must be worth a fortune, Maitri. I cannot accept!"

She gives Viola a withering glare. "Isperia. It's a gift. Take it."

Viola hesitates. The red stone gleams in the early-morning light. It's as if it's come alive with an inner flame. The flickering light dances inside the gem and draws her nearer. She picks up the offered ring and raises it, so the light from the open window spills right over it. "It is beautiful," she murmurs. The glow brightens and begins to swirl. It tugs at Viola as if wanting to pull her towards the strange glowing nebula within. It seems to speak to some forgotten part of her soul, and she can't tear her eyes away from it.

Maitri's hand falls over the exposed stone, and Viola snaps her attention to her teacher. "Watch out, Isperia. You wouldn't want to fall into the void. If you wish to use the ring, you must have a clear picture of where you're going; otherwise, it will trap you in the in-between."

Viola's mouth is dry, and she swallows hard, but Maitri continues. "The magic of the travelling stone ebbs and flows, and sometimes it needs recharging. You can usually do that in places with a high concentration of magic, like the nodes where ley lines meet. At the moment, this stone has enough power for one more trip to The Capital. Then you'll have to leave it at least a week in a place where it can absorb the natural magic around it. There's a grotto in the palace gardens that worked well for me. It's the only one I know of in The Capital, although I expect there might be other places where the ley lines intersect. It's a rather big city after all, and the energies of the land are still bound to the original geography." Maitri retracts her hand and sits back in her seat.

Motoko shifts beside Viola, who glances at the dog. He pushes himself to his feet and tilts his head towards Viola's face. The black nose snuffles in the direction of the ring as the canine twitches his eyes from the gold and red piece cupped in her hand to her face and back again.

"What do you think, Motoko?" Viola asks. "Would you like to travel to The Capital with me?" She turns back to Maitri. "It is strong enough for that, right? The dog can accompany me?"

Maitri nods. "Oh yes, one other can travel with you using the ring. It's quite a powerful one, but you will have to hold onto him tightly. When travelling with another, there's always the risk they slip into the in-between." Maitri's brow ripples into a series of furrows. "You named the dog Motoko, even though he's male."

"What of it?" Viola looks up.

"Well, it's a female name."

With a shrug, Viola clarifies, "I chose it for the meaning: beginning. Choosing to take Motoko with me was a conscious decision to accept what Jo was talking about and to deliberately seek out the peace and harmony I long for. Motoko is my new beginning."

"Fair enough," Maitri concedes, and they lapse into silence.

Viola considers her desire to return to The Capital. She turns the ring between her fingers. Through this little twist of fate, a journey that would have taken months has been reduced to a few hours. Her gut clenches while her heart thumps harder against her chest. *Am I ready for this?*

Then again, if she overthinks the situation, she'll only put it off. She knows herself well enough. *It is simple, really. I have faith. All will be well.* Jo's words echo in her mind, and it's true; since she made her decision on the Startraveller's Hope to do the right thing and stop running, everything keeps working out in her favour. Instead of getting arrested and carted back to Baile, she survived the Leviathan, which in turn destroyed all her pursuers while leaving her and Jo alive. She withstood the fireflies only because she accepted Motoko's company, and now she's able to return to The Capital as intended, but also much sooner than she'd ever expected. "The world works in mysterious ways," she murmurs.

"Indeed it does." Maitri nods. "Are you ready then? I'll need to get you a few provisions, and I think I have an old backpack lying around somewhere."

Viola laughs softly. "I suppose I am as ready as I will ever be for this encounter I have put off for almost thirty years." Her gut clenches again, and she shifts uncomfortably against the hard wood of the chair. "You are sure you do not want me to stay another day or two?"

Maitri's eyes narrow. "I thought you were adamant to leave so as not to stagnate and put it off. You're deflecting. Your fear of confrontation won't serve you."

"Yes. That is very true. I must face this. And dignity is good."

A smile twitches over Maitri's lips. Viola considers she's never seen her teacher as relaxed as she is here in this tiny town on the empire's outskirts. It's strange and yet satisfying. Her mind wanders to Jo and how her apprentice was almost always content. *We all find our peace when we are willing to follow our own truths.*

Chapter Six

Viola focuses all her attention on the plaza outside the imperial palace and follows Maitri's instructions. *No one can portal directly into the palace; there are safeguards against it. Despite your heritage, there is no guarantee the wards will let you through. Avoid getting hurled back into the in-between. It is better to play it safe and simply do things the way I always did. It never failed.*

Maitri's words still echo in Viola's mind as she hurtles downwards. It's as if she's falling through the universe, and although her eyes are open, all is black. She doesn't know up from down. Blind in the relentless darkness, Viola plays over Maitri's parting instructions as they jumble through her head while she tries to keep her focus on the plaza outside the palace.

Her hand is clenched around the scruff of Motoko's neck. She clings to the dog as she might grasp at sanity, for there's nothing beyond her existence, and panic begins to creep into the edges of her stomach. It steadily rises, threatening to overwhelm her heart and mind, but she pushes it down, forcing back the fear. She must keep her thoughts trained on her destination: the main plaza in The Capital.

Time whirls in an endless, immeasurable mass. It extends and flexes, expands and contracts, and all the while, Viola focuses all her attention on achieving her goal: reach solid ground. Nausea ripples through her, but she clenches her teeth and trains her brain to focus on other things. *Remember the plaza outside the imperial palace in The Capital.*

Viola's feet slam into the ground with knee-numbing impact and her weaker right knee buckles. The weight of her new backpack suddenly returns, crushing her downwards. Motoko lets out a pitiful yelp as Viola stumbles forwards, still holding onto the back of his neck. She gasps for air while the world spins around her. She shakes her head and her eyelids flutter in an attempt to steady herself and bring her whole being to rest in this new environment.

With her stomach doing flips, Viola holds her arms out to regain her balance and glances about her. Cool morning air tingles against the exposed skin on her arms. The fingers in her left hand are stiff from holding onto Motoko, and now she's let go, the ache zings through the limb as she flexes. She breathes in deeply as if she might absorb the sights around her. It's been over twenty-eight years since she last set foot in this place—in actual fact, that was the only time she's seen this side of The Capital. In front of her squats a large white building in the shape of a five-storey, eight-sided star with multiple layers at the points. Each tier sticks out with triangular sheets of glass held together by walls of marble. At its top balances a shimmering ball, reflecting the sun's bright light. The solar orb hangs just above the top of the building, and Viola realises it's early morning even though she left Téarman close to midday.

The grand entrance of the white marble and glass star building arches ostentatiously. Gold letters curve over the doorway, and Viola takes in a sharp breath. IMPERIAL GRAND LIBRARY. How has she never known about this place? Well, she'd known it existed, but it's right here, at the heart of the city. This is where all the stories are stored. It's the most complete archive of all written works in the empire.

A thought echoes in her mind. *I want to work somewhere where I can write the stories I have learned and share them more broadly.* Might it be possible she can find a way to work at the Imperial Grand Library? It most definitely fits the idea she's been working on since talking to Jo about these things. *Maybe, just maybe, I can have my feast and enjoy it. But first—*

First, Viola must face her mistakes and end this ridiculous hunt. She turns towards the building on her right. Although it's only three stories high, and the golden dome of the Imperial Audience Chamber at the palace peeks out over its roof, Building 1, as it's called, is still extravagant. Grey stone columns sweep upwards behind a portico crowned with a small golden cupola, a miniature copy of the massive dome marking the centre of the Haldrian Empire.

Viola considers the contrast of this fine building with its lack of a decent name. Perhaps the people of Haldria have given it a name of its own, but confined as she was to the palace and the life within it, Viola doesn't know what that might be. Building 1 spans the entirety of the south eastern side of the plaza. At 135-degree angles, it's bordered by Building 2 on the right and Building 8 on the left.

She takes a step towards the portico and the glass doors winking at her in the early morning light. The soft click of nails on cobbled stone draws her attention to Motoko. The dog is already trotting off in the direction of the building as if he can sense Viola's purpose. She follows and glances around. The plaza is surrounded by other buildings. Most of them are single or double-storey, all low enough that the great dome at the heart of the palace is visible throughout the city.

What surprises Viola, though, is how quiet it is. There are no people milling around. No one is coming and going through any of the glass doors, and she can see into the government buildings that circle the palace. Her last experience of this space was so entirely different. Then, people had teemed in and out of buildings, busy as ants.

As she steps under the portico, Viola's arms prickle in response to the drop in temperature. It's a cool day, but the shaded area is downright chilly. She pulls her cloak around her, shrugging her backpack into a more comfortable position as she does, and welcomes the worn fabric as it glides over her arms. It's a comfort against the strangeness of the abandoned city. Viola studies the streets that open onto the plaza, but there's still no sign of movement. All is still. No sign of clouds, and the air is dry. It's as though the empire is holding its breath, and she wonders if everything is waiting to see what she'll do.

This ought to feel like coming home, but I feel as out of place as ever. The realisation weighs on Viola. After all this time away, she'd thought she would be glad to be back, but the silence and these ostentatious buildings remind her of how much she's changed. *Leaving The Capital was the best decision of my life*, she acknowledges.

She climbs a set of three stairs and pulls on the brass handle of the glass door. It remains firmly stuck, and a rattling complaint from the lock is all Viola hears. Motoko sits beside the entrance, tongue lolling out. "You are no help," Viola grumbles as she turns to scan her surroundings once more.

Have I fallen into a dream? It seems the only plausible explanation for the lifelessness of the city that never sleeps. She rattles against the door a second time, assuring herself it's locked. With a huff, Viola lets her hand fall to her side.

Motoko whines and shifts on the spot, rump wiggling against the cold stone floor. "I know," Viola snaps. "I am not sure what to do about this." She blinks away the tiredness in an attempt to clear her head. She has used a lot of magic today and must be careful or rest soon.

She turns again and sees a figure clad in a blue cloak hurrying up the stairs to the Imperial Grand Library. Before she can think, Viola runs across the square and lumbers up the flight of steps as fast as she can. It still takes her a while to reach the glass revolving door of the library's main entrance. She pushes against the bronze handle and is rewarded by the whisper of an unseen mechanism and the gentle rotation of the door.

Beyond it, Viola comes out into a foyer stretching up the five storeys to the roof and decorated with what looks like floating globes. They shimmer in the half-light, but Viola imagines they might be lamps. A marble staircase with gleaming bannisters rises to the first floor on her left. To the right, she can see a row of glass cubicles followed by shelves. The air is musty and heavy with the scent of ink and parchment. Unable to see where the person she was following has gone, Viola turns in a circle. Directly to the right of the revolving doors, she sees a series of waist-high plinths. Even as she wonders what people would use them for, Viola hears a desperate, pitiful bark from the other side of the entrance.

She's forgotten the dog.

Hurrying back outside, Viola caresses Motoko's head and murmurs, "There, there. I was just seeing if I could catch that person. They have got away, but nevermind. Perhaps there is someone else here at the library who could assist me."

She walks back into the revolving door and steps aside to let Motoko stand beside her as she pushes her way through.

"What are you doing?" A shrill female voice jerks Viola's attention to her right. A woman clad in blue, with a midnight robe billowing around her, comes forwards, her eyes trained on Motoko. "In the empress' name, you can't bring an animal in here! This is the library!"

The dog's forehead pinches into a worried expression, and its eyes dart from the scowling woman, who is a little younger than Viola, to the storyteller and back again. Viola grimaces. "The dog will do no harm." She sucks air into her lungs, realising the terseness of her words. To soften the simmering frustration, she adds while gesturing to the plaza behind her, "I just got back to The Capital after many years abroad. It is so quiet; I was wondering if something had happened around these parts." She takes note of the silver book pin clasping the ends of the blue fabric at the base of the woman's throat. *Ah, so this must be the second in rank.*

"Why would anyone be out at this time on Sachukari? Whatever do you mean? And years? Where have you been holed up for the past several annums?"

Viola smiles at memories of *gift-giving day*, as her friend Eryk called it. She remembers they'd made a ritual of it, exchanging little things, mostly transient ones like flowers, although Viola once gifted him a locket. She shakes her head, imagining the memories being flung from her like droplets of water. Glancing into the long, pinched face of the woman before her. She decides to ignore the slight about her slip-up and instead jibes, "Well, you are out, are you not?" She raises an eyebrow. "Why is that so strange to be out and about on a beautiful day?"

The woman huffs. "Well, *most* people are home or spending time with their families and friends. The bureau," the woman gestures towards the building across the plaza with a swish of her robe, "will only open at tenth circ, for but a short while." She raises her eyes towards the high ceiling. "The library is open, but I didn't expect anyone to be here. It's usually my quiet day of work." There's resentment in her tone when she glances at the dog once more, her eyebrows arrowing into a dark V. "Now, I have things to do. Get that thing out."

Viola holds back a growl. Starting an argument won't gain her any favours, and she has questions—important ones. She forces a smile. "Motoko is doing no one any harm, and I shall be on my way in just a moment. I was wondering, and since you work here, maybe you can help me. How does one go about getting employment?" Viola lifts her gaze, absorbing the grandeur of the foyer with its globes suspended from the vaulted ceiling.

A laugh brays out of the librarian. "You want to work here?"

The woman gives Viola a once-over, her eyes hard with judgement. Viola meets the librarian's gaze, and sadness fills her as she absorbs the disdain in those brown eyes. It was this hatefulness she sought to escape when she ran away twenty-eight years ago. *And now I seek to return, but nothing has changed.* With a wry smile, Viola takes in her worn clothes and sun-darkened skin.

The other woman's voice turns to acid. "Never in a thousand annums would anyone like you work in this, the most esteemed house of records. Begone, and take your fleabag with you." She points to the door behind Viola, who almost expects the librarian's foot to start tapping.

"How curious," Viola holds her tone civil. "You turn people away without asking for credentials." She turns and motions for Motoko to follow. Over her shoulder, she calls, "I am certain we shall meet again and perhaps then you will be less inclined to judge so harshly, Second Archivist."

As she steps into the revolving door, Viola hears the librarian sputter, "How do you know who I am?"

She waves it off and steps through into the cool air of early morning. Now to wait for Building 1 to open for its brief spell. Viola has a purpose, and she won't waiver from it, even if she'd prefer to stake out the library. Well, for what it's worth, she can explore the idea germinating in her mind. *I want to work somewhere where I can write the stories I have learned and share them more broadly*. She remembers saying so to Jo. She lets the heavy backpack slip from her shoulders and drops it at her feet. Settling with her back pressed against one of the cool columns under the portico of Building 1, Viola lets her gaze travel back to the library. Maybe, just maybe, this could be the solution to that part of her dream. And what a beautiful place it is, and steeped in history, too. Definitely, a worthy place for her to hone her craft and share stories with the whole empire.

Her heart flutters. That would be perfection.

Chapter Seven

The sun rises almost to its zenith before a metallic *click* jerks Viola from her daydream. She blinks away the graininess of exhaustion and turns to see the door to Building 1 swing wide. An official in a white suit with grey stripes on the shoulders and hem slips from view.

Viola pushes herself onto her feet and swings her backpack onto one shoulder. As she slides the other arm through the strap, her eyes fall on Motoko. She ought to leave the dog outside, but when she goes through on the other side of the building, she'll need to bring the dog with her anyway. Shrugging, she heads inside and snaps her fingers for Motoko to follow right beside her.

To the left and right of the entrance, corridors with eye-scorching bright lights stretch as far as Viola can see through her squint. Before her, a floodlight beams its rays onto a polished wooden counter behind which stands an official, also with grey stripes on the shoulders of his white suit. More people busy themselves behind him, some sitting in office chairs on wheels, others flitting about with stacks of paper in hand. All wear the same uniform, and she's not certain the person who unlocked the door is the one she's facing now.

The man behind the counter looks upon Viola without emotion. The blankness of his face is disconcerting; she feels as if he's an unwritten page, empty and undefined. However, she also knows she must convince him to let her through.

The blandness isn't restricted to the man's features. Viola is further unsettled by the paleness of his skin. Even though it has a hint of brown in it, his arms and face seem almost colourless. She wonders if the odd shade is a result of his work keeping him indoors all the time. By comparison, her complexion is brown, darkened by long hours spent trudging under the many suns of the empire. There are hints of copper in the tone, making her skin vibrant.

Viola steps up to the counter and lets her arms sink against the gleaming surface. The wood is smooth and cool to the touch. "Good morning," she says. "I would like to request an audience with the empress."

"Name," he says, his tone bordering on inattentive.

"Viola Alerion."

The man pulls a device up from under the counter and presses a button with his thumb. A moment later, the screen lights up, and he scrolls through. A furrow ploughs its way between his brows. He scrolls again and looks up. "There's no record of a request."

"I know," Viola says. "I just arrived in The Capital. I wish to request an audience."

The official's eyes widen, and his mouth falls open. It takes all of Viola's restraint not to laugh at his ridiculous frog look. His lips open and close several times before he collects himself. "You can't simply walk in here and demand an audience with her most exalted highness, Dedopali, empress of

Haldria, ruler of the thirteen spheres and dragon-blessed lady of the stars."

Viola holds back a snort. *He just had to go ahead and list all the stupid titles.* Her irritation mounts, and she has to make a concerted effort to rein it in. How can things be so different from what she was taught about the workings of the empire? She tries again. "Is it not custom for the empress, ruler of the thirteen spheres and dragon-blessed lady of the stars—as you so rightly point out—to grant audiences to her subjects? Please correct me if I am wrong, but there was a time when *her most exalted highness* attended to the whims of her subjects almost daily. Why should I not be granted an audience, especially as it is law for newly-arrived subjects to present themselves, is it not?"

The man's eyes grow even rounder. It's the only sign of any emotion as the rest of his face remains impassive. "The empress doesn't attend audiences daily. Whatever gave you such a notion?"

Viola stares at him, her mind working furiously. It has been close to thirty years since she last attended court. *Much can change in such a long time.* She meets the gaze of the official across the counter. He's younger than her, probably in his forties. "How long have you worked here?" The question pops out of her mouth before she can think better of it.

He presses his lips together as he pulls himself to his full height, still half a head shorter than Viola. She schools her face to an expression she hopes shows interest, pushing down her frustration at this posturing.

"If you must know," he blusters. "I have thirteen annums of experience working in this bureau." His chest puffs out.

"Ah, well, that would explain it. My last contact with her imperial majesty was before your time. So, when may I have an audience with the empress?"

"Not today." The man's tone is final, and he lifts his gaze beyond Viola's shoulder.

She glances behind her to see at least ten more people staring at her. Turning back to the official, Viola leans forwards, and she can't help the flow of sarcasm that bursts from her. "When will the empress, *dragons exalt her illustrious name*, have her next audience?"

"What?" a woman shouts from behind Viola. "The empress isn't seeing people today? But I was told this Sachukari digh is the only audience she'll be holding this segment. I've travelled from beyond the outskirts for this."

Viola raises an eyebrow at the official. She suppresses a triumphant smile as the people behind her press forwards, many muttering or even shouting about the turn of events. The man behind the counter raises his hands in submission, glancing from the broiling crowd to Viola and back. She can see he's thinking fast.

"Settle down, everyone!" The voice booming through the hall is female, and Viola looks around. For a moment, she can't determine where it's coming from until a woman, clad in white but with light brown stripes on her shoulders, walks over to the attendant Viola has been talking to. The newcomer confronts grey-stripe. "What is the meaning of this, Seishiki?" Her voice booms through the hall and Viola almost expects lightning to flash in response to the glare brown-stripe offers her fellow official. "Off, empress damn it. Off!" the woman snaps, and the echoing projection of her voice is swallowed up.

Viola suppresses a laugh at the civil servant's difficulties with the voice projector. Her mirth evaporates quickly, though, when a hushed conversation between the two officials follows. There's much gesticulating and grey-stripe glances repeatedly in Viola's direction. He's definitely getting an earful, and Viola feels equal parts smug and sorry for him. Following her escape from The Capital in her youth, she's steered clear of anyone with the power to force her back home. She has, therefore, always kept her contact with civil servants to a minimum. As she watches the two bureaucrats whisper to each other, her insides churn in apprehension.

After a moment, brown-stripe steps up to the counter. Her eyes flash as she takes in Viola's attire. "I'll see what can be done about your petition. Please step aside and give the others their turn now. I'll return shortly; I must speak with my superior first." Without even waiting for Viola's response, the woman does an almost military about-turn and marches off, disappearing from view through a glass door on the right.

Grey-stripe fills up the space behind the counter once more, glares at Viola and waves her off. She nods her head and steps aside, Motoko faithfully trotting beside her as if glued to her leg.

"You can't have an animal in here!"

Viola turns back to the man at the counter. The whites of his eyes are visible, and the shade of his skin has turned a tone darker. "Have you no respect?" Spit flies. "This is Building One! Not some crackpot office on the Hub."

Viola folds her arms over her chest and stares the man down. Her patience is nearing breaking point, and she longs for the peaceful tranquillity of Maitri's home on Téarman. She breathes in and exhales slowly before replying, "My companion is well-behaved and causing no harm. I suggest you do your job and help these good people," Viola nods towards the muttering crowd, "and I shall wait here as I have been instructed."

She lets the backpack fall to the floor and rummages in it until she finds an earthen bowl Maitri gifted her. She pours water from the drinking flask attached to the outside of the pack, and beckons Motoko, who laps up the cool liquid with a sigh.

Once he's licked the bowl dry, Viola clears everything away and leans her back against the marble wall behind her. Cold seeps into her shoulders almost immediately, but she pays it no mind as she keeps her eyes trained on grey-stripe behind his counter. Motoko sinks down on all fours and rests his head on his front paws. The man gives a long-suffering sigh and waves up the next person in the queue with a flick of his fingers.

Waiting isn't a skill she has refined. As the crowd dwindles, with many of the people ushered through to the corridor on the opposite side of the hall from her, Viola's insides turn into a bubbling furnace. The woman who'd come from beyond the outskirts for an audience with the empress is one of the first to be escorted through by another grey-stripe. Viola takes note of the woman's dark brown dress. If she remembers rightly, brown is the colour reserved for the farming classes, although different shades denote the various types. She can't remember what this particular tone of brown means—

Although, with the weather the way it is on Haldria, chances are the woman works in a plant incubator, the only way to produce plants as far as Viola can remember. Other people follow the woman, and one by one, they're led down the corridor. All wear different colours, and Viola tries to recall the meaning of each, although she finds her memory fails her quite often. Having lived so long outside the strict hierarchy of The Capital has taken a toll on her. What else has she forgotten?

Some of the visitors complete whatever matter they've come for and leave again through the doors onto the plaza. Viola stretches out her right leg. Tiredness tugs at her senses. Travelling between planets using a magical vortex is exhausting, but she stretches her arms out every once in a while and focuses on her breathing in the hopes of staying alert.

After a while of simmering, Viola pushes her fatigue aside

and begins to pace. Her mind traces a multitude of paths and goes over everything she and the official said to each other. She picks the conversation apart over and over while her irritation grows. Motoko remains stretched out against the wall, eyes following her every move. When the hall empties, and she realises no one else is waiting, Viola slings her backpack onto one shoulder and marches back towards the counter.

The man she spoke to earlier has been replaced by another official in the same white suit with grey stripes on the shoulders. This one is a woman with an angular jaw and pinched expression that makes her look perpetually put out.

"I have requested an audience with the empress—"

The woman shrugs and cuts Viola off. "The audience is over. Come back next Sachukari."

"Oh, is that so? I have seen several others granted an audience leave that way," she gestures towards the corridor on her left. "Since none have returned, I can only surmise they are still in audience with the empress. I, too, have a right to be heard. Let me pass."

"I'm afraid the spaces for the digh's audience have been filled. There's—"

"Poppycock!" Viola bristles. "Fewer than twenty people have been guided through that hall," she points out.

Before she can continue, the woman across from her speaks. "There's no need to raise your voice or use that tone—"

"Oh, is there not?" Viola's voice drops. "I was the first person through those doors today," she points towards the entrance. "Although I am nearing fifty, I have been made to *stand* and *wait*. I have been openly lied to by all three people I have encountered in this bureau. You represent the empress. It is your duty to—"

"Don't speak to me of my duty. How dare you?" The woman's hands ball into fists.

A spark of satisfaction ignites Viola at this first real show of emotion. At least it's some kind of reaction.

She ignores the woman's protest and continues, "I know the oath you took to become an official in this illustrious building. From what I have experienced today, I get the impression you do not uphold any of the things you are meant to. You represent the empire. Well, all I see is a group of people who hem and haw while refusing to do their job. You instead find excuses to make the lives of the imperial subjects a living nightmare. That is a disgrace."

Other officials have stopped their work and gather round. One of them snaps, "Who do you think you are?"

Viola grins. "I bet you would like to know that." She considers for a moment. *Giving my true name will not help. If Maitri is right and the rumour mill has put me in an asylum for the deranged, it is unlikely I would be believed. I have to do this differently.* Drawing on her storyteller persona, Viola makes a small bow and says, "I am Viola Alerion, greatest storyteller of the Haldrian Empire and personal acquaintance of her most exalted highness, Dedopali, empress of Haldria, ruler of the thirteen spheres and dragon-blessed lady of the stars."

The group behind the counter mutters and trades dark looks.

"Can I verify your identity?" The pinched-faced woman holds up a small black box and gestures towards Viola's hand.

Taken aback, Viola's eyebrows draw together. What is this about? Something tugs at the back of her mind, a memory from her youth. Then everything falls into place. "Oh, you want to check a tag?" She grinds her teeth. *Why, oh why, did they say I should not get one?* Having a tag would have made things so much easier right now. Although, considering she's been on the run for years, having her identity confirmed in such a way would have made life most difficult indeed for the past few decades. Viola shrugs, "I do not have one."

The woman looks at her as if she's grown two heads. "What? That's impossible."

Viola holds out her hand, and the woman glides the thumb-sized device over Viola's wrist. Nothing happens. She passes it over again. Still nothing.

"Imp—" the woman begins, but Viola cuts her off.

"As I said, I do not have one, but the empress can verify my identity herself. She does, in fact, know who I am."

"Out of the question," someone else chimes in.

The official with the tag reader taps the device against the counter and sweeps it over Viola's wrist again. When nothing happens, she passes it up the length of Viola's arm.

"You can keep searching, but there is nothing to find here." Viola shrugs. "I have never been tagged."

"But no one is permitted to enter The Capital without documentation. Why was the immigration bureau not notified when you disembarked?" The bewildered expression on the woman's face adds to Viola's frustration.

"I did not, in fact, arrive on a ship," Viola admits.

"But that's impossible." Others are also muttering, but Viola keeps her focus on the woman before her, who is shaking her head. Under her breath, the civil servant whispers, "Interloper."

The other officials fall silent. All of them stare at Viola.

"What do you mean, interloper? I have just journeyed to visit the empress and am requesting an audience, as is my right to do. I am an imperial subject. It is, in fact, my duty to present myself. Is there not a decree stipulating newly-arrived persons in The Capital should present themselves to the empress?"

The glares intensify, and before Viola can process the

sudden shift in the air, someone calls out from behind her. "There, that's the interloper. Arrest her."

Viola turns to see the brown-striped official she spoke to earlier in the day flanked by two guards. They wear crimson uniforms, and each one carries a short staff. Viola shudders. The Imperial Guard is renowned for their brutality and the magic staves they carry. The sight of the two men slams Viola back into the moment she and Jo were running away from guards dressed as these—guards whose lives were snuffed out by the viciousness of an immense beast.

She blinks and stalls for time. Then she holds her arms wide and hopes to disarm them with her smile. "For all the dying stars, are you going to imprison me?" Her own staff is packed away in the top pocket of her bag, just out of reach. *I have been getting complacent. Have I not learned to travel with the staff in hand at all times?*

Before Viola can come to a decision on how to deal with the approaching guards, a white streak hurtles between them from the other side of the hall and jostles the guards. The official beside them shrieks.

The bundle of white fur skids to a halt right in front of Viola and barks. Behind Motoko, the guards close ranks again and flick their staves out on either side. The air crackles. Viola's teeth hurt, and she knows the guards have activated their weapons. The dog crouches, and a growl rumbles from his chest. Viola drops her hand to the soft fur of the animal's shoulder.

The guards take a step forwards, moving as if they're a single being. Motoko tenses. There's nothing for it. The full truth must out, or she and Motoko will be in grave danger. Viola knows about the Imperial Guards' deadliness. It is legendary.

"I am Isperia. I ran away from court twenty-eight years—

erm—annums ago and have now returned. I must beg the empress' forgiveness for causing—"

"Interloper!" brown-stripe shouts, while someone else from behind Viola chimes in with, "Impostor!"

Viola shakes her head. "I can prove it!" She calls up a magical shield, cocooning herself and Motoko in the protective bubble. "I wield magic as only members of the imperial family are permitted. I am telling the—"

She is cut off when the stick of one of the guards hits her shield. Sparks fly. The air hums under the assault of the magical baton, but Viola's shield holds. The air fills with the scent of burn. Behind her, Viola hears a clamour of voices. Shouts of *impostor*, *interloper*, and *illegal magic user* are bandied about.

"Oh, for the love of the empress!" Viola exclaims and wills herself away. At least she still has the knowledge and power to flit short distances. She calls up the first place that comes to mind in her immediate vicinity. The palace gardens have always been her favourite place—her sanctuary. She hears the cries of the officials in the bureau of Building 1, followed by a bellowing shout from one of the guards, but she and Motoko have melted away before anyone can react further.

Chapter Eight

With prickles crawling over her skin, Viola materialises on the side of a grassy knoll near a pond. She's relieved everything appears as she remembers it. The sun reflects off the smooth water, unruffled and glassy in the motionless air. The warmth of its rays caresses her skin and dissipates the sensation of pins and needles.

Was that the ward Maitri talked about? Viola suddenly realises her miss-step. *I could have been zapped or caught in the magic.* Then again, if she remembers right, the ward was constructed to keep unwanted magic users out. It's primed to allow members of the royal family through. *Well, whatever the situation, that was risky, and I am lucky.* She hopes it didn't set off some kind of alarm.

Tiredness infuses Viola with lead. She's used quite a bit of magic now for one day and will need to rest soon. *Find the empress, say my piece and then, hopefully, I can fall into bed.*

Her thoughts are cut off by a dousing of icy water. A gasp is all the sound she can make as her insides freeze with the shock. She turns around, and her ears pick up the soft *fizz-fizz-*

fizz of a sprinkler. She watches an arc of water spraying around in a circle. Three steps to her left take her out of the path of the rotating jet of water.

Shaking herself, Viola basks in the warmth of the sun once more and blinks away the remnants of fatigue. *At least that dousing was good for something.* She holds her arms wide to absorb more of the light's heat. It's the perfect sun. Not the incendiary twin orbs of Mshrali where her skin cracked under the ceaseless incandescence. It's also different from the bright, single flare of Téarman with its cloying heat and suffocating air.

The box hedges around the opposite side of the lake are as well kept as she remembers. It's as though she's stepped back in time. A path circles the pond, and white and yellow flowers border it. She's suddenly struck by a memory of the pond needing to be filled weekly because of the incessant sunshine. *Why did that never appear strange before? I have learned so much about rain and natural phenomena since I left.*

Viola's gaze sweeps over the weeping willow. It trails its tendrils in the waters, and she finds it's exactly as she remembers. Even the white marble seat beneath it shines as it did when she met here with Eryk. She wonders what has become of him.

Motoko lopes up to the top of the hill, where a series of bushes has been cut to look like a group of dancers. That's new. Viola remembers them in the shape of five swans. Taking a good look at the gardens, she sees other small changes. The imperial gardens might be perennial, but she realises even this static heart of the empire is constantly changing. There's a beauty to it, and she draws in a deep breath of appreciation.

Upon reaching the top of the knoll, Viola gazes across the network of paths and plants towards the palace building. The north wing stretches out to her left and feeds into a giant cylinder from which branches another wing: the west wing she remembers sneaking around with Eryk and even some of her cousins when ambassadors and delegates from other planets visited the empress. *Oh, the trouble I used to get into*, she muses. The thought reminds her of her purpose. *Find a way in. See the empress. Get this over with.*

Her eyes fall upon the door leading into the north wing, closest to the central audience chamber. That's where she must go, and hope to get past the guards before the empress concludes her audience session for the day. Motoko gambols between the bush-dancers, and Viola considers leaving the dog here.

A commotion near the doorway to the north wing catches Viola's attention. She instinctively crouches down beside one of the bushes and watches. She has to strain her eyes, but the distance is too great. With the need to know burning in her chest, she decides to use a touch of magic to help clarify what is going on. The energy within her races and surges through her blood. It creates a focal point; she hasn't used magic this freely in ages and knows she's sending out a beacon to anyone with a magic detector. The urgency of getting into the audience chamber and ending this whole mess as soon as possible bubbles inside her.

Viola focuses on the doorway. Now she can see that the six red guards usually stationed outside of the Grand Hall have been bolstered by four more. Purple-clad imperial staff are huddled in groups. Apart from the guards, nothing is static. The aggregations ebb and flow with activity. The bustle reminds her of an insect hive—an undulating mass of buzzing fireflies pouring out of a hollow tree. Viola shakes off the memory and focuses on her dilemma.

There is no chance I shall be able to slip in that way. And it is unlikely I can get in through the south wing, either.

She mulls over her options as she watches Motoko, who's slumped on his stomach, tongue lolling. *With all this fuss, I also cannot leave the dog out here.*

Another thought flashes into Viola's mind. If she flitted from Building 1 into the palace gardens, she should be able to do the same from here into the audience hall. Of course, she doesn't know if the interior has been changed. What would happen if she flits into a row of chairs, or worse, one of the columns? Flitting blind is an unsafe practice, she knows. The thought of doing it again makes her think of Maitri and the lecture she'd get.

Maitri is not here, and it is only a matter of time before those looking for me begin searching the gardens. Her mind chimes in with another possibility. *I passed through the wards. That should be enough to prove I am not an impostor.* She considers how the bureaucrats behaved and sighs. *It is likely not worth the effort. Find the empress. That is most important.*

Even as the thought comes to her, Viola notices the large doors to the audience chamber folding open. The brown-clad woman and a few others Viola remembers from her time waiting in Building 1 shuffle into view, looking alarmed at the hubbub around them. The doors close again behind the petitioners, and a moment later, they're hustled out of sight by a white-clad official.

It is now or never.

"Motoko," Viola calls softly. The dog pricks his ears, and when she snaps her fingers, he comes to his feet and trots over.

She gives herself a moment to weigh her options and remembers having been caught unawares by the guards in Building 1. With a huff, she shifts her backpack onto her front and rummages in the top of the bag, pulling out her folded-up staff and the quartz crystal. She slings her backpack out of the way again and assembles the catalyst for her magic. *There.*

Much better. She returns her attention to the issue of flitting into a space she can't actually see.

Viola hears a shout from the doorway. A purple-clad servant is pointing right at her, and she sees two guards pushing their way through the door. Her time is up.

She grabs Motoko by the scruff of the neck and takes the plunge.

Moments later, Viola materialises in the only location she can safely flit to. She briefly notes there's no prickling sensation this time, but brushes the thought aside. She stands upon a raised dais overlooking the audience chamber. Before her stands the golden throne Empress Parveli had installed centuries ago. Beyond it, Viola sees a cluster of courtiers filing out of the chamber. She's too late. There's no sign of the empress.

"Motoko, stay," she instructs as she steps forwards, praying the animal will do as he's told. With uncertainty rearing its head inside her, Viola searches for any familiar figures among the departing group, but disappointment sinks its heavy stone into her being. She glances towards the door on her right. If she'd only thought to flit directly into the audience chamber instead of stopping to get doused by the sprinkler, she would have most likely succeeded in her attempt to find the empress. Can she slip through unnoticed and seek out those who would help her? Or should she try flitting to the empress' chambers? She feels the weight of the energy already used. It would not be advisable to burn it all up.

Before she can take a second step in that direction, a voice calls from the back of the chamber. "There she is! Arrest the interloper!"

One of the guards vaults over the retreating courtiers and lands a few feet from Viola. She sinks into a defensive stance and tries to tune out the mayhem she's unwittingly unleashed. While the courtiers retreat and a dozen guards join their compatriot, Viola tries one more time to reason with them.

"I am Isperia," she calls, hoping the courtiers can hear her. She trains her focus on the men before her. Not one of them even pauses. "You would risk the wrath of this empire and the imperial family? Just give me a chance to prove I am who I say I am!"

One of the guards breaks formation, stepping forwards, his chest coming up against the dais. He's young, probably in his twenties. His short, dark hair is slicked back, and his shirt strains over his chest and shoulders. "How dare you claim to be High Lady Isperia? She died. How can you use that pain and abuse this—"

"What? I am dead now? Hello," Viola waves a hand and quickly returns it to its place on her staff. "I am clearly alive and well. If I were dead, there would have been a funeral."

The guard hops up onto the podium using one hand to lift himself. As his feet land, he grinds out through his teeth, "Lies. All lies. Impostor!" He launches himself forwards, and she has no other choice but to defend herself.

Chapter Nine

Viola pulls up a shield around her, letting it sit tight against her figure like armour. She braces herself for the blow, which cracks against her bamboo staff. The impact sends shockwaves to her elbows, and it takes all her strength to keep hold of her weapon.

Using the focal stone at the tip of her staff, Viola draws energy from the surrounding air as she shifts. In the blink of an eye, she's twisted the bamboo rod around to land a glancing blow to the youngster's head. Upon contact, she allows some of the energy in the stone to zing through the length of the staff and put her opponent to sleep.

The young man slumps to the ground. Viola winces at the landing but knows there was no way to break his fall. Besides, she has other things to keep her occupied. The remaining guards have responded to their comrade's defeat with shouts of dismay. As one, they surge up, and Viola is enveloped in the storm of battle.

Her staff whirls and thrusts, hitting the guards who are pushing in closer and closer. Their overwhelming numbers would make Viola's resistance a short one if not for her ability to put her opponents to sleep. The power in the stone is depleting, as is her own strength, but she strains to use the magic as sparingly as possible. It proves insufficient against one of the burlier opponents, who shakes off the grogginess and re-engages with a roar.

Lightning flashes from his staff, and Viola is forced to duck the blow. The end of the flickering staff connects with the shoulder of one of the guards standing behind her. A scream rings in Viola's ears. She thrusts her opponent's staff upwards and uses the end of her own stick to channel another dose of sleep into the man in front of her. He drops to the ground like a sack of wet sand.

Viola spins around to face the man who'd circled behind her. He's clutching his right shoulder. It's blackened, the red cloth of the uniform seared away. The smell of burned flesh is strong, and her stomach flips. She clenches onto the need to remain focused. With a tap of her staff on the injured guard's head, she sends the last of her sleeping power into him, and he drops, landing with a crunch.

As she turns back towards the remaining two opponents, catching sight of the bodies sprawled out around her, Viola's memory drags her back to the desert on Mshrali when she'd faced off a mob of blightstruck meerkats. Jo's scream of anguish fills her mind. *Stop!* he'd shouted. *Care for all living things.*

She receives a glancing blow to her left shoulder. If it weren't for the protective barrier, her left side would have been crushed. Viola tries to shake away the numbness in her side. From her right, she senses more than sees the crackling arc of another staff aiming a blow in her direction. Her reflexes are too slow, and even as she tries to lift her staff to meet the trajectory of the oncoming impact, she knows it isn't enough.

She braces herself for the outcome and hopes her shield will hold.

Instead of the awaited collision, something jostles Viola from behind, throwing her to the left. The incoming staff whistles through where her head was moments before, and Viola struggles to re-establish her balance. She twists to face her opponent only to find the guard flat on his back, his staff fallen from his grasp and Motoko crouching, hunched on the man's torso, teeth bared. Ferocious growls rumble from the dog, and the man pushes at the creature's chest, holding snapping teeth at bay.

In the next breath, the other remaining opponent lifts his staff and directs it towards the dog. Viola steps in and takes the hit directly on the centre of her staff. It cracks but holds firm. Another blow will leave her with two useless pieces. She struggles to breathe. The intensity of the fight has taken too much out of her. She should have listened to Maitri and given herself longer to heal from the fireflies' burns. She can't keep up this tempo.

Out of the corner of her eye, Viola notices a river of red-clad guards pouring through the doors of the audience hall. She's not going to make this. A sense of futility wipes away the spark that's been driving her defence. Viola becomes hyper-aware of the bodies strewn around her, and the current picture overlays itself onto her memories. She's back in the forests of Téarman, hearing the screams of the dying as bodies litter the fern-covered ground. And at the same time, she's in the sweat-absorbing heat of Mshrali with a tsunami of little furry bodies rushing towards her.

STOP!

Her mind echoes with Jo's scream from that day when the meerkats attacked. His will from then echoes through her. She feels the power of his desire to protect all living things. The energy from that moment in the past courses through her, burgeoning until it might burst. She doesn't know what to do with all the magic straining against her being. Where did it even come from? It's too much. And it demands that all of this stop.

Viola stands, frozen in time. The wave of oncoming guards slows to the speed of cooling lava. The upcoming assault creeps forwards, one painstaking step at a time. The man in front of her has raised his staff, ready to bring it down onto her outstretched bamboo stick, which will crumble before that onslaught. Her opponent will break through her barrier with the blow and cleave into her with the might of his magical quarterstaff.

Beside her is the throne. It shimmers in splendour, a water lily embossed into the centre of the backrest. A few steps behind her, Motoko and the guard still wrestle. She can't see them, but the sense of their tussle is strong within her. Viola can smell the blood dripping from the man's arms where he's been bitten. The fresh crimson mingling with the redness of the guard's uniform.

Red.

Death.

It must stop.

Viola seeks a way to resolve this and still care for all the lives involved. Her mind struggles against the impossibility of such a task. She and Motoko will die, she knows it, and yet a seed of hope lives on in her mind: it could be possible to survive.

Even as she struggles to wrest this waning prospect from the suffocating grasp of her disbelief, she is surprised by a voice calling out from behind her.

"What, by the thirteen spheres, is the meaning of this?"

Viola's eyes close of their own volition. Relief pours

through her at the memory of this voice. Shrill and commanding—always. It's the sound she's spent three decades evading. She can imagine the sternness in familiar dark eyes flashing as they stare down everyone in the hall. Her relief is fleeting. Up bubbles dread in the simmering pot of her stomach.

Turning to face the voice, Viola ignores the man she's been fighting. She must face her fear or forever disintegrate and lose herself. The figure before her stands commanding and regal, but the years haven't been kind to her. Empress Dedopali has become thin, her hair is wispy ivory, and her skin is papery. She stands propped up with the sturdy support of a cane. Despite it all, the sternness hasn't left the empress' demeanour.

She shuffles forwards, her eyes boring into Viola. "Who are you, and why do you cause such mayhem?"

From behind, Viola is jostled, and fingers wrap around her arms. Her shoulders sag, but words pour out of her even though she feels at a loss. "It is good to finally see you again, Mother." Her lips quirk up in a wry smile, for she realises it is indeed true.

"Isperia."

For a heartbeat, there's a combination of softness and contentment in the empress' eyes. It does not last long.

Viola quails under the barrage of lightning that comes to life in those dark orbs. "Yes, Mother." It comes out more like a hoarse whisper than the determined statement of fact Viola hoped for.

"Do you have any idea the trouble you have caused me, young missy?"

Viola rolls her eyes. She's been transported back twenty-eight years as if not a single day has passed since she last spoke to her mother. "Before you go into your diatribe," Viola wrestles her arms from the guards' grasp and holds up a hand in appeasement. "Please call off your guards. They seem to believe I mean you harm."

The empress glowers at Viola. "And do you?"

"Of course not! I just want to talk. We need to work through this." Viola gestures to the space between them.

"Leave us," the empress commands.

"But, Your Imperial Highness," one of the guards steps forwards. He wears a golden pin of two crossed magical staffs on his lapel. He points to the fallen guards around Viola. "My men have been—"

The empress cuts him off. "This is my daughter. Now, begone. I shall summon you should there be any need."

Viola bristles at the dismissal in her mother's voice. *That is no way to treat dutiful guards of the empire.* It brings into focus how much she has changed because, in the past, she would hardly have noticed such condescension. A shuffle to her left draws her attention to Motoko, still hunched over the guard's chest. The dog has calmed, though. His teeth are no longer bared, and the animal even licks the guard's arm as if embarrassed for having caused him injury.

She calls, "Motoko, come." Bafflingly obedient, the dog hops off its victim and glues itself back to Viola's side.

The silence is broken as some of the guards tend to their fallen comrades. She sees relief on several faces when they realise the prone figures are merely sleeping. Understanding flits across the leader's visage, and he meets her gaze. A weight lifts off her shoulders when he bows his head.

No hard feelings? A small smile tugs at her lips.

It doesn't take long for the whole group to fall into ranks and march from the hall. Once the sound of their boots has faded and no longer tremors through the ground, the empress turns to Viola.

"You want to talk. Well, come, let us speak in my chambers." She whirls and is out the side door into the south wing before Viola can take her first step.

I am a changed person. Viola pulls herself to her full height and squares her shoulders. *I do not need to fall into the old patterns. Mother has not changed, but that does not mean these altercations have to stay on her terms.*

Interlude

Monadir grinds his teeth together. Yet another day of fruitless searching has passed. It's been months since he reached Abhainn, but he can't find any sign of the storyteller or her apprentice. Apart from the certainty glowing in his abdomen, insisting they're both alive despite the carnage he witnessed outside Baile, there's nothing. No proof they are indeed alive. Has his intuition failed him?

He hasn't even been able to find another storyteller here. If only Natesari could have remembered the name of the new teacher the boy was supposed to find in this city. He sighs, rubbing a hand over his eyes. Everything seems fruitless. His whole life—pointless. The news of his father's death has weighed heavily on him. His fingers find their way to the locket resting just below the notch at his throat. The cool metal brings to life the dreams he had in his youth; bygone wishes and desires dance in his mind.

With a grunt, Monadir turns away from the alley his feet have taken him to. All his dreams are ashes, and now even his life is on the line. If he can't bring the storyteller to the empress, he knows execution or exile will be his future. He has failed—not only himself but also his family. A life of disappointment is all he's ever known.

Monadir sighs. There's nothing for it. He'll have to go back to Baile and set out for Haldria. A return with his tail tucked between his legs. He won't be able to look the empress in the eye. Then again, the whole purpose of redeeming himself and bringing his father back to court has run like sand through his fingers. Monadir is a failure. Then again, it's the truth. He must accept it. There's no longer any point in continuing this chase.

Turning, he makes his way down one street and then another. Although he's generally heading back towards his quarters near the river, he's aimless and pays little attention to where his feet are taking him.

A crowd has gathered in a small plaza squeezed on all sides by stately villas. There's a fountain at its centre, and the gathered people are focused on something at the base of the water feature. Monadir hears strains of music. Where he'd normally stay away from such displays, something draws the imperial hunter closer. His heart yearns for something, and perhaps this street musician can provide the patch to soothe his invisible wounds.

Every note seems to call to him. It's as if the musician has cast a line to Monadir's heart and is reeling him in. Each step matches every note. The instrument is some stringed thing he doesn't know the name for. The performer, a youth of perhaps fourteen summers. Relentless, the boy's voice and the nimbleness of his fingers draw Monadir forwards until he stands right before the child.

When the song comes to an end, the boy looks up. His eyes come alight when he sees Monadir, and a smile brightens his young face. "You're finally here. Good. It's time we talked, you and I."

PART II
A DREAM BECOMES DESTINY

Chapter Ten

"You wanted to talk, did you?" The empress' voice is smug. Hazel eyes glitter as she turns them to Viola, who is left to stand while her mother settles into a high-backed upholstered velvet chair. The gold upholstery brings out a yellow stripe midway down the skirt of the gown the empress wears. Viola takes in the white long-sleeved bodice and top half of the A-line skirt, which transitions from the yellow strip through several shades of red and then blue. In this empire where everything is structured and symbolically marked, the vibrant, multi-coloured gown is a visual sign of sovereignty. All others in The Capital are forced to wear single colours to denote their station in life: white for imperial officials, purple for the imperial palace's servants, red for the guard—

Viola knows the time to speak hasn't yet come. She takes the opportunity to look more closely at her mother. Beyond the regal bearing, posturing, and haughty flaunting of imperial position and power is a woman of advanced age. It takes a moment for Viola to do the arithmetic in her head. The empress is eighty-four now, her eighty-fifth name day fast approaching. She sits, sizing up Viola as she relaxes slightly into the chair's support. Her right arm comes to rest along the carved frame of the seat, and Viola's attention is drawn to the sinuous and scaled body of a dragon etched into the wood.

The sight brings Jo's faith into stark contrast with the claims of the imperial family—descended from dragons, right to rule by virtue of divinity. Jo's Mother-Father deity is an all-encompassing concept that focuses on love and the worthiness of all. Viola has been vexed by his beliefs and the power of his faith when faced with the controlling and divisive religion of the empire that raises the few above the many and imposes faith as an act of imperial domination. She finds that what Jo taught her resonates more. Viola does not believe in dragons. She's never once accepted the divinity of her line. The imperial family is human and as flawed as any other. However, treating others with dignity, speaking the truth and taking responsibility for oneself and one's own actions—that's something she can get behind. Maybe there's something to this belief system called *The Way*?

The insight sends Viola reeling. How can this be? For more than thirty years, she's been a confirmed non-believer, a denier of all faith. And yet here she stands facing her mother, the head of the Dragon Order and ruler over all life in the thirteen spheres, and Viola sees only a diminished being clinging to importance as her human body fails her.

Viola's heart goes out to her mother, and the response surprises her. She has never felt compassion for the empress, who is overbearing and controlling. Even now, as her mother allows the silence to draw out between them, Viola knows it's all carefully calculated. The empress does not want her to speak. She wants the wayward daughter to think over her transgressions, cower, and eventually grovel.

Well, I have no intention of doing anything of the sort.

Folding her arms, Viola lifts her chin. "Yes, Mother. We need to talk. It is time we work through our differences and live with some semblance of peace. Neither of us is getting any younger, and there is no point in fighting. I am tired of running, as I am sure you must be weary of the failed chase. I have seen much over the annums I have spent travelling, not least the incident from today, indicating things are not at all well in this megalithic bureaucratic structure that is the Haldrian Empire. I fear if you do not make a shift in your approach, this legacy of our ancestors will crumble to dust within your lifetime."

The empress' eyes flash. It's lightning Viola has come to associate with the thunder of a dressing down, and she's not disappointed.

"So typical of you, Isperia. You always think you know better. Have you ever stopped to think that the greatest minds in this empire are at work every day to deal with the endless difficulties The Capital and the colonies face?" The empress leans forwards. "Have you considered the illustrious pedigree behind every decree and imperial strategy? How dare you claim to have greater insights than the combined forces of tradition and the council. The Haldrian Empire has thrived for centuries, and it will continue to do so long after *you* are dust."

Returning to her more relaxed position, her excellency purses her lips while Viola's emotions run rampant. She knows she must fight for what she believes in. She can't remain as she was in her youth, accepting the belittling words her mother throws at her. She must pull herself together and keep on arguing until she manages to get it all out. *Speak the truth as you know it.* The ordinance of Jo's religion seems most fitting here.

Viola's hands move as she speaks. "How often do these experts leave The Capital to see what is happening on the other planets? And with the way you are about things that do not suit you, is there any chance they would honestly tell the truth if it turns out to be less than favourable? I highly doubt it. You have a tendency to exile those who displease you. What did Natesari do to be relegated to overseer in Baile?"

The empress laughs, the sound shrill and devoid of any true mirth. "Poor pigeon, you are so simple-minded."

Viola bristles. This is the first sign of a deflection. She meets her mother's gaze and insists, "What gets an imperial kicked out of the palace and relegated to the most boring backwater of the empire?"

The empress waves her off. "Oh, she wanted an unsuitable match and refused to listen to reason."

"So you exiled her?" Viola has to take a deep breath not to let this moment disintegrate into a screaming match. Her mind conjures up their last altercation when she'd decided to leave and never come back. It started out something like this.

Well, Viola has to hold firm to her desire to work through this no matter how trying her mother is. She sets aside thoughts of her cousin. There is nothing to be done about Natesari's situation for the moment.

"Mother, there is unrest in Téarman, particularly in the outlying areas. There was more than talk of open rebellion. I witnessed very strong signs of malcontent with the empire and its way of running things on the planet. That is not all. Mshrali is a cesspit overrun with blight. More and more people succumb every week. Slavery is rampant in Midnare, particularly the kobold population, even though such practices have been outlawed since the times of Emperor Runveli—"

"Oh, pish posh. You are being melodramatic. Things are fine in the colonies; what is a little sickness here or there? It is how things are. You have lived a sheltered life; perhaps I should have expected more from you as a child. And clearly, your education was lacking."

Viola sucks air into her lungs. How is she going to remain calm through this? What can she say to impress upon her mother the importance of all the things she's seen? She tries to steady her voice when she bites out, "The blight in Mshrali is not some harmless disease. I was there only a few moons ago, and the dust bowl is abandoned. Hundreds of settlements have been relinquished in the attempts to flee the blight."

The empress' fingers drum on the dragon's head carved into the armrest of her chair. "You are mistaken, Isperia. And I resent that you surmise I am oblivious to such things. I do, in fact, know what is going on. I have read the reports about this blight thing. It is localised and is not causing any real harm. The people have moved, yes. But there is nothing more to it. The experts say we need not worry. Stop being so melodramatic."

"I am trying to impress upon you the real state of things. You have not seen what the blight does to people—or to animals, for that matter. It corrupts everything it touches, even the plants. If it continues to spread, the whole continent, possibly even the planet—"

"Isperia," the empress cuts in. "You do not know what you are talking about. You are no expert. This is simply how life is. There are hardships that cannot be avoided. Besides, the mines are what make that particular planet important, and those are working fine. There is no sign of this blight there. It is the way of things. Some people die." She shrugs. "You need to grow up and deal with it."

Viola's hands curl into fists, and she takes several calming breaths before she dares respond. "Mother, I am no longer twenty. I am almost fifty. I have been out in the furthest reaches of the empire for close on thirty years. In that time, you have been sheltered while I have seen and heard things that would make you weep. This empire is not a pleasant place, especially not for those in the working classes. Conditions are abysmal. I was not so sheltered here that I did not suspect some of what I eventually encountered on my travels. The thing is, the reality is far worse."

Memories fill her mind, and she can't suppress a shudder. She can almost see them—meerkats with luminous eyes and purple snouts drawn back to bare foam-flecked teeth. The sinuous dance of death in a forest filled with screams. The stench of burning flesh as the glow of buzzing fireflies fills her vision. Absent-mindedly, Viola brushes a hand over her arm and runs her fingers along the smooth patches of scarred skin.

She has to blink to clear her vision. Her brow puckers at a thought, and she meets her mother's gaze once more. "And do not dare claim my education was subpar! I had the very best, and you know it—you ensured it by selecting the tutors. If the best education in the thirteen spheres is not good enough for you, then I am not surprised I did not match your expectations. " She brushes a hand through her short hair. It's windswept and tangled, not ideal for making a good impression, and she considers the contrast to her mother's hair, which is piled atop her head, although it's thinned over the years. "Can you come down from your high tower for just one moment and consider what I am trying to tell you. I care deeply about this empire and all the people in it. But terrible things are happening, and I feel there is more to be done from The Capital."

"Ah, so you have come here to tell me I am superfluous because you know better how to run this empire. So, shall I abdicate to you then, Miss High and Mighty?" She leans forwards again, her eyes glittering, daring Viola to make another false move.

Viola throws up her hands. "That is not what I said. You are interpreting my words to suit you instead of listening to what I am saying. Besides, I cannot take over the throne from you. Rumour has it I am either insane and locked up in an institution, or dead."

"That, Isperia, is entirely your fault." The empress' voice rises. "You should not have run off. I had no other choice."

"I respectfully disagree, Mother." With her last remaining nerve, Viola clings to her daughterly duty to remain civil. "No one forced you to lie about my whereabouts or state of being. You chose to do that. You could have told the truth—"

"And become the laughingstock of the entire empire? You do not seem to understand the consequences of your actions."

Viola's gut wrenches. She feels the anger surging through her, and she squeezes her eyes shut to keep the pressure of her boiling point under control. She forces her reply through her teeth. "I most certainly did not expect the consequences to be twenty-eight annums of running from your dragon-cursed hunters. Did you ever think about how that has made me feel? Hunted like a rabbit without pause or safe harbour."

"Ah, you and your feelings," the empress interjects. "Have you ever thought about what all of this has done to me?" Her right hand comes to rest on her chest, and she looks up to the heavens. After a brief silence, the empress shifts to focus her gaze on Viola once more. "As for those hunters, much good they did me." She waves a hand in dismissal. "They cost me a fortune and still could not apprehend you."

"What you do not seem to realise is that your decision to send them after me is what has kept me from coming back all this time. If you had just given me the time to see the empire and explore a little, find my feet, and settle my thoughts, I would have been back soon enough. I know you have always needed to be in control, but I am a human being, and all your clinging is suffocating. Even now, I feel as if I cannot breathe—"

The empress rolls her eyes and cuts Viola off. "You keep bringing this back to you. You are aware you are not all-important?"

The pressure build-up is ready to explode. Viola clenches her fists and grinds her teeth together to stop. In the past, this would have been the moment she gave up and ran off to the garden to cool off. Twenty-eight years ago, it was the moment she flitted to her room, grabbed her packed things and left, missing her assignation with Eryk and finding her own way onto the ship that took her away from The Capital and Haldria. She could leave once more. There's nothing to keep her here, and trying to talk to her mother has proven pointless. As Viola sucks air into her lungs and contemplates the possibility of grabbing Motoko and flitting away from the palace, a gentle voice counters the aggressive beating of her heart. *If I give up now, I will gain nothing.*

She takes a steadying breath. The silence between them is broken by a thunderous rumble from her belly. She looks down and feels a moment of shame, but the small voice counters, *If I am hungry, I cannot reach a satisfactory conclusion to this altercation.*

She meets her mother's gaze, measure for measure. "You know, Mother, perhaps I should freshen up and eat something before we continue this—it is not really a discussion, is it? Well, I cannot remain calm while hungry and tired from travelling. Let us continue later, maybe even over a meal."

The empress grimaces. "It is the most sensible thing you have said so far. Go. The staff will be instructed to prepare your former rooms. The fleabag will be escorted to the kennels."

Viola bites back a sharp retort and forces herself to remain civil. "I shall take care of Motoko. He saved my life, and I intend to treat him with the respect he deserves."

The empress frowns but doesn't say anything as she rises, smoothing her skirt at the same time. She turns and heads into an adjoining chamber. From the doorway, the empress commands, "We shall take supper together. I shall send someone for you."

Chapter Eleven

"Her Imperial Highness awaits, High Lady Isperia," the purple-robed attendant says from the doorway.

Viola looks up, her hands still caressing the soft fur of Motoko's head. It's pristine white now after the bath the head of household insisted on. It was the only way Viola could convince the woman to allow her to keep Motoko in her chambers. The dog comes to his feet at the same time Viola does.

She shakes her head. "No, Motoko. Please stay." Viola points at the soft carpet by the leather seat she's vacated. The dog whines. "She will not allow you into the dining hall. It would be better if you stayed here." She walks across wood flooring polished to a glass-like sheen on her way to the door, where the attendant steps aside and bows as Viola passes.

"Thank you," she murmurs and is surprised to see the young woman's eyes widen.

A shiver tingles up Viola's spine. It's strange to be back in these rooms with the sensation of nothing having changed, even though the people are almost all different, and she's become another person entirely. She glances down at the dress she's been made to wear. The bright lemon yellow of the off-the-shoulder top transitions into a white skirt. The sight of her bare arms brings a scowl to her face. They're wiry and hard, her skin aged in the heat of years spent in the sun and wind. She doesn't really want it on display. Her mother will likely have something to say about it. Then again, she is strong and has proven hardy. *That is something to be grateful for.*

Walking down the corridor with its ornate mirrors and ancient paintings draws Viola back into memories of her childhood. She raced through these halls with her cousins and some of the children of lesser nobles. Whenever they were caught, she received the worst scolding of all. *A high lady should be above such things.*

She passes a carved wooden table with an ornate blue and white vase balanced on top. There isn't a speck of dust anywhere to be seen, and Viola wonders for the first time in her life how much work it must take to keep clean this immense palace with its four separate wings.

Out of the corner of her eye, Viola notices the attendant from earlier walking behind her. The woman is quite young, but her head is held high, and there's pride in the set of her features. What is it like working in this place? Viola never gave it much thought before. Of course, the prestige of working in the imperial palace of an intergalactic empire is through the roof—or through the dome, Viola reminds herself. Now she's back in this place that features the most lauded architectural element in the entire solar system, she will, no doubt, be expected to revert back to the imperial family's expressions.

To the dried-up seas with them and their expectations!

But what is it really like to work in this place with imperials who ignore the hard work done and mostly show disdain for those who serve? How does one ask such questions? As Viola Alerion, it's simple to show interest and learn about people, but now she's back into her role as Isperia, and that complicates matters. The intricate lattice of expectations tightens its web around her being, stifling who she is, and the doubts of her youth are back to plague her.

Viola takes a deep breath. This is not why she's here. The intrigues of the court and posturing of the imperials are not what she's after. With everything she's experienced, she knows it is not the life she wants. *But I do have unfinished business. If I do not work things out with Mother, I will not be able to achieve what I long for. I am stuck and must open myself to the possibility of something better.*

One Imperial Guard stands at the arched entrance to what has always been the imperial family's private dining hall. A tremor runs through Viola at the sight of the red-clad man standing beside the doorway with his arms crossed and a collapsed staff hooked onto a loop at the waist of his trousers. The man's eyes are trained on the tips of his black boots. Viola hesitates. For a moment, the memories of the battle fought earlier in the day spill through her and mingle with the tableau of carnage she witnessed outside Baile when this guard's fellows perished. However, the guard ignores her presence, and Viola forces herself to focus on the here and now. She steps through the doorway. Inhale. Exhale.

The imperial family's dining hall is still decorated with soft white carpet underfoot and a massive gold-inlay mahogany table with space for fifty people gleams in the light of a glittering chandelier. The sideboard of cherry wood with a mother-of-pearl top remains unchanged. More than anything Viola has seen since returning to the palace, this view sucks her back into the past with meals spent surrounded by her mother's siblings and their children.

The hubbub of past memories fades away and brings into stark contrast the one change that has occurred. Instead of fifty people sitting around this table, laughing and talking, sending jibes at each other with good humour, there's silence. Only the empress sits, facing the doorway. She isn't even in the place familiar to Viola, at the head of the table. Now, the old woman shrinks into her gigantic chair placed at the centre of its length. The silence is broken only by a knife scraping over the empress' gilded plate. The air is thick with the mouth-watering aroma of baked fish.

Viola gazes at the empty chairs surrounding her mother. Where is everyone? What has happened to the people who are supposed to populate this palace? She remembers hearing about her uncle's passing a few years ago, but surely she'd have heard if more of the imperial family had passed away. Natesari is exiled in Baile, most likely for some trivial transgression. Were her parents affected too? What of the empress' other sister and brothers?

"Do not just stand there." The empress waves her fork before piercing a piece of whiteness from her plate. "Sit." For the briefest of moments, the fork points to the seat opposite before it disappears into the empress' mouth.

Purple robes swirl as the attendant steps up to the chair and pulls it out. Viola wants to protest, but seeing the sharpness in her mother's gaze, she settles into the seat and smooths the shiny white fabric of her skirt.

"Thank you," she murmurs to the man as he steps away from the chair.

Viola's fingers glide over the soft fabric, and she becomes aware of several servants hovering around the table. All are ignored by the empress. She scrutinises Viola, whose stomach growls and brings Viola's attention back to the table. A platter graced with an arm-length fish sits between her and the empress.

Another swish of purple in her peripheral vision draws

Viola's eyes to a thin man who steps up on her right. He bows, and she notices he isn't wearing the robes common to the other household staff but rather the tight-fitting suit of the dining staff. With dexterity, the man wields a golden knife and triangular lifter, and within moments, a steaming slice of fish rests upon the plate in front of Viola. Before she can think, he's replaced the serving cutlery and picks up a long oval bowl of nasi grains. He raises a heaped spoonful of the steaming grains and gives Viola a pointed look. She nods, accepting the helping.

As the server steps back, the empress orders, "Eat."

There's a pitcher of sauce in front of Viola, and she douses her plate with it. It's been years since she had a meal like this one. The first forkful is a delight. Warm food and the perfect blending of the firm fishiness with creamy sauce and soft grain disintegrate between her teeth. Her taste buds rejoice, and even before she's swallowed, the next mouthful is already balanced on her fork.

They eat in silence, and Viola wonders how she's going to broach the subject for this dinner without the rest of her family present. The empress focuses on her food, from which she seems to take great pleasure; although the few times Viola catches her mother's eye, there's also something grim to the satisfaction.

What do you say to your mother at dinner for the first time in almost thirty years? She chooses to sustain the silence, waiting to see if her mother will break it.

When Viola has scraped her plate clean, the server steps up beside her and whisks away the crockery, replacing it with a shallow gilded bowl. She again thanks him but earns a lightning flash of displeasure in her mother's eyes. With a gulp, Viola turns to study the water lily emblem gracing the centre of the dish in front of her. Now she remembers to look, it's everywhere: in the gold inlay on the edge of the tabletop, in the glittering gems dripping from the chandelier, on the backs of the upholstered chairs, even embroidered on the sleeves of the server's jacket. She hasn't seen a single water lily emblem in years, not even in her cousin's ambassadorial palace in Téarman.

It is strange to think the actual people of this empire have no visual reminders of their allegiance to it, while here, where it is least needed, the symbol is everywhere.

Viola is jolted out of her thoughts when a white and blue ceramic tureen, complete with a water lily lid, materialises between her and the empress. She marvels at how she never noticed the subtle uses of magic in the daily rituals here at the palace. Thinking back on her childhood, every mealtime the food miraculously appeared like this, and yet she's never taken note of it, let alone questioned it.

The server is by her side in an instant and bows before lifting the covering. A wall of fragrant steam makes Viola's mouth water, and although she's quite satisfied with the fish course she's just eaten, she's still hungry enough to have this too.

While the empress is being served by her personal server, whom she ignores, Viola breathes in the smells. The crispness of the herbs used takes her back to the last time she ate stew in a run-down inn at the edges of Mshrali's dust bowl. Her apprentice was so thin back then, and he pretty much inhaled his serving.

There is so much Mother cannot see from here. The Capital is oblivious to the plight of the colonies.

The empress clears her throat, and Viola looks up to meet her mother's gaze. With a wave of her hand, the empress sends away the serving people and weaves her fingers together. "So, now that you have finished gallivanting and come to your senses, are you ready to settle down and have a family? You are supposed to provide an heir, after all." She gives Viola a pointed look, judgement dripping from her gaze as she appraises her daughter's sun-darkened arms and the lines on her face.

"No, Mother," Viola keeps her chin up. She's not going to let her mother do as she always does. "That is most definitely not the reason I chose to return to The Capital."

Eyes narrowed, the empress asserts, "You cannot choose to be childfree." She shakes her head, pitying. "Childless women are incomplete, especially when it is your duty to see to the continuation of this illustrious line."

"I beg to differ. I have made my peace; I am past such things. My cycle was irregular at best with all the stress of being on the run, but even so, things dried up completely almost a decade ago."

"Oh, nonsense. These days, with the right treatment, that is totally irrelevant."

"It is relevant. The biological facts of my existence are what they are. I am not going to try to force your will on my body against my better judgement."

"Really, Isperia." The empress throws up her hands. "There is no such thing as biological *facts*, as you call them. Through science, we have proven time and time again that there are ways around the failings of the body. A little nip here and a tweak there, and I can guarantee you, you will be in full working order once more. Just look at me," she waves a hand. "Almost eighty-five, in perfect health, and I can eat as much as I want because, thanks to the Perfect Weight pills," she gestures to a small silver box beside her place, "I do not gain even an ounce."

Viola shakes her head. She has to force down the disbelief fountaining inside her. "It is my body, and I get to decide what

I do with it," She folds her arms in front of her chest. "And there is no way I am going to suffer such indignity to my being. I do not live with the hubris of believing I can control everything, and I most certainly have no wish to exert such shortsighted manipulation over my body. You also do not have the right even to suggest it."

"But what about an heir, Isperia? The empire needs an heir."

Sucking in a breath, Viola leans slightly forwards, "You will have to find one from somewhere else." She hopes her eyes convey the sincerity of her words. "Pick one of my cousins or their children. You have potential heirs aplenty."

"Bah! Not one of them would suit. Besides, they cannot maintain *my* bloodline."

"Well, you should have given me the siblings I asked for when I was a child."

"How can you?" the empress draws a hand to her clavicle. "I provided you *everything*."

Viola gives her head a shake. "You did not. And by refusing me my deepest desire—to learn the art of storytelling—you ended up pushing me away, and I was left with nothing but myself." The empress clears her throat, but Viola refuses to let her interrupt. "Your decisions fuelled my experiences. You refused to listen to me and never gave me any slack on the leash you wanted to control. I am not here to fight about the past, Mother. I would like to see if there is some way we can reconcile. I will not debase myself or go against my personal wishes, but I am willing to spend time with you and try to help resolve the things I have seen. I am here because of what I have experienced of the empire and to help bring changes necessary for the—"

"Do not start with that again, Isperia. There is nothing wrong with the colonies. The whole empire is running smoothly. You are inventing drama to get into my good graces."

Viola throws her hands up in defeat. "There is no point in letting the food get cold over this. Let us agree that we disagree on most things and see what we can work with."

The empress purses her lips but turns her attention to the food on her plate. She ignores Viola for the rest of the meal.

The food thickens in Viola's mouth and dries into a lump, difficult to swallow. All she can think of is the simple fare of life on the road. Pushing aside her half-eaten stew, she glances across the table. Her mother is still enjoying her meal, and Viola wonders at how thin the empress is when she consumes so much. *She did mention she takes pills to stop putting on the weight.* Viola's stomach is a balloon protesting the stretch of the quantity and richness of the food. She dabs her lips, the soft fabric of the serviette reminding her of the comforts she could return to if she decides to stay. Then again, with the constant head-butting she seems to face with her mother, this might not be the right idea after all. The thought of the Grand Imperial Library pops into Viola's head as she tries to ignore the sound of the empress slurping up the remaining sauce in her bowl. *I want to share stories and stay in one location. That library is the perfect place to do so.*

The empress pats the excess liquid from her lips, and the gold water lily embroidered on the serviette catches Viola's eye. She squares her shoulders, ready for whatever her mother chooses to throw at her next. If she can just work her way through the labyrinth of frustration and irritation she knows awaits her, Viola hopes she can find a way to get an appointment at the library. This recently-seeded dream is something she wants; every fibre in her body hums with the yearning for it. But how to achieve it?

When you ask 'how', you can only think from within your under-

standing in the now, Jo's words echo in her thoughts. She strains to catch the memory. What else did he say? *Can you let go of the how? Just because I know it works.*

Things are working out well enough as it is, Viola realises. Although her own plans for how she'd get through to meet her mother didn't work out at all, here she is, sitting at the imperial family's dining table. Somehow, she's going to get what she wants. The sense of certainty lifts the weight of doubt off her shoulders. *I can have this.*

"You are remarkably quiet, Isperia." The empress tosses her crumpled serviette into the bowl and lifts a golden bell.

Viola shrugs. "I am thinking."

The empress' eyebrows climb into her hairline.

"You do not believe I am capable of it?" Viola can't contain the resentment that creeps into her tone.

"Well," the empress shifts in her chair as the serving staff work their way through the task of clearing up much as an army of ants would void a tree of its leaves, "You have not shown a predisposition for rationality. All your previous decisions have been fuelled by impulse."

The last of the servers pushes a small gilded tray towards the empress and bows. Viola notices there's still one wine goblet left before her mother, who dismisses the man with a flick of her hand and draws the item in front of her. Atop the tray, which is no bigger than the flat of Viola's hand, is the small, silver-plated pill box the empress drew Viola's attention to earlier. The empress flicks it open to reveal a little tablet. She pops it into her mouth and takes a sip from her goblet. "So, why have you returned?"

"I have come to clear the air between us and to find a solution to our conflict."

"And why should I welcome you back with open arms? You have shirked your duty, cost me dearly, and now you dance back in here without a care in the world and expect everything to be the same."

"No, mother. You misunderstand. I am not here to return to my life as Isperia. I am not she. I have been Viola Alerion for so long; that is who I have become. I cannot shrug her off as one would a coat. I wished to speak with you because you are my mother. It is not right that we should be at odds for so long over a disagreement. Time waits for no one, and I feel it is important we stop our conflict and find a solution to our differences. I have no desire to be your heir; I never have. There was no need for that with your long life expectancy. The tradition is for a grandchild or great-grandchild to take up the throne. Although any chance I might have had of having a family is gone, I have come to realise it is better to follow the purpose we are meant to achieve than to force a duty."

"What nonsense is this, Isperia?" The empress takes another sip from her wine. "Is this some ploy to seem more suited to the throne?" She narrows her eyes. "You know, I thought I had deciphered your intentions. But you make little sense. I fear you have indeed gone mad."

Viola laughs. "You can see with your own eyes that I am sane. Why is it so hard for you to understand that I simply want something beyond what you have envisioned for me? I am not you, Mother. I require other things to be happy."

"Whoever said anything about happiness? And what of your duty?"

"Mother, you are going in circles here. First, you claim I am no good for the throne, even saying I am mad. And in the next breath, you are trying to force it on me as a duty. I am not the right person to run this empire, but I do know I have a part to play in helping it become what it could be. There is so much potential in this Haldrian Empire. It is being smothered, though. The system is exerting so much control it is suffocating everything that is good and beautiful. You are surrounded by wondrous things, Mother. I fear you have lost sight of the situation beyond your palace walls."

"There is no need to be patronising, Isperia. And you misunderstand me. Your duty is not to sit on the throne but to provide an heir. That, dearest, is your highest purpose." The tone makes Viola sit up.

Who is being patronising? She bites back her retort with a sigh. How can she make her mother see the truth of anything? Her mouth has grown dry, and licking her lips doesn't seem to help. There's nothing for it. Viola has come this far; she must try to clarify her point and break through the walls built around her mother's mind.

"You have to let go, Mother. Loosen your grip. The Empire is suffocating its people. Living, breathing beings need freedom to create. They become unproductive when you smother them. Everything is forced—rigid. This is a failure of the system, but I fear you have become wilfully blind to it. If you could only allow the people the space to achieve their potential. Let them breathe. Give this Haldrian Empire, great pinnacle of all societies known throughout the universe, the chance to foster change and bring about a golden age of possibility."

Viola meets her mother's gaze and tries to impart the importance of her words. "Our ancestors built this empire on the backs of slaves, and now that it stretches across the known universe, it continues to suck the life out of everything. But it does not have to be this way. The garden has been built; now it requires care and nurture so it can blossom. Do not force your subjects to wither simply for living in your shadow. You, ruler of the thirteen spheres and dragon-blessed lady of the stars, can achieve this, and if you did, it could all be beautiful."

Viola shifts and is surprised her mother sits quietly. Now,

perhaps, is her chance to reach through the barrier between them. "Mother, let me share with you what I experienced, what I have seen."

The empress rises, a footman rushing over to pull her chair out and hand her the cane. "First, let us retire to somewhere more comfortable. And then, by all means, regale me with your silly tales."

The next morning, Viola wakes as the heavy drapes are drawn. She sits up with a start. Disorientation tugs at her senses; she's herself, forty-eight-year-old Viola Alerion, but here she sits in the soft lilac room of teenage Isperia. It's like waking up in a dream—well, more of a nightmare.

"The empress requests your presence at your earliest convenience, High Lady."

Viola swings her legs over the side of the bed. Above her, the ceiling catches her eye. How long has it been since she last studied the painting there? Tilting her head, Viola absorbs the sight: a depiction of The Capital along one side of the space, the golden dome of the palace prominent. Beside it, looking upon the resplendent city, is her ancestor, the first emperor. He gestures grandly towards his creation. Behind him rears a mighty dragon; one claw is extended, and from it flows a beam of golden light. She's always been told it's blessing the vision of Pendzach, the first emperor. They say he was descended from dragons.

She scoffs. She doesn't have time to ponder imperial propaganda. It was late when she and her mother finished talking. Being able to share her experiences was cathartic, possibly even therapeutic. Even as the thought nudges her mind, Viola has to admit she wasn't as honest as she ought to have been. She held back the account of the Leviathan, for one thing. A shudder spiders up her spine. There are good reasons for suppressing those memories. She doesn't feel strong enough to confront them under the scrutiny of another, most especially not her mother.

Now she's been summoned again. Time to see if she's been able to sway the empress and if there's any chance of finding her way into that beautiful library. Viola swallows and clenches her eyes shut. *I can achieve this even if I do not know how.*

She glances around the room and sees her clothes from the day before stacked on the dresser in a neatly-folded pile. Her boots stand beneath the dressing table—polished. It doesn't take Viola long to get ready. She's sitting at the dresser and pulling on her second boot when a bark sounds from the other side of the door. Even as Viola wonders how Motoko got out, the barrier is pushed open and the dog bounds in, yipping happily.

The same servant from earlier says, "I took it out to do its business." Her face screws up in a grimace.

"Thank you. I appreciate it." Distaste turns to surprise, and Viola smiles at the change. She strokes the dog's head and realises he must be hungry. Meeting the serving woman's gaze, Viola adds, "I fear I must impose on you for further assistance. Could you please refill Motoko's bowls with food and water too?"

"Yes, that can be arranged, Imperial Highness."

Viola bites back a grumpy retort. She's never liked the titles, but she knows the woman is only doing as she's told. "Thank you," she says and tries to smile. "Where might I find my mother?"

"The empress is in the solarium." She gestures at another

door to Viola's left. "I'll be off then to get that for your dog, High Lady."

"Thank you," Viola says to the flick of purple robes as the door clicks shut. Her gaze is drawn to the door leading directly to the solarium. She and her mother are the only two with rooms adjoining it. Coming to her feet, she heads out, but a whine behind her makes her look back.

"Stay, Motoko," she requests. Reproach shines from the dog's pale brown eyes. He protests with another whine. Viola shakes her head. "You will have more food soon. And you do not want to be near my mother, trust me. I will do everything I can to get us both out of here as soon as possible. This palace is not good for either of us."

The dog lets out a sigh and sinks onto the soft carpet.

"Good dog. I shall be back soon," she calls over her shoulder.

The wood floor of the solarium is in stark contrast to the carpet of her room. The glass dome is supported by curved wooden beams carved to look like dragons reaching into the sky. Viola is struck by the warmth in this room, and her eye is drawn to the garden stretching out beyond the glass doors.

The empress sits on another velvet upholstered chair. This one is a deep blue, which contrasts with the orange bodice transitioning into black skirt that the empress is wearing. She lounges on her seat, and Viola is surprised to see her mother so relaxed. The ramrod impression from the day before has melted away, and even her hair forms a loose frizzy halo around her head.

A servant steps in carrying a gilded tray and stops at a table beside the empress. With a soft *clink*, a steaming cup of kopi is placed within her reach. A second cup is placed beside Viola and she breathes in the fragrance. The scent sparks energy through her and she thanks the server.

"Good morning, Mother."

"Ah, Isperia. Come and sit."

A second seat faces the empress at an angle while also providing a view into the garden. Viola settles into it, and a second cup of the dark brew is placed on a table beside her. The steam sparks life into her system, and she takes a sip, careful not to scald her tongue. While the stimulant takes effect, Viola scrutinises her mother.

Although the empress sits with comfortable and relaxed grace, the tilt of her head shows she's not as serene as Viola first assumed. Concentration ploughs into the empress' brow, and Viola notices the glint of an earpiece. Memories of the endless reports she'd been made to listen to in her youth spring up in Viola's mind. She shifts to better see the greenery outside. *No need to bore myself before I have even started the day.*

She drinks in the beauty of the garden, and her mind wanders. The perfect hedges and tended bushes are lovely, but Viola's overwhelmed by memories of grand vistas and harsh wilderness. Jo looked for beauty in the unforgiving Dust Bowl of Mshrali. For the first time ever, Viola can actually see what he means. The desolation of the boy's home planet has a stunning quality to it, as does the intensity of the jungle on Téarman and many other places Viola visited. She wonders if she was able to impart any of that in her storytelling the evening before. Of all the listeners Viola has entertained over the past several decades, her mother proved the hardest to please. *It is as if she wishes to remain ignorant because that suits her or because it is how she has always done things. How do I get through to her?* If everything Viola shared the evening before could not sway the empress, then what might? *Mother wants control but also does not wish to lift a finger —she may pretend, but I think more than anything, she is comfortable with the way things are.* Viola knows the status quo suits her mother, who will therefore do nothing to create any lasting change.

The empress releases a huff, drawing Viola back to the moment. The furrow on her mother's forehead has deepened. Viola's stomach cramps, and she acknowledges the need for food. Almost as if her desire was heard, a swish of purple catches Viola's peripheral vision, and she looks up to see a server stride towards her.

"The empress does not take breakfast, but I can fetch you something if you'd like, High Lady."

Viola smiles. She finds it strange how much she's forgotten about life in the palace. Although unused to being served hand and foot, it's nice to have every whim resolved with such ease. "Thank you. It is very considerate of you. Something light, like toast, would be perfect."

The man bows and heads out to the main doorway of the solarium. Viola twists in her seat to watch him go and notices another servant standing by the same door. She's never considered how many people ensure the imperial palace runs as smoothly as it does.

Still the empress doesn't move, and Viola's eyes take in the oval room. She and her mother sit in a little nook created by the two chairs overlooking the garden. A short distance away, a set of three sofas does the same, but allowing for ten people to congregate comfortably. A third space is created around a dining table that seats six.

Viola's toast is served, and she moves over to the table. She makes light work of the breakfast, enjoying the satisfying crunch of toast and the sweet tang of jam. She ponders the fact. *Mother doesn't eat breakfast. She overeats at night and starves herself by day. Takes tablets to keep in shape. Definitely not the sort of life that is healthy and sustainable.* Her thoughts are cut off when the empress moves, and Viola wipes the last sticky remains of jam from her fingers.

"Ah, Natesari. What are we to do with you?" The empress shakes her head, the earpiece of her device now resting in her hands. Viola settles back into the chair across from her. Silence hovers between them as the older woman's gaze drifts out to soak in the fresh green of the garden.

Viola takes note of the deep lines etched into her mother's face and the heaviness of the purple beneath her eyes. The empress' bones stick out more noticeably in the light of day, and Viola wonders once again at the contrasts of her mother's vigour and the quantities of food and drink she consumed the night before, with this living skeleton overburdened with the cares of a galactic empire she desperately wants to keep the way it is.

The empress sighs and looks up. "It seems you were right, Isperia." Her shoulders sink into the quicksand of her thoughts, and she lapses into silence once more.

"Mother?" Viola scoots to the edge of her seat. "What is it, Mother?"

The empress startles back to the present. She sighs again, deeper. "The entire Red Guard in Baile has been devoured by some unnamed monster, and now a disease, never before seen, has brought chaos. Natesari has been forced to shut the city gates and has banned all vessels from docking. I cannot believe such upheaval and utter failure could befall the empire during my reign." She shakes her head.

Mention of the Red Guard flings Viola back into the past. Her mind fills with the heavy heat of the tropics, the sound of trees tearing and splintering under the weight of a monstrous body and the air vibrating with the screams of the dying. Her memory hits her with the scent of blood. It fills her nostrils, reminds her of the terror she felt surrounded by death and convinced of her own demise. This is what she glossed over last night. She couldn't bring herself to speak of what she'd witnessed—and survived.

Seeing her mother's diminished form, Viola knows it's time to share what she knows, but still, she hesitates. With elbows propped up against her knees, her chin falls into her hands. How do you speak of the very real existence of mythical beasts? How do you broach the fact that it's all your fault?

The sound of screams fills her head. The scent of iron lodges at the back of her throat. Viola swallows hard against the scratchiness of her throat and slides her face through her hands. Looking at the scuffed toes of her boots, she croaks, "It was a Leviathan—maybe *the* Leviathan. I do not know. But what I do know is that I should have died there too." She looks up and meets her mother's open-mouthed stare. "I was there, Mother. I saw those men ripped to pieces by a monstrous serpent bigger even than the tallest trees in that tropical forest. It snapped trunks like they were kindling, and it tore into the men hunting me. By all accounts, I should be dead, too, rotting on the rainforest floor. I had to use my magic to get out, and I nearly did not manage. I grabbed one of the hovercrafts they had abandoned in their search for me and fled while they died. I ought to have stayed. I should have faced that thing, or at the very least, drawn it away from the soldiers, but I cared more about my life than theirs." The outpouring of words lifts some of the weight of her guilt. It's an unburdening, and she suddenly realises how responsible she feels for all those deaths. She didn't admit it to herself, but now she's said it out loud, Viola knows it to be true. "It was my fault they all died."

The empress leans back into her seat; her eyes are still wide, but disbelief has shifted to curiosity. "What happened?"

Viola forces herself to relive everything from the moment

she escaped the Téarman Imperial Ambassador's palace until she was saved from the fireflies on the outskirts of Bryniau. For some reason she doesn't like to ponder, she holds back and does not mention her apprentice much. While she spoke freely of him to Maitri, she keeps his skills and whereabouts secret from her mother.

When Viola finishes her tale, the empress stares out the window once more. She takes a sip from her cup every now and then; it has been replaced with piping hot beverage at intervals. "And what of this disease, then?" the empress looks at Viola over the rim of her steaming cup.

Viola shrugs. "I left to see Maitri. I did not hear anything about any sickness. Mshrali is full of disease, but Téarman I had not heard of until you mentioned it."

The empress' brows plunge into a sharp V. "But how did you get here without going back to Baile?"

"Maitri gifted me her travelling stone." Viola wiggles her fingers, showing off the red gem glinting from its gold setting. "Granted, I must replenish it, as it is useless right now, but it is a most generous present." The empress' eyes glitter and Viola lets her hand fall back into her lap, so the trinket is no longer visible.

The flicker of greed vanishes from the empress' visage. "I am pleased it has been returned to its rightful owners. That gem should never have left our family."

Viola bites back a retort and focuses her attention on the information about Téarman. "If Natesari has shut down the docks in Baile, what will you do? That is one of the most important stop-over points on the interplanetary shipping lanes."

"I know that," the empress snaps, her frown deepening. The frustration melts away again on the next exhale. "I do not know what ought to be done. I am tired of it all. Perhaps it is time I passed it all on." Her eyes latch onto Viola.

"No, Mother," Viola waves her hands in front of her. "That is not happening. I shall gladly help you, but I am not cut out to be empress, especially not after you spread that rumour of madness."

"Oh, that?" The empress waves a hand dismissively. "The easiest thing to remedy. Medical treatment is so much more advanced now. We shall claim a miracle cure. The people would love that."

"But it is a lie, and recently I have found there is great virtue in sticking to the truth. I refuse to go along with any of this."

"Bah! Virtue is overrated. It does not get you anywhere."

"I have found the opposite to be true, and I shall stick to what little I have. My integrity is one of the things I refuse to part with."

"Pity," the empress sighs. "It would have been a good solution."

"No, Mother. That is a useless solution. I am not the right person to lead this empire. I would just as soon dissolve it and be done with it, reinstating autonomous rule on each of the thirteen spheres."

"Oh, Dragons! Why, in the name of Haldria and all that is good in this empire, would you ever do such a thing? It would bring chaos. Well, it is a blessing I am still in charge, then." The empress studies Viola for a moment as she sips her kopi once more. "But you do have great insights into the goings on —at least on the ground—from a local perspective—" the empress muses.

"Yes, that I do, Mother."

"You could join my council." With a *chink*, the empress sets down her cup onto its saucer. "That would give you a purpose and make your accumulated knowledge useful."

The empress leans forwards and rubs her hands together. Her mother's excitement gives Viola pause. *Would I like this?* Her immediate reaction is viscerally negative. Without a doubt, she wouldn't. It would be stifling all over again. She'd grin and bear it until she reached a breaking point once more, and then she'd be forced to leave again. *That is not what I am here to achieve.* Viola's mind settles on the idea she fomented the day before. Visions of the Imperial Grand Library fill her thoughts.

She meets her mother's gaze and does something she's never done before. "Mother, I feel that path would lead me—us—back to where we started. I shall likely feel suffocated by my duty and eventually run away again. At my age—well, at yours for that matter—I do not think that will be—no, I *know* it will become unbearable for me. I know myself well enough to see that clearly."

"Well then, what *am I* to do with you?"

Viola clenches her hand to stop her reaction to the tone. She takes a steadying breath and continues, "I would love to work in the library. The Imperial Grand Library is the centre of all knowledge in the Haldrian Empire. It is the source of everything known about the thirteen spheres. It could also become the epicentre of information within the empire." Viola tamps down on her excitement. It wouldn't do to alert her mother to how ardently she wants this. From experience, that has never served her. "It seemed a good opportunity to me, considering the rumours you spread. This way, no one outside the palace precinct would need to know that I am, indeed, your missing daughter. And perhaps I can serve you in a position there."

The empress considers, her fingers drumming against the fabric on the armrest of her chair. "I suppose," she says after a momentary pause. "I suppose it could do. Certainly, it would be less of a bother. Eyes and ears right where the knowledge is and with the power to disseminate—yes, I think it could do." The empress tilts her head and gives a surprised laugh. "It just so happens—" She meets Viola's gaze, eyebrows aiming towards her hairline. "Well, is this not a coincidence?" She chuckles again, her fingers flying over the holoscreen she's called up from her device.

Viola watches in silence. Her heart beats so fast she fears it might *thud* its way out of her chest. Coincidences are good. They're what Jo always reckons with. *Please, please, please let this be a coincidence in my favour.*

"Yes, here it is." The empress leans back in her seat as her eyes dart over the words she's called up. "The high archivist sent in a resignation three days ago. A family matter requires their full attention. There is no one suitable to replace them— but now you are here." The empress gestures towards Viola with a flick of her wrist. "You may lack all refinement or sense of womanliness, and I agree you do not suit for the weight of rulership—" She pauses, running her finger and thumb over her chin. "This is a better use for your skills. At least you are not a complete disgrace to our house."

Her fingers fly over the glowing projection before her while Viola bites back a barrage of retorts burning at the tip of her tongue. *Do not mess it up now. Let it simply sluice off. No point in a rash reply and the risk of losing this opportunity.*

The screen blinks out, and the empress gives a satisfied sigh. "There you have it, Isperia. You may report for duty at the Grand Imperial Library as soon as you are ready. You will be staying here at the palace, I presume?"

Viola grimaces and has to control herself to stop her head from shaking. "About that, Mother. I think it may be better if I find lodging suitable to my needs and Motoko's."

It's the empress' turn to pull a face. "Ah, yes. The dog.

Perhaps that is a good idea. I would not want the palace full of hairs and—the smell—well, you know—" She shrugs. "If you can find something, I shall gift it to you."

"Thank you, Mother. That is very generous." For the first time in her life, Viola finds she actually means it.

"It is, rather, is it not? Well, I feel in a generous mood today, Isperia. Make the most of it. What more can I do for my only daughter?"

Viola is on the verge of waving off the offer when a thought pops into her head. More than a thought, it's a familiar face. Could she? She meets her mother's gaze and gauges the empress' mood. Some measure of goodwill radiates from the empress, and Viola chooses to take the plunge. "Erm—since I have been away for so long—um—I have lost contact with most of the people I knew here. I was wondering if I might restore some of the acquaintances I have had in the past. Natesari, I know, is not here at present, but perhaps others are —like Eryk—"

Storm clouds descend upon the empress' face, and Viola's voice dwindles. *I did push it too far*. She prepares herself for the oncoming squall.

"I have never fathomed your strange ways, Isperia. What could you possibly want with the disgraced son of a minor noble? That whole family has not dared set foot in this palace in decades." She waves off the suggestion as if it were absurd. "But I suppose a family do, to reacquaint you with your cousins and welcome you back into the fold, would not go amiss. I shall have a ball arranged."

"Thank you. That would be lovely," Viola grits out and rises to hide her distaste at the thought. The last thing she would ever want to attend is another imperial ball, but saying so would be ungrateful. She holds her head up high and pulls her shoulders back. "I shall leave you then, Mother. I have taken up enough of your precious time and will present myself at the library as soon as possible. It is probably best to get this settled quickly."

"Run along then, Isperia."

With a tight smile, Viola takes a slight bow—no more than her head and shoulders inclined. "Blessings and prosperity to you, Mother." She astounds herself at how easily the formal greeting slips out of her. *I was well trained.* The thought almost makes her laugh.

A few steps later, she's through the door, ready to sink into a happy, exhausted heap, but she's bowled over by a furry mass. Bony legs push into her, and fur tickles its way up her nose. All she can hear are excited snuffles until something wet slithers over her neck. With a squeal, Viola pushes the weight off her.

"Enough, Motoko. Sit!" she exclaims, and then the laughter bubbles up inside her. She's stood up to her mother, achieved everything she'd hoped for when she walked into this palace the day before, and she even has a dog—one individual happy to see her, no matter what. With a contented exhale, Viola considers how perfectly everything is unfolding. *There might just be something to that apprentice and his infernal ramblings about faith.* The thought sends her into another fit of giggles, a weakness Motoko capitalises on as he pounces on her once more to cover her face in doggy kisses, and Viola feels the certainty well up inside her: she will take this dog wherever she goes. He is dear to her, and she will not be parted from him.

Chapter Twelve

"Y ou again?" The archivist's heels click over the smooth stone floor of the library, blue robes billowing around her figure. "I thought I'd made it clear that you and your mongrel aren't welcome here."

Viola looks up. The woman's eyes blaze as she marches forwards. Sensing Motoko's hackles rising, Viola steps between the dog and the oncoming archivist. "Something has come up, and I am now—"

The woman cuts her off. "I don't have time for this. I await the newly-appointed high archivist. Be on your way." She shoos Viola, giving the dog a pointed look.

"Ah, yes. You see—on that note—" Viola holds out the small device she was given when she exited the imperial palace. The purple-clad keykeeper had said it contained the relevant documentation for Viola's new appointment as well as a letter of credit in order to buy a house or apartment in the city.

Shock suspends the archivist, her arms falling to her sides, her jaw hanging open. Eyes wide, she moves her lips, but no sound emerges. She swallows and tries again. "*You're* the new high-archivist? How can this be? I— I was told—" The second archivist bites off the words clamouring in her mind. Her eyes widen even more, showing off a ring of white when she actually stops to take in Viola's brand new, scintillating blue outfit with gold stripes on the shoulders, sleeves and hem. The second archivist's shock brings to mind how strongly she must detest the dog for her to have overlooked the unmistakable outfit.

"As I was saying," Viola smiles. "Here are my papers. I look forward to working in this illustrious building and continuing my work on the histories of Haldria."

The second archivist takes the device, her gaze still glued to Viola. As if in a dream, she clicks on the projection button and reads the missive. Her eyes dart from the words in front of her to Viola and back again. "You— You're *the* Viola Alerion?"

Viola takes a bow and wishes she had her feathered hat on her. It would add so much flair to this moment. *Always focused on the stagecraft.* She bites back a chuckle. *I won't be needing so much of the dramatics anymore.* The thought is strangely satisfying. It's a part of her she doesn't mind moving away from, although it can be fun sometimes—especially in moments such as this.

"I would very much appreciate a tour of the building." Viola sweeps her hand around the hall. "And I will need to meet everyone who works here. Perhaps I could see what my predecessor has left behind in terms of work and focus? As I find my feet, I can see what I will be continuing and what will require delegating. And what do you dedicate your research to? I would love to hear about your work." The second archivist stares—she's a fish out of water. "I suppose it must all be quite a shock, and I apologise for the inconvenience," Viola continues. "But rest assured, I will not keep you long today. I must also find lodgings and will be dedicating the better part of the day towards that."

"Um— I, ah—" The second archivist shakes herself. "Of course you can have a tour of the building. I'm Nevona, by the way."

Much later, Viola concludes that the second archivist is actually quite a sympathetic person. Spending time with Nevona has given her a chance to see the woman's expertise in action, not only with visitors to the library but also with the workings of this centre for all information. The Imperial Grand Library is the depository of all documents relevant to the empire, whether from Haldria or any of its vassal planets and colonies. The sheer quantity of physical data stored in the building and its immense cellars is spectacular, and that's nothing when considering the data saved on the digital repositories.

The quantity of work the former high archivist has left uncompleted is staggering. Thankfully, the second archivist is willing to take on some of the drearier tasks, leaving Viola a chance to focus on getting her bearings. When Motoko whines from the corner of the office, her head is spinning with everything she needs to take into consideration. The dog is doing a little butt-wiggle on the floor. She hasn't taken him out since the morning. How long has she been here?

With a start, Viola glances through the glass walls of her new office towards the outside world, where the sun is high in the sky. She still has so much to do, and first priority is finding a patch of grass for the dog to do his business—a tall order in the city of glass and white plaster.

When she comes to her feet, Motoko does a little dance of joy before joining his shoulder to Viola's leg as if he were a magnet. "Right then, Motoko. Time to find us a home." She smiles as she pulls the flowing blue and gold cape—symbol of her status in this building—from her shoulders and drapes it over the chair she's just vacated. "It will need a garden, will it not?"

The answer she receives is a single, loud bark.

"Shush, Motoko. You are in a library. Besides, do not remind them you are here. They are not very fond of having you, but maybe in time, I shall convince them otherwise."

Nevona stops at the threshold. "Is there anything else I can do for you, High Archivist?" Viola notes the way the other woman's lips purse as her eyes land on Motoko, but she doesn't say anything.

"You would not happen to know of anyone selling a house with a garden, would you? I am looking for a suitable place where Motoko can be happy too, and he is used to being outdoors." Viola expects an unhelpful 'no', but the second archivist surprises her once more. The way she stops to think makes Viola wonder again about the difference in behaviour towards herself as a wayward, unkempt stranger versus being the high archivist and personal acquaintance of the empress. That's all the second archivist knows for the time being. Viola doesn't want to think about how Nevona would behave if she found out the truth of her identity.

"You know," the second archivist murmurs. "I think I might know someone. A friend of mine inherited a cottage from her parents a while ago. I'll have to ask her if she's managed to sell it. It's on the outskirts, so it would mean a bit of a commute to get here, but it's in a nice area and, indeed, has a garden."

"If it is still available, I would love to take a look," Viola encourages.

"I'll have to contact her. It could take a little while."

Nevona's tone switches to apologetic, and Viola nods. "That is quite understandable, Nevona. While you do that, is there anywhere nearby I could take Motoko to stretch his legs and do his business?"

The second archivist pulls a face as she looks at the dog. She glances up and shrugs, "There's a little park near the cathedral, but I doubt they'd be appreciative of the dog. No one really has them outside of their homes and the canine creches. It's very unusual to see an animal accompany a person out on the streets."

Some time later, Viola trudges along a paved lane on the outskirts of The Capital. She's accompanied by Nevona's friend, a young woman in her early twenties. They come around a bend in the lane, and a yellowing lawn opens up before them. It fronts a two-storey cottage hemmed in by leafless trees on all other sides. A dry stalk of ivy rambles upon the grey walls, and dried-out moss dots the steeply-inclined shingle roof. The rounded arch over the door is free from the ivy vines, while the windows would be shadowed by the overhanging plant if it had any leaves on it.

"It needs a little work," the young woman says. "The gardeners are due to come next Tsqali digh and fill up the pond." She bobs her head apologetically.

Viola is taken with the grey stone walls and the dark wood of the door. Dry sticks, indicating there was once shrubbery to her right, and a crooked stone on the step up to the doorway, all add something to the character of this place. It has been a home. It has a history, has been lived in, and she's floored by the feeling she knows this place. "It has character, and the overgrown look actually suits me well." *With some love and care, the plants will give it even more character.*

The owner unlocks the door and pushes. Nothing happens. She presses her shoulder against the wood, but still it doesn't give way. With a groan, she slams her side into the wood, and it falls open, sending the young woman careening through. She catches herself on the doorframe. "It's never been that stuck before. I can have it checked if you would like." The woman twists the hem of her blouse between her fingers.

Stepping through into the gloomy interior, Viola nods. "Yes, that might be a good idea." Her whole being lights up as she comes into the main room. Although it is furnished with garish synthetic fabrics and the counter around the kitchen area is stained with age, Viola can picture how it ought to look. It's exactly as she imagined on the ship, and somehow the appearance of the place has the familiarity of home with its potential for ivy tendrils hanging outside the windows and the late afternoon sunlight slanting in through glass doors that lead out into an unkempt slice of nature. This is *her* place. The certainty hums in her bones.

"It is perfect," Viola whispers, observing a little nook beside a staircase which leads up to the second floor. The hollow looks out over the back garden, and Viola can imagine a desk sitting there with a view of the outside world. She pulls back a bolt on the glass door and pushes it open with a screech of metal hinges.

Motoko gives a bark as he bounds out into the gathering dusk. Viola observes his frolicking. The dog definitely seems at ease here, and as Viola glances around her again, she can imagine the small changes necessary to make it hers.

"Are there any furnishings you would like to keep?" she asks the owner, particularly eyeing the hideous pink and burgundy sofa standing front and centre.

The woman lets her eyes roam over the living room and kitchen. She shakes her head as she gestures towards the stairs. With a nod, Viola follows her. There are two rooms and a bathroom. The slanting ceiling forces Viola to duck as she makes her way to the window of the first room. It looks out over the front of the house, a gable allowing her to stand a little more upright as she peers down below. When she turns, she catches sight of a bed to her right and a wardrobe to her left. The furniture isn't to her taste, but it's nothing she can't fix now she has the salary of an imperial official.

A cursory glance at the bathroom confirms it could do with some new tiling and perhaps more modern fittings. She washes her hands and smiles at the clean water coming from the spigot. It's warm too. Excitement tingles through her blood, but Viola still has much to check. She goes over everything, considering the window sills and skirting boards. On her way down the stairs, she stops on each step to examine just how safe this daily ascent and descent will be.

After her exhaustive examination is over, Viola feels she can let her tingling blood loose. The knowledge this is the place for her resonates within. A hint of doubt gnaws at the back of her mind, pointing out how smooth this search for a home has been. Too easy, in fact. Jo's presence surges inside her, though, almost as if he were right here with her. His smile radiates into her being, and Viola can almost hear him say, *How many cottages do you need?* Viola almost chuckles at the thought. It is true she only needs one, and after all the perfect coincidences she saw unfold around Jo, this seems less surprising.

Viola turns to the owner, who bears a dubious expression as she looks over the downstairs room. Clearly, the woman doesn't appreciate the gem she has in her possession. *My gain*, Viola thinks.

She smiles at the young woman. "I shall take it. When can I move in?"

"Oh, I—well—I suppose—right away," the owner stutters. Viola raises an eyebrow. "Honestly, I've no use for it. If you would like, I can give you the key right now."

"How much do you want for it?"

The woman states a price, but Viola doesn't know if that's the going rate for such a place. She should have done her research and checked the housing prices. She knows there's some work to be done; that will cost too. And how quickly can the empress' financial team make this happen? There's money at her disposal, but is it enough? She didn't think to discuss the exact sums with the keykeeper earlier in the day.

Viola hesitates, but as her uncertainty grows, a new feeling pulses in her heart. She knows this is the right place for her. Motoko, who came back inside while Viola was inspecting the upstairs area, lies stretched out upon the sofa. She struggles to tear her eyes away from the bright pink bulges along the back-rest. They look decidedly like three unmentionable parts straining for freedom from the contrasting burgundy faux leather around them. *That will have to go.*

Shaking her head, she returns to her contemplation of the space, trying her best to ignore the furnishings. Jo's voice echoes in her mind. *We're always granted what we wish for as long as we prove, through our behaviour, that we want to make it a reality. Our thoughts guide our actions, and those direct our outcomes.* Looking around the room and out into the hints of a garden beyond, Viola smiles because everything he's ever told her is proving true.

She doesn't feel comfortable trusting blindly, though. *I could rent the place for a segment.* The thought gives her pause. It would give her time to make sure the price is fair and ascertain that everything is functioning as it should.

The young woman shifts from one foot to the other. Viola smiles, a radiant declaration of her enchantment. "I definitely would like to buy this place, and I will start the process directly tomorrow, but I know that can take some time. I would love to start living here immediately. So, I wonder if it would be possible for me to lease the place from you until the paperwork is in order for me to buy it."

The woman's eyes grow wide. "Why, yes, I suppose that would be fine." Viola notices a glint of greed when she states, "I think forty thousand imperial notes would be sufficient for a segment."

Viola huffs and crosses her arms. "Now I know I arrived recently, but even I am aware that is too high. I suppose I shall have to find another place then." She heads towards the door and calls Motoko to her.

"I apologise, Mistress," the woman calls out. "I misspoke. I meant twenty thousand."

Viola turns to face the owner again. "I'll give you fifteen."

As they haggle over prices and the ins-and-outs of the logistics, Viola can't help but marvel at the perfection of it all. This is exactly what she wants. Her whole world lights up with this knowledge. She also ponders the time she spent with Jo and his insistence on belief. Her eyes wander the room again, taking in the sofa and a table near the kitchen area. In her mind, all the seating spaces fill with guests, the house awash with laughter and humorous banter.

The door shuts behind the owner with a bang. Viola is startled for a moment and then chuckles at her own jumpiness. How many opportunities has she missed in the past years simply because she was on the run all the time, dogged by her fear of capture? Since meeting Jo and opening up to his worldview, she has found everything can be quite simple, provided one has a clear concept of what one wants and allows it to flow while also believing it is possible. Tomorrow, her new life begins and she thinks fondly of Jo. What might he be up to now? And perhaps she can track down the Custodians in The Capital. She still wants to know more about them and how their beliefs have influenced Jo.

Chapter Thirteen

Weeks have passed since Viola moved to The
Capital. Her days are spent in the Imperial
Grand Library, and she feels she's found her place
within the library's system. The time is fast approaching for
her to begin making a name for herself, as every high archivist
is expected to do. The tradition is for the person at the helm
of this great place of learning to steer the direction of research
within the archives as well as providing entertainment for the
people. What she chooses as her first publication will colour
the whole trajectory of her career, and, of course, it's imperative she find something both suiting her interests and readily
accessible to the people—for it's they who will be the judges of
her position as high archivist.

Time is of the essence, Viola knows. If she waits too long,
the hype around her recent and unexpected placement will die
down. She needs to capture the public's attention with whatever she chooses to publish first. The difficulty: what to focus
on. There's so much knowledge sequestered in the bowels of
the Imperial Grand Library that it's rather hard to choose
what to go for. She's studied the previous high archivists' publi-

cations, and each one has a very different focus on subjects Viola finds uninteresting. What will she concentrate on?

After much internal debate, she decides to seek inspiration from the Hall of Unregistered Histories, a cellar room below the main archive that's full of ancient manuscripts no one has had the time or inclination to go through. Viola hopes to find something worthy of her talents as a storyteller that's entertaining but also informative and on a topic she finds interesting. Is it too much to ask? She hopes not. Her career as high archivist depends on finding something that can balance all these aspects, as well as being relevant to the glory of the Haldrian Empire; and so, off to the cellar archives she goes.

What a mess! Viola raises her light-stick to reveal rows upon rows of heavy wooden shelves. She cranes her neck, but the towering stacks vanish into the darkness above her, beyond the reach of her measly light. The shelves are stuffed with parchments, scrolls, and bound volumes, which are jumbled higgledy-piggledy without consideration for the rigid orderliness that characterises other parts of the great library. As her gaze absorbs the extraordinary disorder gripping this particular hall, Viola feels the edge of an abyss opening up beneath her.

How, in the first emperor's name, is she ever going to find the manuscript to earn her the public's approval as the imperial high archivist? She ponders the dilemma of her new position, which does not merely require overseeing the smooth running of the library and helping nobles from the palace find something captivating from the archives. Her duty is also to entertain, to contribute to the empire by producing historical texts worth reading that say something worthy about Haldria or the great intergalactic empire it's become.

How—in all this mess—am I ever going to find the perfect manuscript to secure my future? Picking up a large volume at random, Viola thumbs through it, pausing to read a section here and there. After a short while, she slams the book shut with a resounding slap. While a cloud of dust rises into the air, a matching shudder courses down her spine. *Some people have no concept of storytelling. Plodding through that and trying to make something of it would take a decade, at least. No wonder Nevona and the other librarians avoid the cellar.*

Sighing, Viola wonders whether she should have accepted Nevona's offer to send some filing specialists to bring her a selection of manuscripts. She shakes her head. As she told herself earlier in the day, there's no point in sending some underling to bring her something when she doesn't even know what she's looking for. She turns back to the shelf in front of her and begins searching through the documents it contains. Within a few hours, she's identified the system used to sort the manuscripts. She wants something meaningful to Haldria, perhaps from before the formation of the empire. With her tenuous grasp of the filing system, it takes Viola a little more time to find the period and area she hopes will provide her with a manuscript worthy of her talents. Sure enough, it only takes a few days spent searching before the high-archivist's triumphant shout echoes through the silent hall of musty vellum and parchment. At last, her true work can begin.

Viola trails a gloved finger along the cracked page of the ancient manuscript she's spent days poring over. The ink is faded, smudged in places, and she's reminded the vellum she holds between her fingers is close to a thousand years old. Nevertheless, the issues Elisabeth of Vendale faced in that distant past are the same Viola sees undermining the empire now. The same seeds of resentment and dissent, not to mention disregard for all things living, are visible in The Capital now she's taken the time to stop and look.

Who would have thought a simple fairytale could shed so much light on our time. She swivels in her seat and focuses on the words floating in the air at eye level. There's an error in the transcription. With a frown and a huff, she taps the incorrect word and barks out, "Zibby." *Getting the main character's name wrong would indeed be a nightmare. There could be other instances of the same error,* she thinks. Tapping a symbol at the top of the projected screen, Viola commands, "Search Libby."

15 results, the screen flashes back.

"Change all to—" Viola pauses, focusing on careful pronunciation for the system to interpret correctly, "Zibby."

A ripple takes place in the letters she can see. It reminds her of the wind skimming over the grasslands of Shanti. It takes her back to her years spent travelling and everything she's seen. With a shake of her head, Viola considers the age-worn tome lying on her desk. Just reading this memoir has brought up so much of the truth behind folklore. *The Siblings' Tale* may have been a family favourite, immortalised in collections of children's stories for generations, and here's the proof of it really having happened.

She gently taps the page, and her heart sings with the possibilities. What if there are more such documents stored in the Hall of Unregistered Histories? Perhaps those strange tales have some truth to them, like the one about the water sprite— or even the fable of that princess who married a soldier and helped the forest return to its former glory? In a world stripped of its natural magic and suffering eternal drought, such things might seem far-fetched, but Viola has seen enough in her time abroad to know water nixies and other elemental beings do exist. And she's personally seen the records of the extermination of the elves in Haldria. It's not such a great stretch of the imagination to consider truthful the stories that included all these beings. *What of lion shifters?* she wonders. Her memory tickles with a tale of a young girl alone in the aftermath of war—during the years of conquest, before the empire. Sadly, they have all died out.

Viola shakes her head. *The bloody beginnings have always been sugar-coated.* It wasn't until she ran away that she realised the true horrors of the Haldrian Empire. Perhaps it's her duty to set the record straight and acknowledge the failings of the *glorious* beginnings of this political monstrosity. That could be a task worthy of her talents. Something to be left for another day.

Again she leans over the faded page of the manuscript. Time to continue working. Transcribing a personal account of something even more ancient is hard work but also immensely rewarding. Her excitement bubbles to the surface. Reading Queen Elisabeth of Vendale's words is like stepping into the imperial family's dining hall on Dasruleba day—digh, she reminds herself. Her subordinates regularly give her the side-eye for her provincial ways. Living outside the self-importance of The Capital, she'd forgotten how essential image is to those living here.

Time to take them all down a notch. The people here think far too much of themselves to the detriment of others.

Chapter Fourteen

Viola sits facing the back yard of her home. Just the thought of it sends goosebumps over her skin. In forty-eight years, she's never had a house of her own. The novelty makes her heart race, and she takes a moment to contemplate her gratitude for how smoothly everything went. There had, indeed, been enough money set aside at her disposal not only to buy the cottage but also to improve the plumbing, kitchen counter, and tiling in the bathroom. Additionally, with her salary, she was able to purchase furnishings more to her tastes. Viola could not dispose of the shudder-worthy sofa because Motoko had appropriated it, and she was happy to keep the pink and burgundy monstrosity outside under the eaves. The dog spends the better part of most days lounging in the shade there or slumped over the backrest to keep an eye on Viola's movements inside the cottage.

The living area is graced with a much more tasteful settee. Sleek, elegant and with upholstery in a single shade of deep purple. The whole place is now a reflection of her and everything she loves, like comfortable moments looking out over the garden area or time spent relaxing while reading.

However, although she might inhabit her own personal slice of heaven, all is far from well in the Haldrian Empire. The Capital has turned into a place of nightmare. Less than three months after Téarman's intergalactic docks were shut down, whatever plague they experienced migrated to The Capital. Theories on which ship carried the contagion are fanciful at best. Chaos abounds. The hospitals are overrun with patients no one knows how to treat.

Ensconced in her home, Viola tries to ignore the imperial alerts broadcast into her living room. The most recent distraction from her work is an announcement encouraging all dissenters—something about protests in the streets—back to their homes as the Red Guard has been dispatched to restore order.

"Why would people take to the streets in droves when the one thing we seem to know about this disease is it is airborne?" she mutters.

Viola turns back to her work. She's transcribed about two-thirds of the manuscript, and as she dictates the words, she finds herself transported. Life was so different in that time, centuries ago. Society has changed immensely, and yet some things have remained the same. There are still fathers who mistreat their children and humans who believe only ill of beings with magical powers. She looks forward to finding out how Elisabeth addressed the evils of her time. According to the folktale about her and King Richard, the changes were dramatic, and she was lauded as the saviour of Vendale. With the truth of events at her fingertips, a wave of excitement engulfs Viola, and she turns to the next page, ready to keep on dictating.

The leaf is blank. Viola stops short. Flipping through the remaining pages in the volume, she confirms they're all empty. She holds the book up to the light, but there's no sign of anything having been written past this point. She turns back a page and traces the blue words bled into the animal skin.

Not knowing what the future held, we set off into the darkness.

That's all. There's nothing more. Viola groans. How can this be? It's only half the story. Where's the sojourn with the elves? And what of Elisabeth's triumphant return to Vendale? Viola scratches her head. This cannot be it. The manuscript was the perfect piece of history to resuscitate, but now she's left with incomplete work.

A light scratching against wood jerks her attention out of the disbelief she feels. She looks up to see Motoko scraping his nails over the corner of the door leading into the back garden. With a huff, Viola pushes herself to her feet.

Another alert blares through the house. "All imperial citizens must remain indoors. It is imperative you stay at home and avoid all contact with people outside your immediate family—" The electronic voice drones on, but Viola fades it out, focusing on letting Motoko into the garden to do his business. Her eyes rove over the wild growth of plants encroaching on the flagstone footpath that leads towards a ramshackle arbour dripping with clusters of wisteria flowers. Since she'd brought in a company twice per segment to restore the plants, give them the attention they require and irrigate the back garden, everything has burst into green. Viola reminds herself she needs to have the algae-coated pond seen to before even more odious things make it their home. With open water so scarce, it's a magnet to life. Perhaps she ought to get some fish to keep any insect breeding under wraps. Then again, with the city in uproar and people dying like mosquitoes in a desert, it would probably do to wait before getting the water feature tended.

Viola leans against the door frame, enjoying the cool evening air brushing against her exposed arms and legs, refreshing after the heat of the day. Her mind wanders back to the shock of finding her perfect manuscript unfinished. What can she do? Going back to the Hall of Unregistered Histories isn't an option at the moment, with the whole city shut down as it is. There's been talk of a curfew being implemented, and from what the alerts during the day have spoken of, she's pretty certain no one without express permission to leave their homes would be allowed out. The riots have seen to that. Besides, the shuttles have been deactivated for the first time in living memory. Viola forces her thoughts away from the snippets of news that were aired before the empress declared a state of emergency and shut everything down. The Imperial Guard is out on the streets in full force and the atrocities committed have made her want to gag on more than one occasion. She does not want to think about the continued violence. Better to focus on her dilemma with the manuscript.

There must be something I can do from here. When Viola discovered Elisabeth's personal account of her life, there had definitely not been anything else like that tome on the shelf dedicated to Vendale. In all likelihood, the queen of Vendale never finished her memoir and what Viola found is all there is. *But what to do with it?* Her excitement about the manuscript was having the opportunity to share the truth behind the fairy-tale favoured by so many Haldrians today.

A lightning strike of thoughts sends Viola's mind reeling. *What if?* She strides back to her desk. *Only one way to find out—*

Viola settles into her chair and directs her attention to a black synthetic device with lights flashing over its face. "Call up all versions of the folk tale, *The Siblings' Tale*," Viola commands.

One of the green lights furiously flashes until a *beep*

emanates from the apparatus, and a list of glowing letters is projected into the air before her. Viola taps the first entry, and a new projection is opened beside the first. She skims through the information, swipes it away and examines the next option. By the time she's gone through several versions of the folk tale, her excitement simmers inside her once more.

"Call up the history of Vendale," she directs. The light begins to flash again, and then the device lets out a prolonged *beep*. A list of about fifteen entries appears before her. *There must be more than this.* Viola's heart sinks. How can she piece together the facts from the fiction in the tale if she doesn't have a decent amount of accurate historical information?

Another thought stabs into Viola's mind, and a smile creeps over her face. *But of course. I am not searching the library's database but rather the general depository.* Her position as high archivist provides her access to far more information. Now, to see if she can reach that from home. The thought of having to wait—or request permission to visit the library—grates on her nerves.

Do not be so hasty, she reprimands herself. *Try first. It might just work.*

To the gadget, she says, "Search *history of Vendale* in complete Imperial Grand Library archives."

There's a moment of hesitation, and Viola fears her wish can't be completed, but then the device speaks in a tinny voice, "Confirm identity."

With a sigh, she holds her hand over a sensor on the appliance and says slowly, "My name is Viola Alerion."

The light begins to flash, and she leans back into her seat. Her fingers drum the arm rest as she waits. With her patience beginning to wear thin, Viola considers stopping the search and going through what has been found so far. A sharp *rap* on her front door startles her, and she comes to her feet.

Who could that be? And should I even be opening the door to unexpected guests during these times of plague?

Viola peers through the little glass rectangles at the top of the door. The sight that meets her confirms the hesitation she feels about opening up to speak to whoever it is. The purple-clad individual standing outside is ensconced in what reminds Viola of the space suits of old. A transparent bubble helmet distorts the visitor's face. Their hands are hidden inside thick gloves, and the padded one-piece suit makes Viola overheat at the mere sight of it.

The purple outfit gives her pause. It's the shade worn exclusively by palace staff, and hence this person can only be an emissary from the empress. *What does Mother want? Have I not declined enough messages urging me back to the palace? Did she not understand I am working and do not wish to be disturbed?*

Pushing open the door, Viola folds her arms and stands in the doorway. "I was under the impression there are strict regulations about contact between people who are not family. What do you want?" She can see this ploy for what it is, an attempt to extend control over her once more. *Maybe because Mother can't control the situation out in the world, she is deflecting that impotence by exerting dominion over me.* Viola reminds herself this is not the messenger's fault.

The space-proof envoy raises their hands. A muffled voice Viola can't distinguish as either male or female echoes through the visor. "Her most exalted highness, Dedopali, empress of Haldria, ruler of the thirteen spheres and dragon-blessed lady of the stars, demands your immediate return to the palace, High Lady."

Oh, she does, does she? Just as I expected. Viola considers unleashing her indignation but shrugs it away because this person is only the messenger. She lets her eyes brook no contradiction when she says, "I will have none of that. I am my own person, living in my own home. I am safe here on the outskirts of the city. By all accounts, your presence here puts me in greater danger of contracting this disease than I have been in living on my own."

"I must protest, Highness. Your safety can't be guaranteed. And how will you provide food for yourself without being at risk? Nowhere is safe."

Viola barks a laugh. "I can manage without having to set foot out this door. Never fear. You may tell my mother she ought not to worry about me. I shall be fine, and I shall not put myself in any unnecessary danger. I have absolutely no intention of leaving this house until the sickness has stopped ravaging this city." In thought, she adds, *especially not if my search proves fruitful and I can do all my work right from my own home.* Excitement sparks through her veins at the thought of the search currently ongoing on her device. Soon she'll know if it's successful or not.

"But how will you do for food, Highness?"

Viola sighs. "I am a member of the imperial family. I am also one of the most powerful magic users of this generation. As soon as word reached me of the disease spreading, I purchased an annum's worth of food and stored it by magical means. Whenever I choose to retrieve some of it, those items will be as fresh as if I had purchased them the day before. I am fine."

"I was given an order, Highness—" the voice emanating from the transparent bubble breaks off.

Shaking her head, Viola steps back. "I shall say nothing more on the matter. There is no need to remove me from my home, where I am perfectly safe. I shall stay here. My mother has no reason to insist. Just be sure to have other members of the palace household with you when you give her my answer. I know she won't take it well, but there is no reason for me to come with you." Viola shuts the door and bolts it for good measure. There is not a chance she would willingly submit herself to life at the palace. *After meeting some of the extended family at that ball Mother organised, I am done with them. They are the most boring, snobbish and conniving people in the thirteen spheres.*

Through the glass, she watches her visitor hesitate as if they're going back and forth in their own mind about whether to press the matter further or give up. Several moments of their upper body twisting first away from the house then turning back again are followed by a decisive spin, and Viola watches, satisfied, as they walk away.

She returns to her desk, curiosity blazing inside her. Has she truly been able to tap into the vast resources of the Imperial Grand Library? The list of documents found glimmers above the device on her desk. With a tap of her finger, the list drops all the way to the floor, and Viola sees 498 in the top left corner. It's as if a yule candle has been lit inside her. With a big smile on her face, Viola taps the first entry and gets to work.

Chapter Fifteen

Many, many segments have passed, and things have settled in The Capital. Everything in the Haldrian Empire is once more under control. The sickness has been overcome, ships have free rein of the cosmos, and business is back to normal. Viola spent her time in isolation well, and she has finished writing her book, but the other things she's tried to do have all met with failure. Even after communications with the other planets were re-established, she wasn't able to contact Jo, and apart from his listing among the elite 'hunters' of the Imperial Military, there has been no sign of Eryk either. She's also been unsuccessful in tracking down the Custodians in The Capital. Although that has more to do with her being so busy she usually forgets to make enquiries than for any other reason.

She has not been back to the palace, and the ring from Maitri remains useless to her. Often she considers finding another ley line node to re-energize the gem, but her writing has distracted her from such attempts.

Viola paces in the garden behind her house. She doesn't look at the well-tended lawn or the splashes of colour bordering the flagstone path to the fixed arbour and spotless pond. Her regular garden service is usually the first thought on her mind when she walks here, but for a change, its importance has dwindled. She hates waiting—always has. Her mind nervously runs over the work she's done in the past months. Hours spent locked in her home and working her way through hundreds of documents have paid off, but is her version of *The Siblings' Tale* good enough? Should she have waited a little longer before sending it to the empress for approval? Should she have added more about what happened to Richard and Elisabeth after they defeated Olivia the Witch? What about Koshki Tower and the young women taught there? That was Elisabeth's finest legacy, still functional today and even a key element in the empire's structure for the instruction of sanctioned magic.

What if her mother disapproves, especially of the pointers Viola has included towards the evils perpetrated against magical creatures in the name of the empire?

She shakes her head. There's no point in doubting herself now. The work is submitted, sitting among a pile of other things the empress must go through. Approving a publication, even if it's that of the high archivist, is unlikely to be at the top of the empress' agenda. Viola knows this. More than a year of difficulties brought on by the Kliavi sickness have caused political and economic disaster throughout The Capital. Of course, the worst of it was during the first few segments. After that, some movement was allowed by those who could prove they weren't infected.

At least Viola had no real worries. Once her food supply began to dwindle, things were running well enough for her to go shopping once more, and she stocked up a second time.

Her mind comes back to her book, and she can't seem to dissolve the queasy knot in her stomach. Back and forth she paces, as if her impatience were a caged lion rattling at the bars of this infernal waiting.

You left home with the fear of pursuit. Your fear became a reality, and your thoughts have fed your actions bringing you to this point—constantly foreseeing capture. Jo's voice pops into Viola's head, and in her mind's eye, she sees him the way he was that day, his hair dishevelled from running, his voice breathless, and his eyes flashing with anger. She remembers how he trembled with suppressed rage. In the blink of an eye, Viola calls up another part of that heated conversation. *The Mother-Father doesn't want the children of this universe to experience disappointment or the sense we're letting someone down.* What more had he said? She tilts her head back and closes her eyes, letting the sun's rays warm her cheeks. *Life breeds life. Your heart, your inner voice, can never lie to you.*

He's been proven right. Viola's eyes snap open, and she turns in a circle, drinking in the sight of her cottage, the wall peeking out from beneath a deep green cloak of ivy, the pond a few steps away from her with rocks around it and irises growing in the water. Motoko is stretched out on a grassy patch near the arbour, head laid back, legs sticking in the air. All of Viola's vision has come true.

More of his words filter into her mind, filling her heart with the power of his conviction. *When you give in to fear, you're simply allowing your situation to determine the results in your life, as though you have no power to influence what will happen.*

Air rushes into Viola's lungs. She can dwell on the fate of her manuscript sitting on the empress' agenda for the segment, or she could focus on what to do after her first publication.

What do I want to achieve next? Viola wonders.

She hasn't taken the time to consider this at all. What should her upcoming project be? She ponders her options and is distracted by Motoko, who snorts an almost-sneeze and rolls onto his tummy. Perhaps she should take the dog for a walk? They've been holed up in this house and its yard for an eternity. *I have been so absorbed in my work I hardly noticed. That is not good.* She ought to visit the library soon and see how Nevona was doing. The last time they communicated by messages was some time ago.

"Come, Motoko," Viola calls, striding towards the door.

The dog bounds to his feet and gives an excited bark.

"Yes, let us go for a walk. I have a feeling something is brewing, and I simply need to work out what it is."

Viola is busy at her desk, researching her next writing project. She made one attempt to go to her office at the Imperial Grand Library, but since the success of her first publication, her movements are monitored. As soon as she stepped into the building for the first time after the all-clear was given, the entire city converged on her. Reporters hounded her for an interview, seeking exclusivity for their medium—a new scoop after the fiasco of the Kliavi sickness and news outlets having been shut down to stop coverage of the violent suppression tactics of the Imperial Guard and Military. Viola's attempt to return to work as usual was also foiled by many of the bureaucrats from the government departments surrounding the palace, who crowded into the library to request she sign their copies of her book.

Used to the brief shower of attention from listeners when she performed stories on her travels, this staggering response bewilders Viola. She cranes her neck for a glance out a window. A crowd has gathered. Many huddle, drinking kopi from thermos flasks or travel cups. Parasols turn the shifting mass into something akin to a wart-covered, shadowy beast, undulating in the swish of the wind.

The sun is relentless, but these strange people don't let up. Viola isn't certain how to navigate the situation. She's a skiff being pushed out to sea, and not having the first idea about such things, she's out of her depth. At first, she tries to talk to those who come to see her, but the more she grants access, the more people accost her. For the sake of her sanity, she refuses to see anyone.

My book is a success. That is a blessing I cannot deny, and I will remain grateful for it. The thought reminds Viola of her current work, and she turns her attention back to the bright words she can access from anywhere. She traces a finger over the projected letters. There's something about the regeneration of the environment during the reign of Johara of Erdalbad that speaks to Viola. Her intuition tells her this footnote in the histories is important. More than anything, she wants to find out how it came about. For now, she continues to read the texts that shine light on the life of the people who resided on this continent before Haldria was unified under one flag and became the core of the empire she's grown up in.

Time runs its course, and the commotion dies down. Viola can get to the library once more and enjoys her hours spent scouring the Hall of Unregistered Histories accompanied by Motoko. Perhaps she can find what her heart affirms is a missing link. The information must be somewhere. She draws in on herself more and more. Nevona resigned at the end of the plague outbreak, and the man who replaced her is rigid in his ways and frowns on the dog's presence. Everyone else has come to accept, and even love

Motoko. The new second archivist keeps his distance, allowing a wall to build between him and the high archivist. He does his work but never speaks to Viola unless absolutely necessary, and she avoids the library whenever possible simply for the sake of peace and to stop the dirty looks he casts at the dog. She barely notices how she draws in on herself. She is so busy with her research that Viola spends much time scouring the digital records at home, treading paths of the past. She's consumed by the work, the need to find what her intuition tells her will solve many problems, and she does little else.

A knock on her door brings Viola out of Queen Johara's world. She blinks back the vision of tall towers and abundant farmland, not to mention the immense orchards spoken of in the ledgers of Erdalbadi officials.

A second, more insistent knock pulls Viola to her feet. Who disturbs her at this late hour? She glances out the window. It's a warm evening, but night has fallen, and no one has ever knocked in this way. Even when there were crowds hanging outside her door, not a soul knocked or asked to speak to her inside her home, although on the few occasions she'd stepped over the threshold, they swarmed her, much like a particular hive's-worth of fireflies.

Motoko is asleep on his couch, but when Viola moves towards the door, the dog shifts and peers through the window from the garden. She considers calling him over. *Perhaps I should see who it is first before I get Motoko involved.*

Looking through the window in the door, Viola makes out one person standing under the light on the porch. The man is robust with large shoulders and dark hair. Familiarity tugs at her, insistent but unhelpful. She can't place him. Viola has no recollection of meeting this man since returning to The Capital.

He paces, his hands wringing each other. What could he

want? Viola shrugs away the question. There's but one way to find out, although she's alone and it's dark outside—and she doesn't know this person.

Another knock brings him closer to the door and shows Viola the man's face more clearly. There's something familiar about the straight nose and set of his eyes under prominent brows. He steps back again and twists his hands.

"Motoko," Viola calls. The dog pricks his ears and sits up. "Come, Motoko." The animal bounds through the back door, darts over the living room and comes right up to her, tail wagging, ears faced forwards. "Sit," she commands, pointing beside her.

Feeling safer with the dog sitting to attention by her feet, Viola unbolts the door.

The man on the other side stops moving and looks expectantly at the wooden barrier. Viola pulls it open and says, "Yes. How may I help you?"

Pale green eyes lock onto her, and Viola is certain she knows them. Everything about this man screams at her, but she can't remember ever having met him.

"Viola Alerion," he begins. His voice is deep and resonant, and once again, recognition tickles at the back of her mind.

"Yes."

"I—" his mouth drops open.

With his eyes drawn wide and his lips opening and closing soundlessly, he looks like he's seen a ghost. He takes a step back.

"What can I do for you?" Viola struggles to contain her impatience. She has work to do, and this clown isn't making any sense.

"Isperia," the man whispers. "Is that really you?" His hand clutches something under his shirt, and he rubs his fingers over a spot beneath his clavicle. Viola realises the action is subconscious when the man's expression flits through wonder, frustration, and even anger.

She tilts her head, and her eyes narrow. All of a sudden, she's bombarded with memories of this face grinning down at her. He used to be taller than she, but now they're of a height. The lines on his face and some silver streaks in his hair have changed him, matured him; nevertheless, the structure of the cheekbones and the soft curls framing his oval face are still the same.

"Eryk?" A lump clots in Viola's chest. She's thrown back into the moment she stepped onto a space ship alone, feeling lost and abandoned. Here he is, a lifetime later, standing on her doorstep. What should she do?

"*You're* Viola Alerion?" His hand falls to his side, and Viola notices how his throat constricts around the name. The emphasis on 'you' isn't lost on her either.

"What do you mean? Why does that surprise you—no, affront you so?"

His lips work, but no sound comes out. After a moment, he clenches his eyes shut and lets his head fall back while he sucks air in through his nose and pushes it out through his teeth.

When his eyelids open, he meets Viola's gaze. The intensity pins her where she stands, but his words blast away all warmth from her body and freeze her to the spot. "Twenty-five annums ago, I was dispatched on a special mission by none other than the empress herself. I was to hunt down the storyteller, Viola Alerion, and interrogate her as to the whereabouts of the missing high lady, Isperia. I was told the storyteller was the last person known to have seen the high lady after she disembarked from a starship in Harland."

Thoughts tumble through Viola's mind. The empress lied to him. Why? And why had Eryk not met her as agreed? Why did he leave her to board the ship on her own? Where was he for the three years before he was sent after her, a hound on a cold trail? There are too many questions; she can't focus on any. They run through her head like sand through fingers, and Viola realises it's she who is staring, slack-jawed.

Eryk drops his gaze and brushes a hand through his hair. "I can't believe it was you all along—all this time." His eyes seek hers out again.

He steps forwards, hands outstretched, but a growl erupts from the height of Viola's right hip. In a flurry of white fur, Motoko springs to his feet and steps in front of Eryk.

Placing her hand on the dog's shoulder, Viola says, "It is fine, Motoko. This is my friend." She turns to Eryk. "Come inside. We have much to talk about."

Eryk picks up a rectangular case resting beside the door and follows her inside, closing the door behind him. Once she's prepared some kopi, and they sit facing each other, Viola perched in her high-backed chair and Eryk slumped in the settee against the wall, she nods her head. "Well, start at the beginning. What happened?"

Eryk licks his lips and shifts in his seat. He takes a sip of the piping-hot brew. The silence extends, but at last he seems to find the words to express his tale, and the more he speaks, the more flows from him.

The morning we were due to leave The Capital together, a Red Guard accosted me as I left my room at the academy. I was escorted to the palace, and even though the sun was barely peeking above the horizon, the empress received me immediately. The empress—she was a raging volcano. Where was the high lady? What were her plans? The questions rained down like fire from the heavens.

Terrified, I struggled to find my voice but as the ordeal continued, I chose to hold my tongue. The more she roared, the less inclined I felt to actually speak. You were right, Isperia. You could not have stayed. If you had, your spirit would have been

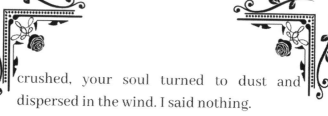

crushed, your soul turned to dust and dispersed in the wind. I said nothing.

By fifth circ when the sun streamed into the room, the city had been shut down. I knew you'd already left, but still I said nothing. They knew from the pack I carried that I'd planned to run off. And they assumed the intention was to join you.

It wasn't until the end of the digh that they considered the ship travelling to Harland.

I was sent back to the academy in disgrace. My father was stripped of his title and given a menial task in Building Three. Everyone watched me. My teachers, the students. One step out of line and I would have been sent to the colonies to work out the rest of my

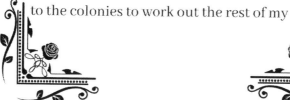

days sifting for Tevisto crystals on Oruna or digging Samuli ore on Mshrali.

After I completed my training, I requested an audience with the empress. Many moons had passed and still they hadn't found you. The word on the street was that High Lady Isperia had lost her mind. I knew that wasn't true. The empress would have dragged you back and made a public display of your disobedience, as she did to me and my father. So I offered the empire my services as a hunter. I'd completed my training—was the best in my class. Since the hunters hadn't found the high lady in three annums, I offered to continue the search in the hope doing so could return my father to his

position.

The empress told me that a storyteller by the name of Viola Alerion had been seen in Harland together with Isperia. They parted ways and no one had seen Isperia since. She suggested if I could track down the storyteller, I would be able to find out your whereabouts.

I was given a single unit and set off in pursuit. In Harland, the trail was cold. People remembered the storyteller, the magic of her words, but no one knew where she'd gone. The original hunters had lost her in the shipping lanes. There were rumours of her on almost every planet in the empire. I followed her to Oruna, only to be sent word

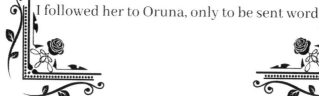

through an alert that she'd been sighted in Aeco City on Daria. She'd disappear for segments at a time before having one great performance somewhere and then vanishing again.

Never once did I hear word of anyone with the high lady's description being sighted. She'd vanished and that terrified me. I'd failed. Hadn't been there to travel with her and protect her. And in the end, I spent my life chasing the infuriating storyteller who refused to be caught. There were many times you slipped through my fingers and I began to fear you might be a ghost, but then the researchers at the academy developed a device to read magic. I started to see a pattern and it became clear the storyteller used the arcane arts to help her move through the empire without people remembering her presence. She used the power sparingly, though. The magic finder would only detect it once every annum or so, but it did make things easier as magic is forbidden in the empire except for certified users and most of those are restricted to Haldria at Koshki Tower and in the Imperial Dragon Sanctuary on the Old Continent.

Every time I thought I might catch the elusive Viola Alerion, I was thwarted. But I couldn't give up. She knew where Isperia was. She was my ticket to redeeming my father who suffered for my slip up. If I'd not

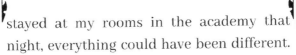

stayed at my rooms in the academy that night, everything could have been different. But it is what it is. I do want you to know I never intended to abandon you that day. It must have been terrifying leaving The Capital on your own.

After another failure on Mshrali I had one last chance to redeem myself. At least I knew which ship the infuriating prey had left on. To think it was you who thwarted me every time!

By the time I reached Téarman, I finally thought I'd won. The storyteller was safely in the imperial ambassador's custody. What could go wrong?

Everything, as it turned out.

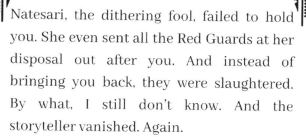

Natesari, the dithering fool, failed to hold you. She even sent all the Red Guards at her disposal out after you. And instead of bringing you back, they were slaughtered. By what, I still don't know. And the storyteller vanished. Again.

I don't know how I knew, but I was certain Viola Alerion still lived. The only clue I had was the boy, the apprentice, who'd performed in Baile and captivated the entire city. The ambassador knew only that he'd been heading to Abhainn. I tried to pick up the storyteller's trail there, but to no avail.

When I was on the verge of giving up, I came across a street musician playing in the rich quarter of Abhainn. He changed everything.

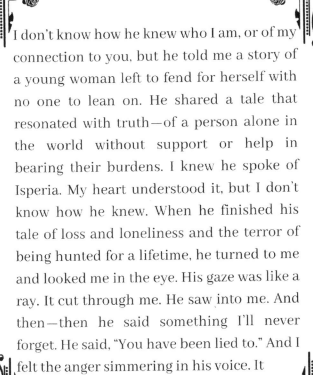

I don't know how he knew who I am, or of my connection to you, but he told me a story of a young woman left to fend for herself with no one to lean on. He shared a tale that resonated with truth—of a person alone in the world without support or help in bearing their burdens. I knew he spoke of Isperia. My heart understood it, but I don't know how he knew. When he finished his tale of loss and loneliness and the terror of being hunted for a lifetime, he turned to me and looked me in the eye. His gaze was like a ray. It cut through me. He saw into me. And then—then he said something I'll never forget. He said, "You have been lied to." And I felt the anger simmering in his voice. It poured over me and then it transformed into something gentle and kind. "Go home and seek out the truth," he said to me. "From the truth, all will be revealed."

As if in a daze, I headed for Baile, ready to step onto the next airship out of Téarman, but it's almost as if the Dragons despise me. Every move I make they shower me with twenty obstacles. Baile was in chaos when I arrived. I was ushered straight to a room in the ambassador's palace and wasn't allowed to leave under pain of death. In the city, people were dying for no known reason. The Kliavi sickness as it became known spread over the whole city. Most people died. The first to go were the elderly and then the medical staff. Natesari barricaded each of the Baile governors into individual rooms in her palace. The cleansing rituals for servants to enter the ambassador's residence were madness, but for some reason it worked and the quarantine system was successful.

I was kept in a room with no contact to other human beings until I thought I might go mad. The only thing keeping me sane was access to information through KnowItAll. I held onto sanity by a thread. We'd been physically cut off from the empire for an annum and a half when word reached us that the Kliavi sickness had turned into a plague to affect almost every one of the thirteen spheres. The solution of an

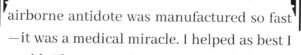

airborne antidote was manufactured so fast —it was a medical miracle. I helped as best I could. The immunisation gas needed to be distributed, after all.

Once the cloud of healing air lifted, the people in Baile who survived the sickness picked up what was left. But there was anger and resentment simmering among the survivors. Baile was the only affected city in Téarman and the speculation is that the disease was brought in by one of the ships. Where it came from, no one seems to know. There were protests and the poverty in that city is great now. With the intergalactic trade network shut down, Baile returned to being a provincial backwater, unimportant and poor. As soon as the docks were reopened, people swarmed the incoming ships, but the newly arrived battalion of Red Guards put an end to that very quickly. Imperial tokens were handed out. Food was brought in. I didn't stay to see how the disaster was managed after that. For many moons I'd been thinking about that boy's words. I needed to get back to The Capital and find out what he meant.

The journey was tedious to say the least and I spent much time wondering how I'd find this truth the boy had spoken of. When I stepped off my transport a few circs ago, I was met with a billboard about a book, The Siblings' Tale by Viola Alerion.

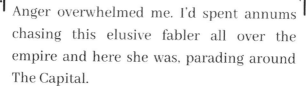

Anger overwhelmed me. I'd spent annums chasing this elusive fabler all over the empire and here she was, parading around The Capital.

From there, every step I took, I saw more information about the book, and it didn't take me long to realise Viola Alerion was the new high archivist of the Imperial Grand Library, appointed by none other than Empress Dedopali. My anger turned to ice. That's when I knew I couldn't go to the empress for answers. It didn't take much asking around to get your address. The second archivist was very helpful after I showed him my credentials.

Eryk's voice drops. "And here I am, only to find out that, indeed, the truth explains everything—and the empress knew all along."

Viola nods. She pours him a fresh cup as his kopi has grown cold. "I do not understand what Mother believed she would achieve by sending you after me like that."

He gives a mirthless laugh. "It was her punishment. If I'd caught you, I would have had to choose sides. Loyalty to the empress and my father, or loyalty to you. To restore my father's name, I'd have had to return you to the palace, but I don't think I could have enacted such a betrayal."

Viola chuckles. "Then it's a good thing I was hard to capture." She looks at Eryk's curved shoulders. The way he clutches the cup in his hands but does not lift it to drink. He studies the dark liquid, and silence draws out between them. *What has broken him?*

Eryk sighs. "Yes, it meant I never had to make that impossible choice. But it also meant my father died in disgrace. I received news of his passing when I was in Ilwych, on Mshrali."

"Oh, Eryk. I am so sorry for your loss." Viola's heart clenches. *How much sadness can a person hold?*

She steps over to the settee and settles down beside Eryk. After a moment's hesitation, she takes the cup and places it on the table before taking his hands in hers.

Eryk exhales after a long silence. His voice is cracked when he speaks, and Viola sees him blinking back tears. "I don't know what to do. I can't show my face to the empress. My family will never speak to me again. The only thing I ever wanted to do was find and protect you, and you don't even need that. You've proven perfectly capable of taking care of yourself."

Viola shakes her head and squeezes his hands. "That does not mean I enjoyed it. It is exhausting, to say the least." She pauses. Her memory calls up a moment sipping kopi with her apprentice on the Startraveller's Hope. *No, I am a loner*, her own words echo in her head. She looks up at Eryk. Perhaps that isn't as fixed as she believed when she spoke to Jo about it.

How much has changed since then? Viola smiles. *Most of all, how much have I changed?*

She squeezes Eryk's hand and says, "For what it is worth, I am glad you are here, and I know everything will work out. You must be exhausted. If you do not have a place to stay, you are welcome to use my spare room. I know I cannot replace the family you have lost, but I am here for you. Stay for as long as you need—or want."

Chapter Sixteen

Viola has managed to unearth the personal notes of Princess Johara—or should she say, Queen Johara of Erdalbad, Jewel of the Forests and Seas. The subject is fascinating, although Viola can't find the apparent missing link. How did Johara rejuvenate the land? There are clear indications she achieved this feat, but there's no reference to the actual ritual or whatever magic she unleashed. It's as if that part of the story was so apparent to everyone that mention of it was considered pointless. And now she sits poring over documents in the hope she can find the solution. Whatever plagues the planets of the Haldrian Empire seems similar to the phenomena mentioned in Johara's records. Although, when she looks closely, Viola can see the current situation in Haldria is on a much grander scale. Is it possible whatever Johara did could be repeated to restore some of the productivity of the land and stop the complex insanities tied to the need for plant incubation and water extraction from the air?

Perhaps she can find more? Or, at least, going to the place might give her some insights. The ruins of Erdalbad aren't that far away. Seeing the towers and walking the cobbled streets of the city that once overlooked the sea might arrange the pieces for her. The bound volume sitting on her desk is what Johara herself put together from her grandfather's correspondence. What might it have been like to live in those times?

Viola turns back to her work. There's so much to do, and she's not going to leave this particular manuscript to the other members of staff to transcribe. She feels it in her bones. This is the key. Just as *The Siblings' Tale* proved the catalyst for her very successful rise to prominence, this information, centuries older even than the Vendalen queen's memoir, could be the missing link for her own personal search. She knows that what she saw in Mshrali and on Téarman, not to mention the sickness that reached The Capital and spread chaos in its wake, are all signs the magic is out of balance. If she can find out what it is that has gone wrong, there's a chance the empress will help to set things right.

Viola's fingers fly over the keys. Previously she'd tried dictating, but when she did so at the library, the other archivists forgot their work to listen to her voice. For the sake of a smooth-running library, she's decided to make use of older forms of technology. It's a small price to pay. No one bothers her work anymore, and she proceeds faster too. Since speeding up her typing, there are also fewer mistakes in her transcriptions. *So much for the superiority of machine intelligence.*

The day whirls by in a flurry of words. Viola takes a break, stretching out her back. Her eye falls on the glass case beside the door. She smiles and takes in the sight of the original manuscript—her personal gem. She thinks back on the success of her book, *The Siblings' Tale*, which provided the information in this unfinished memoir as well as her findings about what happened to the characters after.

She smiles at the age-hardened pages. It's a miracle such a thing could survive centuries for her to revive and return it to the people who have forgotten the true story behind the tale. She opens the case and caresses the ancient vellum. It was all so opportune, as if the universe wished for the whole empire to know the truth, to understand its humble beginnings on the Old Continent and come to terms with a path lost. There's also a deeper message, Viola knows all too well, but she pushes thoughts of her mother aside—that can wait.

As she returns her attention to her writing, a shadow falls over her desk. "High Archivist," the familiar half-whisper of the second archivist demands her attention. "A commoner wishes to speak with you. Should I turn him away?"

Viola's eyebrows inch high into her forehead, "No, of course not. Did he give a name?" Her tone bites, and she can't help smiling, baring her teeth.

The second archivist flinches and shakes his head. "I— I— Forgive me," he stammers. Viola misses Nevona. Her replacement is taking time to get used to, especially since the man doesn't have Nevona's flair for finding things.

Rising from her chair, Viola gestures him away. *Why do they all think I care about the ridiculous intrigues of the imperial court where commoners are looked down upon?* Since the outbreak of Kliavi sickness, the empress has ceased to accept audiences, a centuries' old tradition. She shakes her head at her mother's disregard for the people of the empire. *Commoner or noble. Who cares? People deserve to be heard, and those in power should listen—at the very least.* A person wishing to see Viola these days is rare enough as it is since her fame has waned. Too much time has passed since she published her book.

Striding through the high shelves ensconcing her office, Viola picks out a tall man standing just within the entrance of the library. Sunlight streams through the glass behind him, obscuring his face. She does notice that he twists a cap in his hands, and a huge leather rucksack is propped up against the glass wall behind him. His boots are coated in a thick layer of dust, and the pungent smell emanating from him brings another twitch to her thin lips.

No wonder they did not want to let him in, she laughs to herself. *But who would come here, like this, to see me?*

Her brisk strides echo on the sheer floors, and as she comes closer, the sight of his thin face with high cheekbones sends a shiver of recognition down Viola's spine. He's about twenty years old, and his features have matured. However, it's the deep, chocolate eyes and the glowing flame within them that slaps her with a whirlwind of memories. Viola stops short.

Oh my! Can it really be?

The young man's face lights up in a familiar, cheery grin with a dimple on the left side, and it dispels the last shred of her doubt. Striding forwards, Viola exclaims, "Oh, my dear boy! You are a sight for sore eyes."

Pulling Jo into her arms and holding onto his solid frame brings a lump to Viola's throat, and she feels tears pricking at the backs of her eyes. She takes a deep breath and steps away. With him there before her, she suddenly realises how much she missed him and chastises herself for not making a greater effort to retain contact after she left him in Abhainn.

He laughs. Jo's deep voice—or at least, deeper than she recalls it—echoes through the silent library, eliciting scandalised stares from all around. Viola feels her face crease, showing off innumerable folds in her ageing skin, as she gives off a true smile.

"I cannot tell you how happy I am to see you," she reiterates.

"If I'd known you'd become sentimental in your old age, I wouldn't have dared to come here," he throws back, a mischievous glint lighting up the depths of his gaze. He throws his hands out to encompass the building around them. "So, how do you fare in the place where tales come to die, Storyteller?"

Her frown only extracts another peal of laughter.

Viola grabs his elbow and pulls him through the sterile shelves with their neat rows of labelled books towards her desk, the antithesis of orderliness. "You will not believe what I found last week," she gestures towards the ancient manuscript, which occupies the only cleared space on the metal surface.

"This is more proof the tales are based on truth, as I kept telling you." She notices him studying her, and involuntarily, her smile returns again. Her exuberance, held at bay in front of her serious underlings and their expectations of how the high archivist ought to behave, bubbles to the surface as she regales Jo with her finds and what she plans to do with this latest one.

To finish, she adds, "Would you read it once it is done? It seems providence has sent you to me, and for what other purpose?"

The look on his face arrests the torrent. She feels a big question mark rise on her face. "What?"

"I cannot believe you forgot you never taught me how to read and write!" His laughter booms again, and it's joined by her own giggles. Viola sinks to the floor, clutching her sides as tears stream down her face. When silence returns, she holds out her hands to him. "Help me up, will you?"

"Well," she says, once upright, "I suppose that means your lessons begin in the morning." She stretches her lower back. "As you once learned to speak using my words, you will now learn to read from the pages I produce." He nods, his eyes serious. "Come," Viola adds. "We need a drink! And you owe me a tale—or two." She claps him on the back as she turns and leads him out of the library. It's a relief she left Motoko at home to keep Eryk company for the day. It's almost as if she knew today would be different.

In the main hall, Jo collects his backpack, and a light green staff Viola didn't notice before. And together, they stride off into the late afternoon sun to enjoy the warmth of good memories.

Viola and Jo are ensconced in the booth of a restaurant on the divide between the blue and white districts. The clientele is a mixture of people from both groups. Viola considers the strict divisions between people that the imperial system insists on maintaining. *Where do those laws even come from?* For as long as she can remember, and even from her history books, this is the way things are in The Capital. Viola's kept herself to her home or the library and hasn't had much opportunity to see the divisions in action.

Around them, there are only people in the white outfits of the bureaucrats working in government and those in blue outfits from the municipal services. The servers and owner she can see behind a counter all wear grey, denoting serving class. Jo is the only one not wearing the appropriate colour, and Viola wonders if he'll have any trouble for it, but then again, he's with her, and she notices the glances people at other tables throw her way. The golden stripe on the hem of Viola's blue cloak and along the sleeves of her tunic are a beacon of her position. As long as Jo stays with her, he'll probably be safe from informants—she hopes.

Looking at him, Viola takes in the dark brown hair that hangs into his eyes and the smile playing on his lips, deepening the dimple in his left cheek. Jo isn't looking at her. His eyes roam the room, observing the people sitting at the open tables. She notices his gaze light up as he sees something in a booth along the adjoining wall. She shifts in her seat so she can see what he's looking at.

Her eyes fall upon a couple furiously kissing, and Viola immediately turns her back on the sight. She suppresses a shudder and steadies her breathing before muttering under her breath, "They should get a room."

Jo's attention snaps to Viola. "Why do you say that?"

Viola huffs, trying not to roll her eyes at the innocence she sees written on his face. "Because it is indecent."

Jo shakes his head. "Oh, Master," he sighs. "That," he gestures towards the booth with his head, "is one of the most beautiful things I've seen since setting foot in this city."

Viola's acerbic retort is cut off when a server sets down a steaming plate of stuffed lobster on a bed of nasi grains. The smell of baked cheese mixed with herbs and the salty tang of lobster rises on the steam. Viola sits back and waits for them to be alone again before she picks up her cutlery, raises an eyebrow at Jo and demands, "Elaborate, Apprentice."

Jo grins, revealing his pearly teeth. He breathes in the fragrance wafting from the plate in front of him and digs in. After the second mouthful has disappeared, before Viola has even finished cutting the first piece from her meal, he chuckles softly.

"As always, the best food is to be found around you, Master."

Viola grunts and slowly chews while Jo sucks on a leg. After finishing, he sits back and sighs as he dabs his fingers on a serviette. His gaze travels over to the booth where the couple have risen to their feet, and he watches as they exit the restaurant. From the corner of her eye, Viola follows the sight of the two men, walking arm in arm. She's about to shake her head again when Jo's solemn expression draws her attention to him.

Nodding his head in the direction of the couple strolling

away behind him, Jo says, "This is why I think that relationship is beautiful."

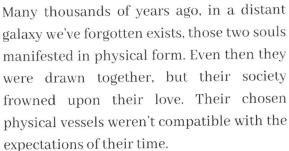

Many thousands of years ago, in a distant galaxy we've forgotten exists, those two souls manifested in physical form. Even then they were drawn together, but their society frowned upon their love. Their chosen physical vessels weren't compatible with the expectations of their time.

Separated, heartbroken and alone, two females, a human and an elf, drifted. Each followed a different path of doom and their lives were black gaping holes of longing. One of them passed on, leaving the other to pine away for centuries more before eventually succumbing. Dissatisfied, the souls yearned for a chance to experience

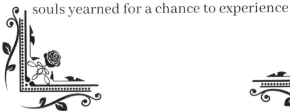

physical life together. An opportunity arose for them to take on form once more, and they returned together to walk their planet. However, the physical bodies they each chose brought only pain and separation. Again, they were kept apart because of a society that frowned upon their desire to be together.

Again and again they tried. Lifetime after lifetime their efforts to exist in harmony with their world and be together were thwarted. Their pain and suffering was immortalised in art and poetry, it even gave rise to movements for change where others like them were granted what they themselves had been denied: the freedom to

 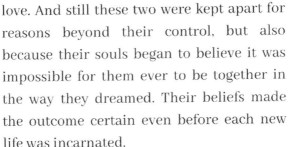

love. And still these two were kept apart for reasons beyond their control, but also because their souls began to believe it was impossible for them ever to be together in the way they dreamed. Their beliefs made the outcome certain even before each new life was incarnated.

And now, here they are. Haldria is a new planet; the empire provides a world filled with freedoms. Here, at last, after so many times trying, they're free to be. And for once they embrace it and exalt.

What a wonderful time this is to be alive where so much is allowed socially. Things that have never been possible before in any

place are freely permitted. I also saw a glimmer of light hanging over them, as if this life is a gift for having dutifully done the Mother-Father's work in previous incarnations. But those details are irrelevant. When all is said and done, that love deserves to be flaunted. It ought to be shown publicly for all to see and everyone should celebrate it. It's pure and deep. And it's entitled to be.

"Very inventive, Jo," Viola says with a gentle shake of her head. "It is a good frame for a story. With a bit of work and some elaboration, it could become the next great tale. Star-crossed lovers over multiple incarnations. There is definitely a market for it," she muses.

Jo clenches his fists and glares at Viola. All humour has evaporated in the heat of his frustration. "No, Master. You don't understand. Their love is so strong I can see glimpses of their past lives hovering around the edges of their physical forms. They have been longing, striving, even fighting to be together through multiple lifetimes and yet they've always failed until now. This isn't the lust-filled dance of hormones. It's so much more. These two—they're special. Throughout all the hardship and strife, they never truly gave up. They kept on trying again and again and again. And finally, they can simply be. Just look at them. What you saw here is an outpouring of love. It's the celebration of all that's good and meaningful in life. It's why they're so open about it. Their souls are imprinted with the memories of furtive moments stolen away from the prying eyes of society. That's why they flaunt it so here, where they're freely permitted to love."

"What do you mean, you can see their past lives?"

With a huff, Jo throws up his hands. "It's hard to explain. It's something I only learned how to do recently and is beyond your understanding and belief. What I see depends on the person. With those two, it was their past lives, but I think there's more to it than that. I get the feeling that particular couple is intricately tied to me and my people. I sense I can see their past lives so clearly because those incarnations are directly linked to how my people ended up in the Haldrian

Empire. In a way, they're spiritual ancestors of my clan. That's why I see them so clearly. Or perhaps it's the strength of their past yearning and the beauty of their being together now. I can't be certain."

He pauses and looks around at the other patrons in the restaurant. "From other people, I usually don't see past lives. I'll see other things, though. Meaningful aspects relating to their souls or their magic. Tepocacoatl said my ability will improve the more I use it."

There are so many questions Viola wants to ask. But instead of focusing on the story he's told or this information she struggles to understand, she decides to shift focus and asks, "Tell me, what have you been doing these past years?"

Jo shrugs. "Learning."

Viola looks at him. She uses the unrelenting stare perfected in her role as Viola Alerion, the itinerant storyteller, but Jo glares back.

When he doesn't give way, Viola settles more comfortably into her chair. Perhaps another approach? "Why did you come here to The Capital, then?"

Jo traces the synthetic top of the table. "I, um— I wanted to find out more about the people in *The Last Warrior*. It seems to me there's more to the story than the Orundian tale provides."

Viola can't help the catty smile coming over her. "Oh, is that so? You do realise that will require assistance from the library you so eloquently called a graveyard of stories?"

Jo has the decency to look chastised, but his chagrin lasts for less than a heartbeat. His smile returns, as does the bright glint in his eyes. "Then I must revive stories, just as you're doing." He winks.

Laughing, Viola adds, "You are welcome to stay with me for however long you need to achieve that."

They leave the restaurant soon after, and Viola takes notice of Jo's staff. She can feel magic coursing through the device, but it's nothing like her own collapsible quarterstaff she still has a habit of wearing attached to her belt. The one he carries is made of some green stone and is carved with intricate designs difficult to make out in the half-light of the buildings' long shadows. Unlike her own staff, which channels existing magic, Viola can tell this one contains its own magic. How that's possible, she cannot fathom.

She tries again to coax anything about Jo's recent life from him. He remains closed-mouthed and gives monosyllabic answers at the most. He's more than happy to talk about other people and places, regaling her with wonderful tales, but as soon as she tries to steer the conversation to him, he deflects.

Irritated, Viola snaps, "Now I remember why I thought you were a vexation."

Jo gives her a long hard look before replying, "And I remember why I always found you so aggravating." He stretches out his arms, and the disgruntlement falls from his features as he says, "Stop focusing on the things that close your mind. Open yourself up to possibility. The glimpses I get from you show me much has changed since we parted ways outside Abhainn. Hasn't everything you dreamed of come true?"

Another smile tugs at Viola's lips. He's absolutely right; she won't deny it. "That and more, dear boy. Too true."

Chapter Seventeen

Viola and Jo have almost reached the shuttle terminal to catch a transport to the district where her home is, when Jo stops. He gazes into a brightly-lit alehouse. Viola walks a few more steps before his silent staring stops her in her tracks too.

"What is it?" she asks.

Jo tilts his head as if listening past the thumping music pulsing through the windows and door. "I—" He takes a step towards the establishment. "The Mother-Father requires something of me here. Please can we stop for a moment? I must see what this is about."

Viola glances at the time on her pocketpiece. Eryk will be wondering where she is. "Well, you go ahead then," she says, nodding towards the door. "I have to leave a message." She holds up the device. "I shall join you in a moment." Viola taps the pocketpiece and selects the message function. Speaking into the recorder, she lets Eryk know Jo has arrived in town and they'll be back at the cottage later.

She enters the gleaming alehouse. She's never actually set foot in a place like this in The Capital, and she's surprised at how uncharacteristically clean the establishment is. She settles onto a tall seat beside the long bar counter, noticing how Jo's eyes rove over the assembled patrons. He looks almost as though he's absorbing all the details of the place, cataloguing everything there is to know about it. While he soaks up their surroundings, Viola orders a drink. She hasn't treated herself to some real firewater in a long time, and she's eager to take a sip. Jo declines when she offers to get him something too.

A young man with short dark hair and wearing a white uniform stumbles forwards and almost knocks Viola from her seat. She watches in dismay as the glass in her hand tips, and a fountain of amber liquid is unleashed upon the bar.

"Get out of here, oaf," Viola growls as she shoves the youth away from her. "Brainless dolt," she adds, stretching towards a container of paper serviettes placed strategically on the bar counter. The offender stumbles off with an unintelligible, mumbled apology while Viola yanks several of the towels from their holder and dabs at the stain spreading over the counter in front of her.

"What a waste of a good drink." Viola shakes her head, thinking of the price of it. Such things have always been expensive, but even more so since the Kliavi sickness ravaged The Capital. Why couldn't the plague have eradicated idiots instead of taking the elderly and infirm? She sighs. *That was an unworthy thought. No need to be unkind. Besides, it was an accident.* Taking a deep breath, Viola lets the frustration blow out on her next exhale. She looks around in the hope of finding the young man to apologise for her irritable response, but he has disappeared among the crowd of patrons.

Viola allows her mind to wander. From the corner of her eye, she takes note of how Jo perches on his barstool and studies the room and everyone in it, but she's not interested in the patrons or the décor. She simply wants to enjoy her drink.

Even as the thought settles in her mind, the barman steps up on the other side and holds up the flask with the amber liquid in it.

"I saw what happened, High Archivist. Please allow me to refill your drink."

"Why, thank you. That is indeed kind of you." She breathes more deeply. *I can be this way, too. There was no reason to fall into my old habits like that.*

The man bows his head and pushes the glass back towards Viola. "Thank you for your patronage," he adds.

She raises her glass to him and returns to the paths of her thoughts as they wander the strange occurrences of the day and especially Jo's claim that he can see past lives of the people around him. In the background, Viola barely listens to the beat of the music or the chatter of many voices. Her mind is consumed by how she responded to the simple accident and that she wants to move away from such vicious reactions. Perhaps she has been too snappy in other situations too?

Jo brings her back to the present when he asks, "Master, the tale *Warring Lions*, has its origins here, in The Capital, am I right?"

She looks up and blinks away her tumultuous thoughts to focus on the question. After a moment's consideration, she replies, "Yes, I believe it is a tale from Haldria." She shifts, her mind going over her history lessons. "But I have no knowledge of any lion shifters ever really existing in this region. If I remember correctly, there were shifter clans in Daria at some point before they were eradicated." She pauses, tilting her head as if the angle might help her remember better. "You know, it is strange because I am sure *Warring Lions* is set in the Plains of Rumput, which is the name of the flat place where this city is built."

Viola considers further, rubbing her nose as she does, but

Jo jumps to his feet. He grabs his staff and strides past a group of tables between the bar and the wall. He stops in an open area where a few couples sway to the beat and raises the jade-green rod, bringing it down once on the ground.

A spark jolts through Viola, and she notices a ripple go through the crowd. A hush falls, and even the drumbeat coming through the speakers goes silent. All eyes turn to Jo. Viola observes a grin spreading over his face and notes the mischievous glint in his eyes. He briefly glances over at three patrons sitting in a darkened booth against the wall on the other side of the dance area. Then he takes a little bow.

"Ladies and gentlemen. I'd like to offer some entertainment for this evening."

"Oi!" The barman interjects, holding up a finger. "What do you think you're doing? Stop harassing my patrons." A mutter goes through the crowd, and several people shift in their chairs.

Jo raises a hand, and Viola almost laughs at the froggy look on the bartender's face. *The boy has gumption*, she thinks and leans back to see how he'll play his cards.

"I think you can humour me, just this once. I promise it will be worth your while." He looks to Viola, but she refuses to encourage him—or discourage him, for that matter. Jo shrugs and turns to the patrons in the bar. "Please allow me the opportunity to share a tale. It's a glimpse of the time in which all of this," Jo gestures around him, "began."

He launches into *Warring Lions,* and Viola is swept away on the wings of his words. She feels the young lion-shifter's fear, can almost taste it. The young girl's desire to become her true self is overwhelming, and it calls to Viola to dig deeper and also seek out her own truths. She considers the work she's been doing on the life of Queen Johara, but there's something else that tugs at the back of her mind. Something about

Vendale, not Erdalbad where Johara reigned. Viola struggles to find what pulls at her. The stream dragging at her is relentless, but it's unclear, and she feels frustrated by the knowledge there's something she ought to know or remember and her inability to do so.

She is jolted from her thoughts when Jo comes to the end of his tale. She notices she's enveloped in gentle undulating light. His power shimmers and lights up the whole room in magical sheets of dancing colours. No one else seems to be aware of the strange phenomenon. The other patrons are rousing themselves, but they still seem lost in the world of the tale, not yet able to focus on the here and now.

The silence holds for several moments, and in that time, Viola watches the magic dim around Jo's form. In the instant it winks out, the spell on the spectators is broken, and people start to move again. There is applause, and several people shout over the din to ask if Jo will be performing somewhere else soon. He grins and shakes his head. Viola hides her smile as she takes a sip from her drink. *He has come a long way.*

"Granted," the barkeep calls from his corner. "That was a good tale. Now, run along and stop bothering my patrons."

Jo nods and catches Viola's eye. She smiles at him, her chest swelling with pride as she considers how masterfully he performed the tale. He takes a step towards her when a scream echoes through the room. Jo's eyes dart to the booth he examined earlier, and Viola follows his gaze.

Three lions, one male and two female, struggle to keep their large bodies on the cushioned seats. Strips of white fabric litter the seating and floor below them. Their golden eyes roll around, expressions of confusion evident in their furred faces. One of the females scrabbles on the upholstery, her claws shredding the grey fabric while huffing grunts pour out of her in a string of sound that could almost be interpreted as expletives.

Panic-stricken shrieks fling the entire bar into pandemonium. Chairs scrape and tip, glasses smash on the tiled floor, and terror claims every human voice in the bar as the patrons stampede for the tiny door. A splintering crash shakes the room when the cannonade of human bodies spills out through the window beside the door.

The lions growl and moan, their own panic fuelled by the fleeing people around them. The male is pressed into the corner of the booth as if he's trying to disappear.

Jo places his staff on the ground and opens his arms wide. Viola's heartbeat thumps in her throat as she watches the boy approach the beasts. The sounds of distress increase, and Viola observes as the second female slips on the seating, landing on the floor beneath the table. The creature launches herself upwards in a clumsy attempt to walk and hits her head against the underside of the table with a thud followed by a moaning grunt.

Viola can see the three animals are on the brink of a hysterical frenzy. In a bewildered daze, she wonders how they even got there. Her thoughts and the rapid pace of her heart slow when Jo begins to hum a tune. The soothing tones reverberate through the room, and the three lions settle on their haunches.

The animals are beautiful. The luxurious golden colour of their coats captivates Viola, and she struggles to pay attention to the panicked crowd. Jo is right to focus on the lions, she thinks; they're incredible creatures. Unique. Unlike anything she's ever seen. Lions are extinct in Haldria, after all. Such creatures haven't been seen in these parts since the imperial zoological gardens were forced to close once fresh water became too scarce.

As he takes another step forwards, Jo's humming subsides.

He leans further in, and Viola hears his words, even though his voice rises barely above a whisper. "I can imagine this must be overwhelming. But this is who you are. Alanna's tale is your birthright. These lands were taken from your people through brute force, and you were made less-than. Your true nature and the phenomenal capacity of your real selves was hidden away, confined by the expectations of white suits." He gestures towards the shredded pieces of fabric littering the seats and floor around them.

Viola gasps. These people are lion shifters? In a whirlwind, everything coalesces. Jo's choice of tale, his focus on these three people since he set foot in the bar, and the fact that he revealed their true nature. The boy's words from earlier echo in Viola's mind. *The Mother-Father requires something of me here. Please can we stop for a moment? I must see what this is about.* He was called to set these people free from whatever magical binding contained their lion forms. Viola can't deny the truth of what she sees, but at the same time, it means everything she's learned about the founding of the Haldrian Empire is a myth. If the tale of Alanna and her tribe of lion shifters is the true version of history, then it tilts everything she's ever learned onto its head. The idea sparks a question: *What more lies have we been fed?* A shudder courses up her spine, and although Viola wants to reject the thought, she squares her shoulders and steels her resolve. *I will do my utmost to find out.*

Speak the truth as you know it. The ordinance of Jo's faith resonates through her being, and seeing it in action inspires Viola. This is where she can truly make a difference as the high-archivist of the Haldrian Empire's Imperial Grand Library.

The lioness sitting on the upholstered seat to Jo's left stretches herself out, taking up the entire couch in one smooth, graceful movement. Viola bites back a cry of dismay when Jo reaches out and runs a finger over one brown paw.

His voice is gentle when he speaks, and Viola's heart constricts at the words. "You are who you are—golden. And just as Alanna was who she was, you can be too." Jo pauses for a moment before addressing all three lions, "Embrace it and open yourselves to the possibility of the power you possess simply by virtue of being you."

The sound of boots stamping in the street outside draws Viola's attention away from Jo and his little group of lion shifters. Red uniforms flash in the pool of brightness from a streetlamp, and Viola's heart rate kicks into a gallop.

"Jo," she says. "Trouble is coming."

The boy looks over his shoulder, takes in the guards approaching the mess of broken glass outside the establishment and frowns. He turns back towards the lions and hushes them as his right hand seeks out the green staff he'd laid on the ground earlier. Very slowly, he lifts it upright and taps the ground.

A ripple goes through the air as if it's being sucked towards Jo and the three lions. Next, glittering light condenses around them in the shape of a dome. Viola gapes at the protective shield he has erected. She's never come across anything quite like the scintillating bubble of light. Her arms prickle, and she can tell this barrier is strong.

"What's going on in here then?" The first Red Guard steps through the damaged door and sweeps his gaze over the area. He has a gold stripe on his uniform, indicating he's the captain of the unit.

Viola takes in the overturned tables and abandoned drinks. Shards of glass litter the floor where rampaging people knocked things down. Six guards in total march into the bar. From behind the counter, the barman's head appears. His motions are furtive, eyes glancing to the booth with the lions and over the wreckage of his place. Dismay melts into relief when his gaze lands on the guardsmen striding in, to the accompaniment of the glass crunching under their boots.

The barman straightens his grey outfit and lifts aside a segment of the counter to step through. He glances over at Jo and the lions before lifting his eyes to the Red Guard's captain, and Viola doesn't like the look she catches in the man's gaze. She turns to face the group of guards, hoping her position as high archivist will help mitigate the escalating situation.

"That boy," the barman exclaims, accusation dripping in his voice, "has used illegal magic to summon these creatures here and cause mayhem. I demand restitution!"

The leader of the guards turns his head to take in the situation. Viola notes the way his eyes widen and jaw sets at the sight of the three lions and the dome of magic around them. Taking another step forwards, she makes sure she's in his line of vision and is relieved to recognise the face. He was definitely among the guards in the skirmish at the palace when she arrived. Perhaps he remembers her as well? She can hope.

Not giving anyone a chance to make matters worse, Viola pulls her shoulders back. "As witness to the whole affair and having seen and heard things the barman could not—for he was there," she points behind the counter, "I would like to make a statement. This young man," she gestures towards Jo, "is my apprentice. He arrived in The Capital earlier in the day. Yes, he has magical powers, but in my position as high archivist of the Imperial Grand Library and," Viola meets the captain's eyes, "through my deeper ties to the royal family, I affirm the activity is sanctioned."

Viola is satisfied. Recognition flashed in the captain's eyes when she mentioned the imperial family. *So, he does remember*. She sweeps her arms out and smiles. "My apprentice is undoing a dreadful curse. It will not take much longer, and we will ensure all is set to rights here as well." Viola nudges a toe against a piece of broken glass lying at her feet. "Now, I request that you allow us to finish."

When the guard captain nods, Viola thanks him and heads back towards Jo. As she approaches the barrier, the hairs on the backs of her arms stand on end, and she stops. There's a soft crackle in the air, and over it, Viola can just make out Jo's soft words to the lions.

"—precisely as I described it in the story. You open up your mind to your other form, and it will come to you as easily as changing clothes."

Viola sees a ripple in one of the lionesses who pushes herself upright, fur and whiskers retracting, tail shortening. There's a crack and a pop, and then a woman with long blonde hair lets her legs slide down the seat until she's sitting once more. For the blink of an eye, she's naked, and Viola wants to avert her gaze, but before she can do so, white clothes materialise on the woman's form. Still struggling to fathom where the clothes came from, Viola watches as the other two lions step away from the booth and shift back into their human forms. Their bodies are clothed even faster than the first. When Jo pushes himself to his feet, Viola notices all the scraps of fabric that had littered the floor have vanished. *Did he just re-materialise the shredded fabric?*

Jo smiles at the three people before him. They're stretching out their limbs, and he pats the man on the shoulder. "You've been lied to. You're naturally magical beings, and containing your true nature by magical means causes great harm to your spirits. Go home and seek out the truth, for from the truth, all can be revealed."

He turns, and as he does so, the glittering dome around him and the three shifters disappears with a pop. The three lion shifters look around the room, and Viola sees them taking in the destruction and then the six Red Guards. She jerks her head towards the door, and they leave, glancing over their shoulders at the guards. Two of them hunch their shoulders as they walk past. The third visibly trembles.

The attention of everyone remaining in the room is on Jo, though. He swings his head from side to side and takes in all the damage. He taps his staff against the ground and murmurs, "Well then, time to clean up."

Wind whirls through the bar when his staff knocks against the ground for a second time. Viola has to squint to see through the blast of air and brings up a hand to shield her eyes. Just as suddenly as the gust appeared, it calms, and the place is spotless. The barman turns in a circle, his mouth opening and closing in silence.

Jo takes a theatrical bow before addressing the barman. "Thank you for your assistance in removing that dreadful *curse* —" Jo flicks his eyes to Viola, and she sees a twinkle there before he continues. "You've done a great service."

He takes a step towards the door, but the captain of the guard holds out his hand. "Not so fast. I'll need to file a report. What happened here?"

Viola swallows. The thought of having this incident officially reported makes her insides crawl. Her whole body rejects the idea, and Viola knows her intuition well enough to follow when it has such a strong reaction.

"May I?" She holds up her pocketpiece for the captain to see. "I can send in my report directly to the empress."

The man nods, and Viola steps aside into one of the booths lining the wall of the bar. She flicks to the recording section and speaks into the recorder. As she talks, she notices the guards retreating. Only the captain remains inside. He seems to be trying to engage Jo in conversation, but the young man's monosyllabic answers apparently irritate the officer as much as they habitually frustrate Viola.

She moves closer to the guard, tapping a few buttons on the device. Viola hears the tell-tale *whoosh* indicating her missive has been dispatched, and she looks up to the guard standing before her. She nods. "It is done. Her Imperial Highness will have it first thing in the morning."

"Very well." The captain inclines his head and turns on his heel.

"Thank you for your assistance, Captain," she calls after him and watches as he marches out. She turns to the barman and hands him a token. There are enough imperial notes on it for him to renovate the place entirely if he wants to do so. Viola hopes it will keep him quiet about the strange events. "Thank you for your discreet and loyal service," she says.

The barman gulps and nods. "Absolutely, High Archivist. You're always welcome in my bar."

She smiles. "Thank you. I hope you do not get many more cursed patrons in here."

"Well, I sure don't want to advertise it as the place to get un-cursed," he chuckles.

"Your good sense and discretion are valued."

"Wishing you a good evening." The man bows his head.

"And to you also," Viola replies.

When she steps outside, she finds Jo staring up into the dark sky. He shakes himself as Viola's footsteps click on the stone. A wry smile plays on his lips.

"Less than a day, and you have already brought trouble with you." Viola holds back the laughter. "What am I to do with you, boy?"

Jo grins. "Nothing to be done but go with the flow. The Mother-Father wishes for their children to be set free. Those three lion shifters were bound, and their magic trapped. I merely did the Great Parent's bidding." He falls into step beside Viola.

She pulls out the device from her pocket and removes the report she sent to Eryk. How lucky the guard's captain didn't check she actually sent her invented report to the empress. Viola chuckles to herself. Sometimes all the bureaucracy can be helpful.

The shuttle arrives the moment they step up to the terminal, and Viola marvels at the perfection of all the coincidences. *We walked past that bar exactly when the lion shifters were there. The patrol was captained by someone who knows I am Isperia—*

Jo shifts in his seat, and the grin is back on his face. With a knowing glint in his eyes, he leans towards Viola and whispers, "There are no coincidences." He winks. "Everything is part of the Mother-Father's plan. When we do their bidding, the Way opens."

Viola nods. "I am beginning to see that, too."

Their banter soon falls to silence as Jo turns back to his interest in everything. Viola can't shake the feeling he's absorbing information, although she also wonders at how tired he must be after having used so much magic. She doesn't ask him, though. For some reason she can't quite explain, she doesn't want to pry, and the way Jo continues to rebuff her attempts to find out what he's been doing for the past several years makes her pause.

The evening is cool by the time Viola and Jo walk towards her home from the shuttle stop. There's a peacefulness to the air, and Viola breathes in the freshness of the night.

Her home comes into sight, and Jo whistles. "Now, that suits you, Master."

Before she can answer, the door to the cottage opens, and a white streak hurtles towards them. Viola manages to raise her hands before Motoko barrels into her. The dog jumps up and licks her face several times.

"Enough, Motoko," Viola snaps. "Get down."

Contrite brown eyes look up at her, little triangles peaking above them.

"Yes, I know. I missed you too."

Whine. Motoko's bum wiggles on the spot as his tail starts thumping against the dirt road.

"Well, you talk to Jo about it. I was out because of him." She jerks her head towards her apprentice.

Jo chuckles, and Viola notices him acknowledge Eryk with a nod of his head. "I'm happy everything is as it should be," Jo states with satisfaction.

Viola meets his gaze and sees him looking from her to Motoko to Eryk standing in the doorway to the cottage. She narrows her eyes. "How much did you have to do with all of this coming about?" she asks.

"Me?" Jo raises an eyebrow. "I had nothing to do with it, Master. This was your wish, wasn't it?"

"It was," Viola admits, gesturing for him to go towards the house. "Although, some details are definitely better than I ever imagined."

"That means you did the work right, Master. The Mother-Father provides what you ask for—and more. It's all between you and them."

Viola chuckles, "So you say, boy. So you say. Although I get the definite impression you helped move things along in your own way."

All she gets in reply is a cheeky grin as Jo steps over the threshold into her home.

Chapter Eighteen

Viola struggles to fathom the skills Jo exhibits. His drive and dedication astound her, but it's his achievements that make her head spin. In an impossible single segment of twenty days, Jo learns to read. Following this accomplishment, he spends his mornings reading in a corner of her office at the library while she continues with her research. In the afternoons, when Viola writes up her findings, Jo can be found curled up on the settee in her home, or when the cool of the evening sets in, sitting outside on the grass beside the pond. He listens to audio versions of the texts he's working on and follows along with the words projected from the device Viola has loaned to him.

One evening, Viola, Eryk and Jo are sitting around the table in the kitchen area of the cottage. Motoko is somewhere outside. Eryk serves the root vegetables he's spent the afternoon preparing, and Jo's nose twitches as it always does when food is being served. Viola absorbs the moment. She's especially appreciative of Eryk and how perfectly his presence fits into her life and keeps her heart full—not to mention he actually knows how to cook, which is brilliant.

"How was the empire founded?" Jo asks just before the first forkful of food vanishes into his mouth.

Viola considers her answer and watches how another three mouthfuls of his meal disappear. A thread of disapproval gathers her brow into several folds. "Jo, you do not have to eat like that anymore." She gestures to his half-empty plate.

Wide-eyed, he places the fork down with a *clink*. "Sorry," he mumbles around a mouthful of food.

"I understand things were different when you were a child," Viola softens her voice. "But as an adult, living under my roof, you are permitted to enjoy your food. And I would prefer it if you ate a little slower while you do so."

"Yes, Master." Jo takes a big breath and slowly exhales before he picks up the fork again and takes a deliberate stab at one piece on his plate.

"Thank you," Viola smiles. "You can call me Viola, you know. I would prefer it."

"Yes, Master."

Eryk snorts. "It looks like that's too much to ask of him, Vi."

Viola shakes her head and turns to Eryk. "And thank you for the tasty meal."

He nods his head in acknowledgement. "It's my pleasure. Dig in."

While Viola chews on a baked carrot, she considers Jo's question. She swallows and turns to him. "The Haldrian Empire has its roots in the Haldrian Confederation, which was a trading partnership between the Kingdom of Vendale, the free cities of Cronia and the Queendom of Erdalbad. I think there were negotiations ongoing with the peoples on the northern parts of the Old Continent, but I struggle with the details."

While Viola chews her next mouthful, Eryk adds, "Wasn't

there a big war that led to the unification of all Haldrian peoples and the founding of this city here?"

Viola nods. "Yes, although I forget the reason for the war. Most of my history lessons focused on the time of the First Emperor—I honestly cannot remember his name right now."

"Pendzach," Jo offers through a mouthful.

"Yes, exactly." Viola waves with her fork. "Pendzach brought peace after decades of warfare and declared all Haldria an empire. The technology for space travel was developed a few annums before he was proclaimed emperor, and that is when things moved really quickly. In the space of a few decades, most of the spheres had joined with the empire. We could offer new technologies and wonderful opportunities for trade." She pauses over her next mouthful of food. "Although, apart from that, I do not know the specifics of how the empire came about."

Jo shifts in his chair, and Viola notices he still has a few vegetables on his plate. She's pleased to see him take one at a time and chew properly. When he swallows, he tilts his head and his gaze shifts. He stares into space, perfectly still for a moment, before he turns back to Viola. "There's something about that war. The energy of it still lingers—or, at least, I think that's what it is. Something gave rise to all the fighting. And I feel I must find the root of it."

Viola shrugs. "Well, I do not know the details. If I remember correctly, the Haldrian army was formed in Vendale and swept throughout the Old Continent from there before crossing over to this side of the planet. Back then, there was an ocean separating the Old Continent from this region here, where Erdalbad and the Plains of Rumput used to be and The Capital is now."

Eryk frowns. "Why did they form the Haldrian army?"

Viola shakes her head. "I do not think that information ever featured in my education."

After dinner, the three crowd around Viola's desk and begin the search, but it reveals nothing. Days go by, and still they have no answer to the question, with more and more queries added to the pile. She spends hours in the library with Jo, trying to find records of the years leading up to the empire's formation.

The Haldrian Confederation formed a century before the declaration of the Haldrian Empire, but there's no information about the Great Upheaval. There's proof it happened with references to the dates the Haldrian army brought cities into the fold, but apart from that, there's nothing. They study what remains of the old texts without result. Viola descends into the bowels of the Grand Imperial Library and scours the Hall of Unregistered Histories, but the answers elude her.

After another fruitless day searching the historical records for any reference to the formation of the Haldrian army, Viola enters her home to find all quiet. It's a sunny afternoon despite the wind being a little nippy, and she checks through the window into the yard. There, sitting with his arms propping him up and his legs stretched out in front of him, Jo relaxes with his eyes shut and face turned to the sun. Viola is stunned by the tranquillity breezing through her, and she joins him to settle down in the grass.

They sit in companionable silence for some time before Jo speaks. "All the records indicate Vendale was a pre-industrial society before the Haldrian army appeared. The Vendalens had firearms, but they were nowhere near the level of development of what came out of Vendale a few years later when the Upheaval began. How did they go from flintlock systems to firing several hundred rounds without stopping?"

"That," Viola sits up, "is a really good question. How

indeed?" She thinks on everything she knows about the society of the early empire, and more things stand out. "Motor vehicles at the time of the emperor's coronation," she murmurs.

A snuffle is the only warning Viola gets before something wet slides up the side of her cheek. She pushes herself to her feet with a squeal. "Motoko, off!" The dog gambols away with a bark and does a little dance. "I suppose that means Eryk is home, too?" She wipes her face.

"Yes, I'm here," Eryk calls from inside the cottage, and Viola's heart leaps. She can't stop a smile from taking over her face.

Jo pushes himself to his feet and dusts off his trousers. As they step through the door, he says, "I have a feeling we must travel to the place where it all started. I have an inkling, a hint from the Mother-Father. The answers we seek are to be found in what was once Vendale."

Chapter Nineteen

The small craft glides above empty sands. Viola sits beside Eryk, who pilots the glider. She looks down at what used to be the seafloor centuries ago. The endless expanse of beige, interspersed with the white bubbles of plant incubators, is ghastly. She hasn't seen any sign of life for hours, not since they left The Capital behind. It's as if the city, the heart of the Haldrian Empire, is a white oasis ringed in a little green, but more concrete and glass than anything else. The rest of the continent is bare—as is the desert below her. In all likelihood, the incubators are run by machines, so few humans have ever seen this abomination.

From the back seat, Jo's voice drifts over to Viola. She looks over her shoulder to where he sits, crammed in the back of the glider with his arms flung around Motoko's neck and tears streaking down his cheeks. A keening song, torn up by ragged sobs, trickles out of him. Shifting in her seat, Viola places a hand on his knee.

Jo looks up. "You know there's supposed to be water down there?" His voice trembles.

"I know."

"It's wrong."

"Yes."

Jo wipes his cheeks with the palms of his hands and sniffs. Motoko gives a gentle nudge with his nose and plants sloppy kisses all over Jo's face until the young man laughs. Silence fills the cabin once more as they all stare out the windows again.

Viola thinks about this destruction. She's always known about it. No one in The Capital keeps it a secret, but she's never before seen this barren wasteland that was once the ocean. It makes her think about all the twisted ways the empire keeps itself going even though it ought to collapse. Food is produced in plant incubators and meat labs. Water is extracted directly from the air, which she now understands must be the reason the streams, rivers and seas dried up over time. *And it is also why there is no rainfall in Haldria.* Her mind plays over her experiences of getting drenched on Téarman, and she wonders at the immensity of what Haldria has lost.

After what feels like an eternity, a smooth wall of rock appears on the horizon. Viola's read about the cliffs in all the ship documents that were part of her research. There was a time when those walls were invoked as a blessing, for they marked the end of a long journey at sea. She racks her brains, but she can't remember what the cliffs are called.

The glider swoops on the air currents and is pushed up. The view steals her breath away. A massive range of mountains looms behind the cliffs. It's as if their feet were shorn off, leaving the last ridge to plunge straight down. Viola can't imagine what it must have looked like with the ocean's waves crashing against that stone barrier.

Grey peaks march northeast in an unending column of jagged outcroppings and triangular teeth. The mountains are immense and beautiful, and it doesn't surprise Viola in the least that they were once called the Spine of the Dragon.

Eddies of air buffet the glider, but the jolty ride turns smooth again as they're pushed into a valley. The tall sentinels of the mountains parade to left and right, and below stretches a landscape Viola struggles to interpret. There's vegetation, as well as some signs of life, but most of the trees are leafless, and there's almost no indication of other living beings. She's aware The Capital has served as a magnet. Most people from Haldria have been drawn to it, but Viola hadn't ever thought this meant the rest of the planet has been left practically unoccupied. That couldn't be right, could it? It seems unbelievable to have a single enormous city and nothing else on the whole sphere.

Some glints of red and gold catch her eye. Most of the trees on the mountain slopes are bare, but enough are cloaked in bright leaves to tantalise her.

"I have read about the leaves changing colour," she whispers as she strains her eyes to see more of the fiery hints. "Can we not land and take a stroll in the autumn forest, Eryk? It would be like going back to the tales of Queen Elisabeth's time."

Eryk chuckles and peers down. "I can't see any places to land. But the light won't last much longer; we'll have to find a good place to set down before nightfall. Do you know how far up the valley we need to travel?"

Viola shakes her head. "No. It was five days' hard ride on horseback, but who knows how far that is in leagues."

"Then I think we may need to stop for the night and continue in the morning." Eryk peers down, swinging his head from side to side. "The glider is much slower than a hovercraft, but there was no way of getting permission to borrow one of those from the military. This was all I could get."

He's still searching below them, so Viola asks, "What are you looking for?"

"A place to land."

Viola looks below them. Apart from a dark streak following the valley floor, there's no sign of any useful landmarks. She wants to keep going; her drive to reach their destination pushes her forwards. She looks at the position of the sun. It has already dipped below the mountains behind them to their left. The valley is cast in shadows.

"How long have we been travelling?" Viola squints against the dimness on the ground. "It cannot be more than half a day, so there should still be quite a bit of daylight left."

Eryk shakes his head. "No, we're much further to the north now. The light is affected by that, too, and with it being autumn, the sun sets much earlier than it does in The Capital."

"There's a tower with green fields around it," Jo pipes up and points.

"That must be Koshki Tower, the famous institution for training women with magical ability. Could we land there?"

After a moment's hesitation, Eryk grunts in the affirmative and pulls out a lever to slow down the glider. In lazy circles, he brings the mechanical bird closer and closer to the ground. It jolts as it comes into contact with the earth and skids to a halt over a grassy patch to the south of the tower.

Viola tries to push herself out of the hatch Eryk lifts up, but she finds herself stuck in the position she's been sitting in for hours. Her back protests when sparks of pain flare at the base of her spine. With a groan, Viola tries to stretch out her muscles while Jo and Motoko tumble out of the craft.

Eryk pops his head back inside. "Do you need some help, dear?"

Viola sighs. "I wish I did not, but this body of mine fails me."

He chuckles and helps her up, supporting more of her weight than Viola would like, but the strength and warmth of his arm is welcome. When, at last, she comes to stand a few steps away from the tower, she lets her eyes travel up the white marble walls. The blue sky and the dramatic mountains make for the perfect backdrop. In the half-light of the afternoon, Viola makes out etchings on the walls of the tower. They're difficult to see, and she can't discern their pattern, but her eyes are tugged to the indentations. They draw her gaze in and refuse to let her go. The top of the white pillar is capped with a green-tinged conical roof.

Motoko bounds up beside Viola, and she looks around. Behind her is the glider, and in front of her, the tower. Eryk is checking the machine; she imagines he's making certain all is ready for their departure in the morning. It takes her a moment to find Jo.

The young man kneels on the ground a short way behind the glider from where she stands. His hands are raised up to the sky, and he rocks backwards and forwards as words tumble from his mouth. At that distance, Viola can't make out his utterances, but she recognises the position well. He's praying—fervently. *But why?*

Viola shakes herself. *I have spent too much time wondering why he prays the way he does.* She turns towards the tower instead and takes measured steps in the direction of the arched door at the foot of the building. The place looks well cared for, but all is quiet. Where are the young women who are supposed to attend this school?

She hasn't even taken three steps when a figure cascades down a few stairs that lead to the doorway. The skirts of the newcomer's dress ripple around her body as she strides forwards.

"Welcome to Koshki tower," the woman says, spreading her arms wide. "Please, come and dine with us and share your news. Travellers are rare these days, and even less frequent are visitors with magical ability. Khoshki Tower has been left to dwindle away. I thought we were completely forgotten, so it seems a miracle to have you here."

She steps aside and lets Viola, Eryk and Jo pass.

The next day, the journey in the glider continues. Viola and Jo work their magic to lift the vessel up, and once airborne, it follows the expert guidance of Eryk at the helm. Viola is relieved to have Jo with her because the cost of using her magic would otherwise make her fall asleep for the rest of her journey. Sharing the burden allows her the opportunity to see the landscape unfolding below them.

It also gives her a chance to consider the strangeness of their brief visit to the famous tower where young girls have been taught the art of magic since the days of Elisabeth of Vendale. The abbess admitted that every decade there were fewer and fewer children with talent brought in, and the dwindling number of students affects the working order of the tower complex. There was hardly anyone there the night before. And the abbess' stories about the reduced number of mages able to combat the Leeching, as she called the loss of natural magic in the region, were heartbreaking.

After a while, Viola latches onto the silence around her, and she looks at her travelling companions. Eryk is focused on flying, and Motoko lies fast asleep in the back seat. Jo stares out the window. His face is grim—as if a heavy black cloud is settled around his head and shoulders.

"What is it, Jo?" Viola ventures.

The young man shifts and blinks away whatever thoughts weigh him down. On the tail end of a sigh, he says, "There's so much death weighing on this land." He looks weary all of a sudden.

"People's deaths?"

Jo shrugs. "It's just the feeling of it hanging in the air, creeping through the earth and floating through All That Is."

Viola notices lines under his eyes and the way he rests his head against the glass of the glider's window. "Is there anything I can do to help?"

He unleashes another even heavier sigh. "I think the only thing that will help is to find the source of the wrongness. Just like I did on Mshrali, I must cure this place."

"What happened on Mshrali? Are you talking about our time there together?"

He shakes his head. "I went back. I was there up until I came here to see you."

"So, what happened?"

Jo shakes his head. "I can't talk about it yet. You're not ready."

Viola glowers at him, but his tone is dark, and she doesn't want to push him. She crosses her arms and grumbles, but Eryk interrupts her dark mood.

"Did I ever tell you about the time I was hunting down this storyteller, and she got away just as I arrived at the docks in Ilwych?" Eryk grins.

Viola slaps him.

Laughing, Eryk regales them with some anecdotes of his time travelling the empire. It doesn't take long for the mood to lighten with his funny stories and Viola's chipping in with tidbits from her escapes.

Soon, Jo calls out. "Stop. We have arrived. I can feel it."

Viola blinks and looks out. Beneath them are patches of open ground between swaths of spindly trees with bare branches. There's no sign of a city having stood anywhere below them. The mountains have closed in, and Viola sees only jagged rocks to left and right. Ahead of them, the valley dwindles into a deep gorge.

Eryk mutters, "There's nowhere to land safely."

Jo clutches his staff, and dancing lights curl like ribbons from him. "I can bring us down," he says and begins the descent before Eryk can say or do anything. The glider touches down much more gently than it did the evening before, and Jo bolts through the hatch before the vehicle has come to a complete stop.

Viola pulls herself out, still stiff but in a much better state than the day before. Less time sitting still is a blessing she won't soon forget. She looks around. All about them, the ground is uneven and covered in yellow grass stalks and the dried brown remnants of moss. The trees stand close by; their twisted trunks and arm-like branches give Viola the shivers. They are mostly leafless. Jo walks with purpose towards an outcropping at the edge of the tree line, and Viola wonders at his vigour. If she'd used magic the way he just did, she'd feel like a dried-out husk until she ate or slept. The air is chill, and goosebumps prickle up Viola's arms despite the thick cloak she's wearing.

Eryk's arm circles her waist, and she leans into him just as Motoko lets rip a throaty growl. Startled, they both look around. There doesn't seem to be anything about, but Motoko keeps up the deep rumbles.

Jo stops short and holds up his hands. "We mean no harm," he calls into the forest.

Viola can't see who he's talking to. She disentangles herself from Eryk's arm and tugs him with her as she makes her way over to Jo.

The strength and determination in her young apprentice's voice surprise Viola when he says, "I have come to help."

There isn't a sound in answer to his words. A shiver runs down Viola's spine, and the hairs on her arms rise as if they're feelers, able to detect what her eyes and ears can't. Even though it's the middle of the day, darkness creeps out of the woods. The shadows deepen, and she squints to see better. Not a sound comes from the forest, and memories flood her mind of trees standing silent on Téarman, only for the stillness to be ripped apart by the serpent of death. She draws her cloak more tightly about her, but the warmth of the fabric does little to calm her trembling nerves.

Motoko has sunk his belly to the ground, and Viola can barely hear the continuous growls coming from the animal. She reaches for the collapsed staff she keeps attached to her belt, and twists to extend it. Beside her, she notices Eryk unclip a magical firearm from his hip. *It is a good thing we came prepared.*

The shapeless blackness increases in size, and with it comes ice that eats its way into Viola's bones. No sound reaches her ears, and she almost wonders whether they've stopped functioning. It's as if a wad of invisible cotton has descended around her head. Jo stands tall, holding his green staff in one hand, and when he speaks, the loudness of his voice makes Viola jump and almost lose her footing on the uneven ground.

"Much is wrong with the land. I'd like to help set it right, but for that, I must speak with you. Please, don't throw lives away. Let's talk." He turns to Viola and Eryk. "Put aside your weapons. We come to bring peaceful change."

From the shadow of a tree, Viola catches sight of two small gleaming copper rounds. They are about the size of marbles, and she strains to see better in the gathering darkness surrounding her, but the luminous orbs wink out, and try as she might, she can't see them anymore. The memory of the last time she stood in terror facing a nameless beast in the dark builds her fear in this moment of silence.

Motoko lifts his head, and lets rip a bone-curdling howl. Viola's heart races faster, and she almost drops her staff. She's thrown back fully into the moment when the Leviathan tore past, decimating the people who'd followed her on Téarman. As she struggles against the fear and darkness of her memories, the prickling on her skin intensifies. She suddenly becomes aware of many, many more glowing orbs. What are they? Why does she feel terror at the sight of them? There is no Leviathan on Haldria, is there?

Over the thundering drumbeat of her blood, Viola strains to see past the flashes of memory. She tries to pull herself into the present to understand what she is seeing. Something shifts in her perception, and she suddenly realises the glowing orbs are eyes. Everywhere she looks, more golden and copper gleams show themselves.

Out of the darkness, a voice rumbles in an intimidating bass, "You say you come to help. We seek none. Begone."

Jo stands firm. "The land cries out for help. From this place, it screams for assistance. I heard that plea and have come."

"Who are you?" The voice is less reserved, and the weight of the darkness lifts somewhat.

"I am the Messenger, harbinger of the change that must come."

The voice grumbles from out of the shadows. "The agent of such news is the Bird of Fire, but I see no wings of flame on you. Who are you?"

Frustration blooms in Jo's tone when he answers, "I am the Bearer, restorer of the balance that was lost."

There's a hardness to the unseen voice when it replies,

"The one who brings equilibrium is the Judge, but I see no scales in your hand. Who are you?"

Viola watches as Jo's grip clenches harder around the staff in his hand. Through her heart-pounding fear and the dimness around her, she sees him close his eyes and breathe. The action reminds her to do the same. One breath after another, and the darkness lifts even more. *You have got this, Jo*, she thinks, and in the same instant, a warm tingle courses through her.

Jo's voice is firm when he speaks. "I am who I am, Messenger of Change, Bearer of Balance, and Wielder of this Ray of Creation."

He thumps the end of his staff against the rock beneath his feet, and the valley lights up so bright it burns Viola's eyes behind her reflexively-shut eyelids. Warmth and lovingness spill from around Jo's feet and envelop everything, sending heat and light through the trees, chasing shadows until they're obliterated in the luminescent wave.

When the brightness subsides, Viola peeks out from behind her arm and is met with the sight of hundreds of wolves standing in a circle around the clearing. Motoko lifts his head and howls. Hundreds of wolf voices join the haunting call, and Viola feels Eryk tense beside her. She turns in a circle, but the four of them are completely surrounded. The wolves' howls crest in a wave of sound and fall away in unexpected silence.

A twig snaps, and Viola startles, turning her attention to the trees ahead of her. One man steps forwards from among the trunks. He's tall and broad-shouldered with a full beard. His clothes are made of leather, and in his hand, he carries a sword. The blade is ancient as far as Viola can tell, but the edge still gleams, and from the look in the man's eyes, she considers it prudent to think of the weapon as sharp and lethal. He comes to a stop and raises the sword in a defensive stance.

The man stares at Jo in silence, and the challenge in his massive frame and strangely yellow eyes is unmistakable. Everything about this man's behaviour sets Viola's hair on end, and she wants to speak, but before she can formulate what to say, another figure totters its way out from among the trees. This person is bent with age, but there's something about the eyes, peering out of the folded skin, that gives Viola pause. Power radiates from the person's gaze, and it makes her tremble. Did this ancient individual bring out the darkness and the cold and fuel Viola's fear? The newcomer shuffles over to the big swordsman and pats him on the forearm, which is at their shoulder height. With an exhale, the swordsman relaxes his stance and lowers the weapon.

The newcomer continues their shuffling advance, but Viola is distracted by the wolves who all sit down, some even stretching out their paws. Their heads are still up and alert, but the threat they held in their bodies has dissipated.

Jo closes the distance to the hunched figure, and Viola follows him. Despite their age, the newcomer's voice is strong when they speak.

"You claim to be the messenger, bearer and wielder, and you've brought light to conquer the shadows. Why are you here, Son to All, Child of None."

Viola bristles at the tone. *What is with this person? Why do they speak to him this way?* The words Son to All, Child of None also grate on her. Viola wants to stand up for him and defend him. He has suffered enough. Considering the way his family treated him, it's not his fault he doesn't belong. But there's also resonance in her heart that he does indeed belong. *He is mine. I claim him.*

However, before she can say anything, Jo quips, "I have

always been a child of the Great Mother-Father." There's conviction in his voice, and it calms some of Viola's reaction.

"Most people claim parentage of a living, breathing being," the wrinkled face says, but there's now humour in the tone. "You're the one we've waited for: the Unclaimed Child who will bring both the Lost Child and the Misguided Child to us. Is that not so?" Beady eyes fix on Viola before twitching towards Eryk.

Viola takes in the figure. They wear animal skins, and there appears to be strength in the limbs even though, from what she can see, the person is no more than skin on bone. Viola considers the enigma: ages old but childlike, neither male nor female but something in between, unnameable, incomprehensible, and immensely powerful. Nevertheless, they exude a strength and power Viola can't quite place.

"I'm Zeni, lorekeeper in this forest."

Jo bows his head. "My friends call me Jo; it's a pleasure to meet you, Zeni." He jerks his head towards the others as they shuffle closer. "Viola. Eryk."

"Welcome," Zeni nods and offers a toothless smile, adding, "Come." The lorekeeper turns, leading the way into the dying trees. "Let's eat, and you can tell me of your purpose." Zeni turns and walks back into the leafless forest, and Jo follows without a glance behind him.

Viola notices Motoko sticking close; he brushes up against her with every stride—almost glued to her leg. She watches as the hulking man falls into step behind Eryk, and a knot tightens in her stomach when the wolves file in behind him. Uneasy, Viola looks around, but apart from the odd wall or pile of moss-coated stones, there's nothing. The tall peaks and the cool air tell her this is most likely where Realtown once stood. She casts about again. How can a thriving city, the heart of a kingdom, vanish so completely? Why was it even abandoned? And who are these two people who command wolves?

Eryk steps up beside her and whispers, "What are we going to do? We're totally outnumbered. If they want to take us prisoner or kill us, there's no way we can stop them. We're at their mercy."

The knot in Viola's gut clenches tighter, but then her gaze falls on Jo. He looks around with curiosity and walks beside Zeni, chatting confidently. Viola smiles at Eryk. "I have learned to trust Jo. No matter how much trouble he gets into, he always manages to get out of it." She chuckles, remembering how he helped her uphold a ruse on the road from Baile so many years ago.

Eryk shakes his head. "I hate to rely on him like that."

"You will have to learn to trust him. Everything I have known him to do has always been a step in a perfect dance. He is a vortex, yes. But he is also a river, and travelling with him, the flow will carry you to marvellous adventures. I cannot explain it properly, Eryk, but he is right. We can have faith everything will work out as long as we listen carefully and act in accordance with what our intuitions dictate."

She glances over at Jo. There's a lightness to his step, and she marvels at how carefree he can be. It reminds her of their time travelling through Mshrali together. He has always been so joyous, exalting in life. Viola is happy this fact hasn't changed, although he's far more serious now.

Eryk sighs, and Viola glances over at him. A furrow creases beside one of his eyebrows, and Viola can't help the chuckle that escapes her. "I know. I really do know." Eryk gives her a sideways glance, and she nudges his shoulder with her own. "I felt that way too. Everything he says sounds backwards when you compare it to what we were taught from the cradle. And yet, when I started listening, I found the results are proof. He gets everything he wants with ease, simply because he believes it possible and only wants what he truly knows to be right and good."

The trees give way to a clearing bordered on one side by a wall of grey rock. Children play with some pebbles close to an overhang in the cliff. A group of youths climb in the trees nearby. Every few paces, there's a stone circle and a cooking fire within it. Many have pots over the flames with fragrant steam rising into the afternoon air. A few women stir their pots or perform other tasks. Their clothes are made from hides and pelts, and Viola is stunned by the primitive conditions of these people. But most puzzling of all, there are no men to be seen anywhere.

The thought hasn't even fully formed in her mind when the pack of wolves arrives. There are so many she considers it could be an army of claws and teeth, but none of the women react to the incursion by the animals. It's as if they're used to seeing this phenomenon. Some of the children stop playing and run over, flinging arms around furry necks.

Her brain has already solved the conundrum when the first wolf melts into human form. It only takes a moment for the man to step into a pair of breeches folded under a rock Viola hadn't noticed in her quick scan of the area. Shirtless, the man steps over to one of the cooking fires and turns a skewer with roasting meat on it to the hiss of fat sizzling on the rising flames, sending the heavenly scent out on the air.

Viola shakes her head. For decades, she's believed the claim that all magical creatures have disappeared from Haldria. And yet, here she is, among the peoples of folklore—shifters, able to take on animal form at will. She looks on in wonder, observing the hundreds of transformations taking place around her, when her gaze falls on Eryk standing beside her.

The former imperial hunter gapes at the males around him.

Viola's always thought Eryk has a stunning physique, but he's got nothing on the rippling pectorals on show in this clearing. She wonders if it makes him feel old. Then again, she's always appreciated his calm ways, how he does what must be done and always tries to make her smile.

Eryk shakes his head, and there's a hardness in his eyes when he says, "This isn't possible. What illusion is this?"

Viola snorts as understanding from his perspective dawns on her. "Believe it or not, this appears to be the hideout of a lost clan of wolf shifters. After seeing three humans turn into lions in that bar a few weeks ago, nothing much surprises me. Jo has a knack for finding the impossible." When Eryk continues to shake his head and clenches and unclenches his fists, Viola settles her hand on his upper arm. "Look at me, Eryk." After a moment, he complies. The shifting sands of a changing worldview flit through his gaze, and the toll it's taking is evident.

"Eryk, I need you to breathe," Viola says as calmly and with as much conviction as she can muster. Air goes in. "Good, now let it out slowly." When he complies, she smiles. "Do you trust me?"

Eryk's eyebrows shoot to the top of his forehead. "Of course I do."

"I trust Jo," Viola continues. "He knows when things are dangerous, and he behaves very differently in those situations. There is nothing to fear here. I am certain of it. If you can, just revel in the experience."

The sun dips behind the mountains, and Viola sits back to study her surroundings while patting her mouth clean, the taste of roast wild meat still rich on her tongue. Most of the assembled people have eaten their fill. Eryk wrestles with a group of youths, each one easily able to overpower him. All the boys preen as they tease the top cadet of the imperial military academy. Viola leans back with a sigh. *At least he has eased into acceptance.* She smiles at the sight of Eryk and the group of children. There are few youngsters. Now that she thinks about it, Viola can see about two dozen under the age of sixteen. There are even fewer babies, less than a handful. *Very strange.*

Pink light glows off the mountain peaks to her left and lights up the few golden leaves still clinging to the branches of their trees. The air hums with laughter and conversation in the wolf-people's dialect.

Viola realises she hasn't seen Jo in a while, and she jumps to her feet, searching for him. Her motion is too abrupt, and dizziness spirals through her. Tumbling backwards, she knocks into the tree stump she was sitting on. She teeters, on the verge of tumbling further, when she catches her balance at the last moment. Breathing hard, she eases herself back onto the tree stump and looks around again. *I need to watch out. Unexpectedly getting up is not an easy feat anymore.*

Jo isn't sitting by the fire talking to Zeni as he was a little while ago. Zeni isn't visible, either. Turning in a circle, frantically searching, Viola's gaze settles on the man with the enormous sword. He stands near the tree line on the opposite side of the clearing from where they were led into the area. Motoko bounds up, much more at ease now most of the wolf people have taken on their human forms.

"Motoko, where is Jo?" Viola asks, and the dog tilts his head and cocks his ears. "Can you find him?"

Yip.

"Will you show me the way?"

Ruff.

The dog trots off towards the large man standing with his back to the forest and his eyes trained on the clearing. As Viola approaches, the swordsman's dark eyes centre on her. A few steps from him, Motoko sits down and wags his tail.

Viola bows her head. "I am looking for Jo. Did he pass this way?"

"Young'un and Lorekeeper go to sacred place."

Intrigued, Viola peers into the gloom of the late afternoon forest. The trunks are thick, and the branches intertwined enough that it's almost dark despite most of the leaves already having fallen. Something tugs at her. She really wants to follow wherever Jo has gone.

"May I join them?" She ventures.

The man's face remains impassive as he shakes his head. A tingling sensation prickles Viola's skin. She has to follow. The feeling is overpowering.

"I feel this is important and something I need to understand. My instinct says I must go there," Viola points into the trees behind the man.

He starts to shake his head, then stiffens. His eyes grow wide, and then he mutters something in his own language. His features tense before he gestures with his head while muttering, "Lorekeeper say you go."

He steps aside, and Viola glances all around them in an attempt to work out how he was given permission. She shrugs and passes, still unsettled. With Motoko by her side, she calms quickly and only looks back once, hoping Eryk will be okay on his own. A sense of calm washes over her, and she accepts he will be safe. *I believe there is no danger here, so I do not need to worry about Eryk. And I can feel the answers are close—I can sense my searching is coming to an end.*

The certainty of her hunch makes her walk with purpose as she navigates the twisted roots and stones underfoot. Motoko leads the way along a path—

With no living plants burgeoning on either side, she's unsure. Everything is barren and dry. Viola considers their trajectory and studies the ground again. She isn't well enough versed in such things to know for certain if it is indeed a path. *At least Motoko seems to know where he is going*, she thinks wryly.

She also considers the landscape. The place where they landed was bare of trees, a flat expanse of nothing, but here the trees are centuries old and sturdy, if leafless. Why has the open area not become overgrown? Where are the remains of Realtown?

Something changes in the atmosphere. All of a sudden, it's much darker, and Viola realises there are no more trees. A dome still curves above her head, but it isn't made from branches, and there are no signs of any tree trunks around her. Looking back, she makes out the last of the trees a few paces behind her.

The path ahead is dark, and she needs light, so Viola digs out the quartz crystal she keeps in her pocket. "Antebas," she murmurs, and the rock glows pink in the dimness of the not-forest. Holding up the quartz, Viola looks around. She appears to be in a tunnel, but the mountainside is behind her. She thought she'd been walking away from the cliff. For a cavern to exist, there would need to be a mountain, but she can't remember anything like that in this position when they landed.

Soft fur brushes under her hand. Viola jumps and looks down into Motoko's soft brown eyes. "Is Jo here?"

The dog turns around and heads into the deeper shadows.

After her experience with the freaky darkness creeping out of the forest earlier in the day, Viola is surprised she doesn't feel more anxiety going into this unknown place filled with shadows and stillness. She's calm and curious. What little of the structure she can make out around her is stone, but there's also something smooth and shiny that reflects the light from her quartz every now and then. Following Motoko, she ventures deeper.

At last, brightness shines ahead, and she hears voices distorted on an echo. Excitement is audible in Jo's tone when Viola is close enough to overhear his conversation. "—is amazing. And you say it crashed? I suppose it isn't possible to get it back out into space?"

Zeni's answer is muffled, and Viola walks into a massive cavern. It is far larger than any cave ought to be. Soft green light emanates from Jo's staff, and there are signs of other light sources filtering across the ceiling of the cave. It's not sunlight. Some strange, artificial lighting glows high above. The wall to Viola's left is covered in tribal paintings of the forest and of animals, mostly wolves, but there's also a streak of orange that looks like flame. There's earth under her feet, but it feels strange—it even smells odd in a stale way—and she can make out what seems to be an intact highrise building. It is reminiscent of the early dwellings built in The Capital during the first years of the empire. It stands to one side of the wide open space but does not quite reach the top of the cavern's dome.

"What is this place?" Viola asks.

Jo's eyes gleam in the light from his staff. He looks like he was expecting her. So does Zeni when Viola glances at the ancient lorekeeper.

Jo twirls around, holding his arms up. "This is what caused the Great Upheaval."

When he stops talking, Viola gives him her trademark *go on* look.

Chuckling, Jo winks at her. "We are inside the spacecraft that crashed into the Vendalen capital close to six hundred and fifty years ago."

What?

Jo looks around again. "Isn't it amazing?"

"How—wait, what—no, I mean—" Viola throws up her hands and huffs. "Start at the beginning."

Zeni gestures for them both to sit. "I'll recount the legend we've passed on from one generation to the next and recorded in this sacred place." The lorekeeper gestures at smudged paintings on the walls of the cave, and Viola considers how much more articulate Zeni is than the sword-wielding hench-man. She brushes the thought aside and focuses on the images depicting what looks like a city perched among the crags, but the cave wall is mostly cast in darkness, and she can't see what follows after that image.

Jo plonks down on the soil, and Motoko collapses next to him while Viola perches on a boulder she finds nearby. Zeni leans on the walking stick and begins.

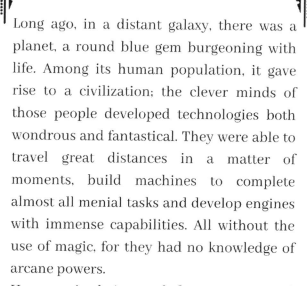

Long ago, in a distant galaxy, there was a planet, a round blue gem burgeoning with life. Among its human population, it gave rise to a civilization; the clever minds of those people developed technologies both wondrous and fantastical. They were able to travel great distances in a matter of moments, build machines to complete almost all menial tasks and develop engines with immense capabilities. All without the use of magic, for they had no knowledge of arcane powers.

However, in their search for ever more and better things, they destroyed the living world of their planet, leaving it a desecrated

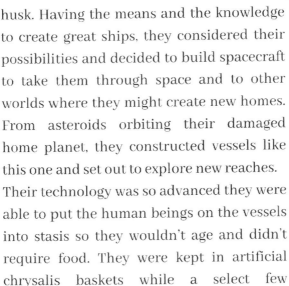

husk. Having the means and the knowledge to create great ships, they considered their possibilities and decided to build spacecraft to take them through space and to other worlds where they might create new homes. From asteroids orbiting their damaged home planet, they constructed vessels like this one and set out to explore new reaches.

Their technology was so advanced they were able to put the human beings on the vessels into stasis so they wouldn't age and didn't require food. They were kept in artificial chrysalis baskets while a select few remained awake to tend them. Together with an army of machines and over many

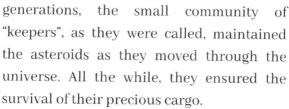

generations, the small community of "keepers", as they were called, maintained the asteroids as they moved through the universe. All the while, they ensured the survival of their precious cargo.

They arrived at a promising planet and the decision was made to revive the sleeping cargo but something went wrong. Instead of going into orbit, the ship crashed into the planet.

"**A**ccording to my ancestors who have populated these mountains and valleys for millennia, the survivors of the crash stepped out of the wreckage of their asteroid, gathered together the few humans from this area who survived and marched west, collecting more and more people to their banner. It didn't take them long to create an army that swept through this continent, and then further afield, in search of resources to establish a new world order run on the technological discoveries of their old planet."

Zeni lapses into silence. Viola glances around. She can't quite make out what this cavern was, but something about it feels strange. She thinks about Zeni's story and considers the size of the dome curving above her. Her mind latches onto her memory of an asteroid impact site she saw during her time travelling the empire.

"If what we are standing in was an asteroid repurposed as a vessel that crashed into this planet, why is there anything left of the ship? Or the mountain, for that matter? On entering the atmosphere, the rock would have burned up or left an enormous crater where it impacted. I did not notice any indentation big enough, and there were still signs of human habitation back where we landed our glider. This makes no sense."

"Your scientific knowledge is sound, child."

Viola stiffens but bites back a retort. This is not her mother, and Zeni would not mean it the same way the empress does. It also makes Viola wonder how old Zeni might be.

The lorekeeper continues. "However, the Kingdom of Vendale was also home to a group of the most powerful magic users known to humankind, the Vendalen Royal Circle of Mages. They did everything in their power to protect their city from the incoming shooting star—that's how they interpreted the falling ship. They slowed its velocity sufficiently for this asteroid to squash the city rather than obliterate everything from here to the ocean." Zeni shrugs. "They died trying to save their people, and indeed, they did save most. My ancestors survived. People living in villages a few leagues away thrived in the years following the crash. The mages of the Vendalen Royal Circle saved the lives of almost all those aboard the vessel, people who would have been obliterated if the asteroid had impacted under the full force of its incoming velocity. They were unable to save the people in the city, which was indeed turned to dust upon the impact of the starship. There wasn't enough time for an evacuation."

Viola realises her hand is in front of her mouth and drops it into her lap. "Oh, my," she breathes. "What a tragedy."

Jo comes to his feet, drawing Viola's attention. "And the people who survived were of a mindset that made Haldria theirs to own and to exploit. Instead of living in harmony with the planet, they plundered it, extracting water directly from the air until there was no more rain. The oceans dried up, and the forests died. From there, changes had to be made, so everything previously performed by nature was done by mechanical and synthetic means. Seeds are manufactured in laboratories instead of grown in the soil. Everything is backwards because of the way the people who were on this ship thought." He sighs, and Viola feels the weight of his cares. Jo shakes his head as he murmurs, "And so many people died. I can feel it through the soil. Not just the deaths caused here during the crash. Since setting foot on this continent yesterday, I have felt the pain and the terror unleashed from this focal point. The group who left here brought death with them. Anyone who refused to join them was brutally killed. Whole cities were decimated. It may have taken place centuries ago, but the memory of the horrors unleashed is still rooted in the soil. No one cleansed the energies. No one restored the balance. And the entire planet is in turmoil because of it."

Zeni nods. "You're a very perspicacious young man. Yes, my people have been watching the disequilibrium become more pronounced with every passing year. In the centuries since the Haldrian Empire was formed, natural—or should I say, unnatural—disasters caused crop failures and other difficulties for the farmers in these lands. Many fled across the sea—well, what is now desert—and joined the burgeoning city, while others starved."

"But your clan has survived and even thrived," Viola points out.

"'Tis true." Zeni sighs, "But we're paying the price now. Food grows scarce, and there are few cubs born."

Viola considers the hundreds of adults she saw gathered around their fires for their meal that afternoon. *There is only a handful of children.*

"The imbalance is also affecting our magic. It's exhausting to transform, and few of the younger generation do it. Those who can wield more, as I can, struggle to maintain it. My illusion of darkness to scare you off this afternoon made hardly any impression at all."

Many questions simmer in Viola's mind, but she latches onto the one that seems most important. "What can be done to reverse these effects?" Her thoughts race over the research she's done about Queen Johara's feat some eight hundred years ago. "I have found evidence that it is possible."

Zeni's head shakes. "If you mean performing the Sacred Challenge or some other offering of magical and human blood, the time for that passed many centuries back. A Guardian ought to have made a call for the Sacred Challenge half a millennium ago, but none ever came. Few believe in the Old

Ones these days, even in these parts. They have been forgotten and have lost their power because of it. I doubt the Forest Father even walks these woods anymore. There has been no known sighting of him in over a thousand years. And without a Guardian, it's unlikely anything can be done."

Jo pipes in, "Don't give up hope just yet. There's always a way. We must just find it." A smile lights up his eyes, and Viola can't help but nod. She believes with every fibre of her being that there is indeed something they can do to reverse the imbalance ravaging the planet.

Chapter Twenty

It's chill when Viola wakes, and she takes a moment to register where she is. Above her, leaves stick out through the interwoven boughs, and she remembers Jo constructed a shelter for the three of them on the outskirts of the forest clearing near the wolf clan's fires. He sang to life some of the dead branches, and now she looks in wonder at the dome curving above her head. She also remembers he didn't show any signs of fatigue after performing the feat.

Sitting up, Viola takes in the nest of pelts around her as frigid air caresses her bare arms. With a shiver, she grabs her tunic folded on top of her cloak right next to her sleeping place. As she slips into her clothes, Viola glances around the otherwise empty shelter. The only signs of Eryk and Jo are a jumble of furs to either side of her sleeping place.

She tries to push herself to her feet and groans. Everything aches. Her back is a bundle of knots. She rolls over and pushes herself to her feet only to get a reprimanding twinge from her knee. *I am too old for this business of sleeping on hard ground.*

She shuffles towards the edge of the shelter and ducks under the pelt that hangs as a door covering. Bright sunlight forces her eyes shut, and she has to blink a few times until the clearing by the foot of the cliff comes into view. It is beautiful in the early morning light.

She scans the wolf clan's fires and looks over to the cliff where she was shown a hidden entrance under an overhang. The wolves' cave home is impressive, but remembering the intense stench of dog makes Viola shudder.

Ruff! Motoko lollops to Viola's side.

"Morning," she replies gruffly and searches the area nearby. A few members of the wolf clan are going about their early morning business. The children and youths are sitting in a semi-circle close to the cliff's foot near the entrance to the caves. Viola squints, but she can't quite make out what they're looking at.

"There you are." Eryk draws Viola's attention to her left, where he's sitting on a tree stump near a fire. She hobbles towards him while he pours something into an earthenware mug from a pot with a spout. "I hope you slept well," he adds, handing her the cup.

Viola grunts and mutters, "If I never have to sleep on the ground again for the rest of my life, I shall die a happy woman."

Eryk chuckles as she accepts the offered cup.

The fragrance from the dark brew zings into her next inhale, and Viola clutches the warm cup tighter. She takes another deep breath and allows the aroma to enliven her spirit before she lets the first sip tingle over her tongue.

Reinvigorated after her kopi and some bread with leftover slices of meat from the night before, Viola once more focuses her attention on her surroundings. The sun is just peeking over the mountaintops behind them, and this side of the valley is cast in shadow. The air is crisp and hints at the coming winter. The children still sit where she saw them before, and now she makes out Jo perched atop a boulder beyond them. She smiles as she walks over to the group, stretching out her stiff muscles with every step.

Jo's audience is entranced. Upturned grimy faces pay rapt attention to his word-weaving. None notice the swirls of light dancing around his figure, for they are spellbound by his tale.

Viola studies the undulating shimmers. They're different from what she saw when he was younger. The light used to look like the aurora borealis but with more colours. Now, it's almost as if vines of brightness stretch out tendrils to caress the people sitting around him. *It looks as if he is blessing them.* Viola's heart squeezes at the thought. *Is that even possible?*

When his tale finishes, there's silence. Viola savours the breath—the stillness where eternity hangs suspended for all to experience. It's her favourite moment of public storytelling, and when she looks at Jo, she sees a glint in his eye. *He's clearly basking in this*, Viola chuckles to herself.

The spell is broken, and the children scamper off in search of new entertainment. Jo bounds to his feet, picking up his green staff from where it leans against a rock, and grins at Viola.

"You spend a lot of time with the children," Viola observes.

Jo's grin widens, and his eyes sparkle. "they're the best audience. Children never doubt, and they can suspend all belief and simply enjoy the tale. *Dragons' Daughter* was the perfect tale for these wolf-children. Fernanda's transformation didn't bother them in the slightest." The happiness melts from his face. "Children are also invariably wiser than adults." Seriousness exudes from every pore when he adds, "I felt something when the sun came up. It's been tugging at me ever since. I'd like to explore over there." Jo points towards the peaks on the other side of the valley, not too far from where the ancient spaceship's wreckage lies.

"What is it?" Viola looks at the bare trees and grey mountains capped with a cape of fluffy clouds.

Jo shrugs. "I don't know, but something tells me it's important."

Eryk sidles up. He looks from Jo to Viola and back again before asking, "Are we heading back to The Capital today? Did you get the answers you were looking for?"

Jo shakes his head. "There's more. I can feel it crawling in my bones. Today is going to be an incredible day."

He strides forwards and weaves through the cooking fires. Viola follows, and Eryk falls into step beside her. Motoko bounds up and joins them on her other side. They walk in companionable silence until Jo turns at the tree line.

"Motoko, stay," he commands.

"Why?" Viola lays a hand on the dog's head.

Whine.

"Because something tells me where we're going won't be good for him. I've learned to trust these notions I sometimes have. Motoko must stay."

Viola pats the dog's head and nods. "Motoko, stay," she repeats.

Jo joins her and crouches down in front of the dog. After a moment of silent conversation, the young man rises, while Motoko slides to the ground on his stomach.

"Good," Jo comments and heads into the forest.

Twigs crack underfoot, and above, the branches whisper and creak against each other. The air warms under the sun's gentle touch, but no birds welcome the morning. The forest is silent. Just like the lifeless desert on Mshrali. Precisely the same as the rainforest on Téarman.

The thought sends a shiver up Viola's spine. Silent forests are the worst kind. She glances around more and more often and strains her ears against the soundlessness. What horrors await them now?

Quiet—both insidious and oppressive—creeps into her mind. It bears down around her, tugs her into the dark and terrifying place where silence explodes in blood, and she tastes fear on the end of her tongue.

"Jo," Viola whispers. Her voice is dry. Cracked.

Eryk's hand brushes against her arm, and she jerks away. "Are you well, Vi?" There's concern in his voice, but the silence of the forest is drowned out by the *thud-thud-thud* of her heart. She can't breathe. Everything is closing in, squeezing tighter. Even the slightest motion is an agonising fight against the steel-tense fibres in her body.

"Isp—Viola," Eryk's voice is more urgent, but she can't respond to him.

In her mind, Viola is in the vortex of fear and screams and spraying blood—death—whirling between the trees. She is subsumed by the memories, trapped in the coils of the past.

"Master." A gentle voice offers a beacon of hope in the terrifying darkness. Viola remembers that timbre. *He* was there, too, that day. The boy. She saved him. The death and destruction she relives are in the past. She can set it aside and live this moment for what it is, not allow that occurrence to colour everything she sees.

"Master."

There it is again. Kind, sweet boy. Apprentice. The one who would have died if she hadn't done what needed to be done. The one who survived. Her one. Hers.

Viola opens her eyes. The light is bright, and she blinks. Behind her, Eryk stands, holding her upright. Flustered, she steadies herself, jostling into Jo, who stands in front of her.

"I am fine," she mutters, nudging both away.

"You're afraid," Jo states.

"Silent forests terrify me." Viola tries to push past, but Jo's stare stops her.

"You need not fear, Master. I went back. The Leviathan has been set free. It will trouble no one anymore."

She shakes her head. How could this little boy, this only-just-man, face off that monster? No. He must be saying it to calm her.

Eryk steps up behind her again, his arms encircling her waist. "What is this? What do you mean, Leviathan?"

Viola wants to pull away. She doesn't talk about this. Reliving it in her nightmares—and waking memories—is traumatic enough. No need to raise the monster intentionally as well. It was bad enough glossing over it for her mother. She shakes her head and tries to wrench free from his grip.

"I am fine," she growls.

"You don't look fine," Eryk points out.

Jo lays a hand on her shoulder. "You haven't spoken of it?"

Viola shakes her head.

"To anyone?" Jo's pitch rises.

She shrugs.

"Well, no wonder silent forests scare you." Over her shoulder, he glances at Eryk. "In Téarman, outside Baile, we encountered an ancient creature, a Leviathan. The destruction of its forest twisted it into a bloodthirsty being—well, it's that no more." His eyes meet Viola's. "It won't harm anymore. You're safe."

Eryk's arms tighten around her waist. His voice is hoarse when he asks, "Was that what killed all the guards in Baile? I saw the—remains—after."

Viola shudders.

"Yes," Jo says. "That was the Leviathan. But it's gone now."

Viola can't begin to imagine that possibility, but Jo's tone is so firm, and his face radiates conviction. *Did I not say just yesterday that I trust him?* The thought is reproachful. She studies Jo's face for a moment, exploring the sincerity in his eyes.

"But how?" she asks at last.

Jo grins. "That's not the question." He winks at her, and a grin spreads over his lips.

Viola tilts her head back, bringing it to rest on Eryk's shoulder, and sighs. Rolling her eyes, she parrots, "When I ask how, I can only think from within my understanding in the now. That is why I need to relax my mind."

Jo's grin widens with every word, deepening his dimple, and his eyes sparkle. "You did listen." There's surprise and pleasure in his voice.

"Of course I listened," she grumbles. "You did not give me much choice in the matter." Viola rights herself again and squeezes Eryk's hand. "I am all right now. No need for either of you to worry."

Jo raises an eyebrow as he appraises her. Viola waves him off and sidesteps him. The young man twirls theatrically and falls into step beside her, pointing with his staff towards a clearing a short way ahead.

After a brief incline, they come out into a large area devoid of trees. Moss-covered stones are scattered all around, and Viola makes out the remnants of walls. Most aren't more than knee high, but there's enough to recognise the residue of a large building. She glances around her, but there's very little to go on. From this vantage point, the mountain peaks to the east and west encroach on the area, ringing it like a crown.

She takes in the slight dip they traversed to get to this spot, her brain working on piecing together the picture of what building might have stood in this place. There's nothing to indicate where in the old Vendalen city they might be standing. Nothing is as Queen Elisabeth described it in her writings.

Something glints gold in the early morning sunlight. Viola walks over to it, stepping over a large curved stone—marble perhaps. Vines are latched onto everything around her, and she wades through the dark green heart-shaped leaves.

Her toe rams into something hard, and Viola bites back the pain. She looks down at the offending item and finds something made of gold. Bending over, she examines what she's found, ripping away the creeper plant.

The sun shines on the white marble head and single golden antler of a stag—the remains of a statue. She casts about, but there doesn't seem to be anything else remaining of it. To her left, the area is bordered by the rounded stone. On her right, there's nothing but sand. When she looks closer at the area, this strange phenomenon is visible throughout the clearing. A swath of sand with glints of glass cuts through the ruins as if a baker tossed some flour in a streak upon a baking tray.

"This must have been the place of impact," Jo murmurs from nearby. He points with his staff, marking the trajectory towards the crashed spaceship's hull several leagues to the northeast. The leafless trees are shorter in this segment of the forest, and there are signs of regrowth that have withered and died since the rains stopped.

Viola looks again at the remnants of the stag statue in her hand. Her mind jumps to the description of the Vendalen Royal Palace from Elisabeth's memoir. *There was a statue of a stag outside the palace, inside a fountain*, she recalls. Her mind chooses this moment to remember another piece of trivia. The stag: insignia of the royal house of Vendale and symbol of kingship, righteous rule and grace. She remembers there's more, but her mind can't unearth what it is. She shakes her head.

Jo has moved away from what she assumes are the remaining walls of the once proud palace. He moves to the east and continues his search. He reminds Viola of a sniffing dog. After a while, he calls, "Over here," and steps between some overgrown boulders. In the next moment, he disappears.

Viola hurries after him, and Eryk joins from where he was poking around the rocks on the other side of the clearing. When Viola reaches the place where Jo disappeared, she pushes against the plants and her foot slips on a loose rock, sending her forwards, flailing her arms to keep her balance. She catches herself and calls out, "I am fine."

She looks up over her left shoulder to see Eryk skid to a halt and snap his mouth shut. He nods, but she can see he's breathing hard. She gives him a smile before turning her attention to her feet. Her right foot has fallen down, leaving her left foot at the height of her right knee. There are two uneven stone steps between her feet, and when she looks down past where Jo went, she sees a flight of stairs that look like crooked teeth.

Jo is several feet below her on a curve around to the left. Slowly, Viola follows. With each step, her heart pounds louder in her ears. The exertion of climbing down an overgrown, time-worn staircase is part of it, but her mind is also running down these stairs in the memories from her own book. The folktale about Elisabeth of Vendale mentions a staircase leading to a secret grotto beneath the palace. Could these be the same stairs close to eight hundred years later? In those ancient days, it was common knowledge that the grotto beneath the palace existed, but how many people outside of the royal family of Vendale ever set foot in this place?

Excitement mounts. It's an ever-growing bubble lifting Viola's spirits. Finally, she's living a fairytale. Viola rounds the wall to her left and comes out in a dark west-facing cavern. The cave is small, and the air tingles, prickling over her skin. There's wonder in the atmosphere. The whole place sings with magic, and she traces over the rough stone walls and the cracked remains of a basalt altar at the centre of the area.

Jo stands beside the altar, examining something, and he glows. Viola looks again, and she shakes her head in wonder. *He is definitely glowing.* She blinks and realises she doubts her own eyes.

"Is he shining?" Eryk's query makes Viola want to laugh. She nods, suppressing the mirth because this is a holy place. She can feel it. Eryk doesn't seem to sense the sacredness, though, because he asks, "Does Jo usually glow like sunlight? Or are you refusing to comment?"

Viola whispers back. "He is glowing. I have no idea why. But it does not seem right to speak here." She steps forwards to see what Jo is looking at.

The young man's right hand traces over etchings in the stone. His left hand clutches his staff, which also glows—bright green. Viola looks over her shoulder. Perhaps the glow is coming from outside and is just reflecting on the boy and the staff. There's no sign of any sunlight coming into the grotto. Looking out over the valley and the western Fyall mountains, Viola thinks about her description in *The Siblings' Tale*. There's no way morning light could filter into this chamber. *So, I got that wrong. It is impossible for the sun's first rays to shine here. But then, what light could it have been that revived the queen? Perhaps it was not this chamber? Could there be a second grotto?*

A voice echoes through the chamber, and Viola whirls around to see where it comes from because the tone is wrong for both Eryk and Jo.

"I bid thee welcome, strangers from distant realms."

The voice makes Viola think of the ancient stone in the mountains and the endlessness of the forests. It's deep and old and resonant. There's no indication of where it comes from, though. Viola glances at Eryk and then Jo. The former is bewildered, also looking all around the grotto, frantically searching out the source of the voice. The latter speaks.

"Thank you, you're most kind, Ancient One."

Viola frowns. How does Jo know that? Then again, the voice sounds ancient.

"And it is a gift to make thine acquaintance, Wordmage." There's a pause as if the speaker is struggling to breathe. "For aeons, I have waited and tended these lands," it says, the words echoing in the chamber, "but never did I dream this day would come." It pauses again. "It is a solace to know I do not leave this world without a champion remaining to continue the work that must be done."

The voice seems to come from everywhere in the chamber, and Viola now turns in a circle in hopes of finding the owner. Apart from her, Eryk, and Jo, there's absolutely no sign of any other living thing in the chamber.

As if reading her mind, Jo asks, "Could you show yourself? It will be easier for us to talk if you take on your physical form."

The voice sighs. "I have not taken on a form of flesh in many long cycles. No one believes in me and mine anymore. It seemed futile, and I fear I may have forgotten."

"What form did you take? I could help you," Jo offers.

The creature snorts. "I suppose thou mayest, Wordmage." It pauses. "But I think I shall make an attempt of mine own first."

A glimmer appears above the altar, and Jo steps backwards to give the speaker space. Viola watches in awe as the little spark of light grows until it's a ball the size of her hand. The orb expands further, and with the next heartbeat, a white stag sits atop the altar.

Wonder fills Viola. This is the white hart, the creature whose statue stood outside the walls of this palace, the symbol of the Vendalen royal house. But now she also remembers more. The white stag is the Guardian of the forest, one of the ancient ones, believed by many early peoples to be gods.

But before her sits no deity. The animal is thin, its fur matted and patchy. In some areas, the pinkness of hide is visible where the hairs have fallen away. The rack of antlers that ought to be majestic is missing. A pair of pedicles remains. All other signs of this stag's grandeur have been lost to time. It's a ragged, pitiful creature. And Viola has no doubt it's dying.

"You're a Guardian?" Jo ventures.

"Aye," the creature wheezes, its whole body shaking under the exertion of each breath.

"And you are the Guardian of the Forest." It's a statement rather than the question Viola expects.

"Aye." The stag turns obsidian eyes onto Viola. "Thou hadst a query."

More than one, surely, she thinks before focusing her mind. She glances around the grotto again and absorbs the west-facing entrance. "In the folktale about Elisabeth, there is a description of her being laid on an altar in a grotto beneath the Vendalen palace and revived by the first ray of sunlight. But," she gestures around her, "that is not possible here."

"Indeed," the stag nods. "'Twas not the sun's ray. Magic can become visible." The stag's chest expands as it draws air into its lungs. "To most, it is so like sunlight it is nigh impossible to distinguish the difference—for a ray of magic bears warmth too."

Involuntarily, Viola sucks in air. It's painful to watch this majestic creature struggling with such a simple act. Her mind goes over all her questions and latches onto the one that's been haunting her for several segments. Maybe she can find an answer here.

"I have been researching the reign of Johara of Erdalbad. She was called the Jewel of Forests and Seas because, during her reign, the land somehow regenerated. Do you know how she did it? I take it there was magic involved."

The white hart chuckles, sputters, and then coughs. Viola considers the strangeness of an animal behaving in such a human way.

Once the hacking subsides, the stag rasps, "Do I ever? 'Twas I who oversaw her offering in the Sacred Challenge." The creature falls silent.

"What is the Sacred Challenge?"

The stillness draws out, and Viola is on the verge of repeating her question when the white stag whispers, "The Sacred Challenge is the ritual used to renew the magic in these lands. It requires the blood of a human and that of a magical being."

Eryk steps forwards, eyes blazing. "What do you mean? A blood sacrifice? Such barbaric practices have been abolished for centuries!"

Jo raises his free hand and shakes his head. He looks pointedly at the stag but says nothing.

After another interminable silence, the stag wheezes, "It *is* a blood sacrifice, but the quantity of blood spilt is proportional to its potency."

"What does that mean?" Eryk's tone is angry, and Viola lifts a hand onto his shoulder.

Jo looks up at Eryk. "It means that a person with strong blood—maybe spiritually or magically strong—can use a drop or two in the Sacred Challenge, and it will do the same as all the lifeblood of a person who is weak of mind and spirit."

"Precisely," the stag echoes. "It must also be given freely. Such a gift can never be taken by force."

"So anyone can do this?" Viola asks. Her heart races at the

thought. She can contribute to fixing this situation here and now. Excitement races. *If this can be achieved today, so much pain and suffering could be averted. If only my ancestors had known about this, then none of the destruction would have happened.* Another thought latches onto her consciousness. "If it is this simple, why have you not initiated this Sacred Challenge before things got to this stage?"

The stag sighs. "Renewing the magic was due five hundred years hence. When the time came, no one on Haldria with strong blood believed in fantastical beings or cared for the state of nature or magic." Another heavy gasp shudders through the stag before it continues, "The elementals and other beings with an affinity for the natural realm were under assault from all sides, and their eradication has sped up the deterioration in the natural world." It struggles to breathe for a moment but still forces out, "There are pockets where things are better, but throughout the land, there is suffering, and until today, there was no one to step up and put things to rights."

Jo shifts his weight and leans towards the stag. "How do we do this? I can—"

Large eyes twitch to him as the animal shakes its head. "Thou canst not do this, Wordmage. It would not be right."

"What? Why?"

Viola hears the frustration in his voice, and she settles her hand on his arm.

The stag sighs. "Thou art not of *this* sphere." There's a weight to its words. "And thou art too magical. The ritual of the Sacred Challenge requires the blood of one *human* and one magical being tied to the land."

Jo shakes Viola's hand off him. "But then I can stand for the magical being, if that's what you're saying I am. And either Master or he," Jo gestures from Viola to Eryk standing behind her, "can provide the human blood. We can fix this now! Let's not put this planet through more horrors."

Shaking its head again, the stag wheezes, "Thine purpose is greater, Wordmage. If thou becomest a Guardian now, thou wilt be tied to this realm and the waxing and waning of its magic, as I have been." The head sinks to the stone below it, and the stag shifts its whole body to lie flat on the hard black surface. "Thine purpose is greater, Wordmage."

"But then how—" Viola starts and glances from Jo to the stag. "Who should do this? I can provide the human blood. I would gladly spill all of my life force if it could re-establish the balance. But who will provide the magical blood? As you said, the elves and elementals are all but destroyed. There has not been word of a goblin sighting in centuries—unicorns are confirmed extinct. How can we renew the magic on Haldria if all the magical creatures have been exterminated?"

"Thou seest," the stag rolls its eyes to look at Jo. "The Sacred Challenge requires more than strength of blood. Always remember the desire to bring change is the biggest catalyst. It strengthens the blood a thousandfold. This one," the eyes flick to Viola, "will need but three drops added to mine own lifesblood for the renewal to take effect." It stops, its body motionless except for the diaphragm, which heaves with every breath.

After struggling for a moment, the stag whispers, the sound filtering into Viola's mind rather than flowing through her ears, "I am the last. The other Guardians have faded away. Olwen, Brynna—I have not heard from either in centuries. Bethany—dissolved in the wind, I presume. Mine time hath come. Spill the last of mine blood and bring on the regeneration."

Viola stares at the stag. *We have to kill this creature?* Her essence objects. She wants to save the stag, not sacrifice it. "No, there must be another way," she argues. "Renewing the magic should help you regain your strength as well. It would, would it not?"

The stag's whisper is softer than a puff of air. "Must hurry. Time runs out— Must spill blood. Hurry—"

Viola meets Jo's eyes, and his expression is solemn. "Do you have a blade?" His question makes her shudder. When she shakes her head, Jo turns a questioning glance to Eryk, who shifts and retrieves a hunting knife from his belt.

Jo takes the hilt as Viola steps backwards, giving him space, and then Jo turns towards the stag whose breathing is coming out more laboured and ragged with every exhale.

"Is there really no other way?" Viola whispers.

Shaking his head, Jo mumbles something Viola doesn't understand, but she feels calm settle over the grotto. It's as if his words have brought another presence to oversee the proceedings, and she feels calmer, although still affected by the thought of sacrificing the stag.

The blade slides through the skin of the white hart's neck, and green liquid spills forth onto the altar. The sight of leaf-green blood makes Viola take another step back. A surge of bile threatens at the level of her solar plexus, and she averts her gaze while she bites back the reflex. Studying the sand-stone at her feet, she realises the basalt altar must have been brought to this location. Looking at the massive stone with the white stag lying easily upon it, Viola wonders at such a feat. She's also surprised at the trivial thought, but it keeps her grounded, and she maintains her focus on it.

Jo steps back from the dying creature, and Viola has a full view of the sickly animal's body, covered in sores and scabs, its pristine white fur tinged green from the liquid rolling down its side and pooling in a channel carved into the stone. Jo shifts where he stands, and Viola sees the knife in his hand. A green trail runs to the tip of the blade and forms a single malachite bead.

Viola claps both hands over her mouth at the sight of it. She also realises the air smells funny; the Guardian's blood doesn't reek with iron. It's more like a condensation of forest —loam and moss with an undercurrent of tree.

Peeking over her fingers at Jo, Viola asks, "Could we clean the knife before you cut me?"

Jo wipes the blade on his sleeve and shrugs. As Viola squeezes her eyes shut, trying to suppress a shudder and thinking, *That is not quite what I had in mind*, Jo steps towards her.

"We need to hurry. I don't know how much time we have before your blood needs to be added."

Viola takes in a deep breath of forest-tinged air and readies herself. *I can do this. It is just a few drops of blood, after all. Nothing serious.*

Eryk clears his throat, and she meets his gaze. He holds his hand out to Jo, who hands over the knife.

"Vi," Eryk clears his throat. "Are you certain you wish to do this?"

Squaring her shoulders, she nods and holds out her hand. "Do it."

Eryk grasps her fingers. His touch is warm and gentle. Viola is so focused on him that she barely has time to notice the zing of pain before it's gone.

A crimson bead wells on the tip of her finger, and she moves forwards, holding her hand over the altar's channel containing the green fluid. The drop splashes, and for a moment, Viola thinks, *Red and green make brown*. But the crimson spatter retains its colour, hanging within the darkening malachite.

The second trickle flees her finger and embraces the green.

A third drop follows close behind and lands right beside the other two globules swimming in a sea of emerald.

Even as the fourth droplet pearls on her finger, Viola notices the white stag's dark spruce-coloured blood begins to lighten. A glow coalesces around the three droplets of red, and as the fourth splashes in beside them, the green brightens even more. The transition through shades is faster than Viola can follow, and with the next inhale, she realises it's become the colour of newly sprouted leaves. The spring verdure intensifies further, and as a fifth drop lands in the liquid, it explodes into gold.

In wonder, Viola stares at the pulsating ball of light that rises off the altar and hovers above it. She's barely conscient of Eryk's hand pulling hers closer to him and wrapping her finger in some cloth. From very far away, her mind wonders where he found a bandage, but in the next heartbeat, the thought is blown away. The pulsating ball of light lances a ray through the eastern wall of the cavern. Almost simultaneously, another ray slices right through Viola and she jumps aside, checking herself. There's no sign of any damage. It's just light. Or is it? The white hart's words echo in her mind. *To most, it is so like sunlight they cannot distinguish the difference—for a ray of magic bears warmth too.*

Viola dips a finger into the beam of light and confirms it's warm, just like a ray of sunlight. *I am looking at magic*, she thinks as she glances up. Four more radiant streaks have appeared, north and south, as well as perpendicular to the cardinal directions.

In the next instant, Viola senses a gathering of energy. The ball at the centre of the streaks of light pulses, and a blast of energy pushes her backwards several steps right to the entrance of the grotto. She watches the energy course out of the grotto, following the light, which casts its line westwards.

The drumbeat of the energy explosion pounds into Viola, and the impact knocks her Self apart. Everything that makes her Viola Alerion evaporates. She is. And she is part of everything. From the smallest living organism to the top of the highest peaks in the Fyall mountains, Viola feels all—sees all—becomes one with All. Beneath her feet pounds the steady heartbeat of the land. It swells and grows into a thrumming rhythm, overpowering, all-encompassing—the very breath of the mountains.

As it radiates out from the golden core at the heart of the grotto, Viola can almost hear the powerful horn call of the magic announcing itself through the valley. Echoes of the sharp, distinct bugle bounce off the peaks and gather all living things to follow the summons.

In the whirl and dance of gentle strings, she senses the plants along the slopes answering the summons. At first, it's soft, tentative, but as the music of magic gathers and builds, the vegetation responds, eager and filled with joy. With her whole being, Viola experiences the wave of growth as it charges through the valley. The magical music strengthens and roars into a glorious burgeoning crescendo—a celebration of life.

The sublime expansion of All That Is condenses into Viola's being and snuffs out in stillness. Although she knows her physical body is still standing within the grotto beneath the crumbling remains of Vendale's one-time royal palace, Viola finds the stillness in her heart is in some other place. Almost bone-white tree trunks spread out around her, forming tall columns that branch into a vaulted canopy high above her. The intertwining branches are so dense that only the smallest tendrils of light filter down to the mossy ground at her feet. She's barefoot. The freedom to walk on the soft earth and absorb the beauty of the living world fills Viola's heart with tranquillity, the likes of which she's never experienced before.

The stillness is complete, and it tingles over the skin of her arms. It brings another wave of calm with it. The place fills her heart with peace, and there's something about the coolness of the air and the deep hush that surrounds her—if she didn't know better, she'd say she was in some kind of chapel. As Viola watches, light travels up each of the column-like tree trunks. The golden brightness reaches the intertwined branches and flares, racing along the length of the natural ceiling and lighting up the space beneath.

Golden sparks rain down, and wherever they hit the ground, tendrils of light sprout, followed a moment later by green spears pushing their way through the soil. After the grass, a surge of colours explodes the place into bloom. The intensity of the golden light emanating from the canopy subsides and gives way to a softer green glow as glittering peridot leaves unfurl from the dome above. Throughout it all, she feels the reverberations and swells of music.

A movement between the tree columns draws Viola's attention away from the combination of magic and natural growth around her. She looks up into unblinking obsidian eyes. A mere three feet from her stands the towering figure of the Forest Father with a full rack of antlers. The white stag's coat is healed and appears white as snow, shimmering in the gentle light of the magic around them.

I thank thee, the hart's voice echoes in Viola's mind. It steps up beside her. *Thou hast performed a great service to this land. Thine blood is indeed potent, and with the help of the Wordmage, the shift will become permanent. If only we still had a phoenix in this realm—but her lack of faith was part of the fall. Perhaps humans will now allow themselves to embrace their true nature as expansive beings and bring goodness and light to the world.*

Viola looks into the endless dark of the stag's eyes. She has so many questions and doesn't know where to start. At the same time, she feels an unprecedented level of calm, and something tells her these questions don't need to be answered at this moment.

The stag rests its head upon her shoulder. *I wish also to give thee thanks for setting me free. I have walked this realm for aeons with never a moment's rest. Now, at last, I may find peace and rejoin the Maker in the Endlessness.*

Viola presses her hand into the soft fur on the Ancient One's neck. She's filled with loss even as the symphonic rejoicing all around her reaches a euphoric moment of exaltation. Tears burn streaks down her cheeks.

Come, do not weep. Look upon what thou hast achieved. The stag leads her to a doorway she hadn't noticed before in the chapel-like place. *See the mountains clothed once more in their mantles of autumnal fire. Hear the laughing song of the rivers rushing to the sea. Soon the birds and the beasts will bring this forest back to life with the magic of the little folk, and as the magic in the elements grows, thou mayest yet find the folk of rock, wind, water and flame regenerating their physical forms and tending to their charges. All will be well. As a parting gift, I wish to bestow upon thee a part of mine remaining essence. Mayest thou always find peace. Mayest thine heart find its courage. And mayest thou ever trust in the potency of thine blood. I thank thee.*

The voice fades, and Viola watches as the stag becomes ever more transparent and fades into the air that tingles with life and change. It vanishes into light as surely as a puff of breath dissipates into the air.

Viola blinks and finds herself standing at the arched entrance to the grotto. Her tears cling to her cheeks, and she brushes them away while looking out over the landscape. Before her lies the valley of Vendale, and the mountains are indeed cloaked in reds and golds. The peaks' majestic heads smile down upon the new life at their feet, and Viola is filled simultaneously with extreme grief and intense jubilation.

Life.

Beauty.

Meaning.

Gratitude.

It surrounds her and fills her, washing away some of the loss.

As the chimes of the magical music begin to wane—or perhaps it's Viola who loses the ability to hear it—she becomes aware of another tune being sung. A human voice hums an echo to the magical tune she can't hear anymore.

Viola looks up. Jo stands on the other side of the grotto's opening. Music pours from his lips, and she can almost feel how it races to join the melody she was able to hear before. Jo's song pushes the magic further, and she can tell it will help renew what was damaged and broken. Together they've achieved the impossible: revived a planet.

Chapter Twenty-One

A short while later, Viola finds herself crammed into the passenger seat of the glider with Eryk beside her and Motoko behind, cuddling with Jo. Her apprentice smiles and talks as he hasn't done since his arrival in The Capital. His eyes shine brighter than she's ever seen them.

Since the events in the grotto, something has shifted in Jo. For the first time since she met him, he opens up and shares his life story with her. His tale angers and pains her in equal measure, but she also hears the gratitude in his voice. Everything he's been through has had a purpose, and Viola comes to understand how much he means to her. *If he had not been forced to leave his people when he did, I would never have met him.* The thought is sobering and makes Viola consider the idea of destiny.

She looks over her shoulder at the brightness lighting up Jo's face from within. *It is not destiny that makes us. It is we who make our own destinies through our choices.*

Jo meets her look with a knowing smile, and Viola chuckles.

Eryk breaks the moment by pointing out the window when he exclaims, "Wow! That's the ocean!"

Sure enough, far below them, sunlight glitters off the great blue expanse.

"How is that even possible?" Viola wonders out loud.

Jo pipes up from behind her, "Anything is possible as long as you believe it to be so and take action to make it become a reality. You, of all people, have lived this now, Master. There are possibilities and opportunities, nothing more."

"And we make our own destinies with them both," Viola murmurs.

Jo grins.

They're silent for a while, contemplating the miraculous waters below. Viola is deep in thought, comparing this expanse of glittering blue to the gentle turquoise of the only other ocean she's ever seen. Jo jerks her from her musings when he says, "I'd like to perform for the empress the story I researched about Princess Silvana of Oruna."

Viola turns around in her seat. "What?" *How did he know I was thinking about my travels on that planet?* She meets his gaze and realises this is yet another coincidence. Jo did not read her thoughts; he wants to share the history of Oruna in the early years of the empire when Silvana was crown princess.

"I wish to perform my findings for Her Imperial Highness," he reiterates.

Viola swallows. "I—I suppose it ought to be possible—"

"Of course it's possible."

"Yes, I know anything is achievable, but you would have to do this the right way, and the bureaucrats are pretty tricky to get around. They have a notoriously difficult system for getting an audience. Just look at the fiasco I went through when I arrived back in The Capital!"

Jo shakes his head. "Why do we have to play their silly

game? There are other ways to get to perform before the empress—there must be."

"Well, I do not know of any other. Either you go through Building One or not at all."

Eryk pipes in, "Isn't there some silly rule that new arrivals must present themselves to the empress?"

Viola sucks in air, "Yes, there is, and it must take place within the first segment. Otherwise, the individual is considered an undesirable and is removed from The Capital."

Eryk frowns. "But then, why haven't they come for the youngster yet?"

Jo looks up. "I resent that, Eryk. I'm twenty years of age." His eyes glitter, though, and a smile plays on his lips.

Tutting, Viola waves off Jo's levity and fixes her gaze on Eryk. "He got away with it because no one knows he arrived. He did not enter through a city gate or disembark from a ship. He arrived on his own." Viola considers the details Jo shared earlier in the day about his voyage to Haldria. It's both fantastical and unbelievable, but she knows him well enough to understand he wouldn't tell an untruth. *He claims to have ridden a dragon to travel between the planets. Once again, I am faced with the impossible having been done. Get used to it. With this boy around, there will be more of that, I am certain.*

She shrugs and focuses once more on Jo's request. "I suppose we can present you in Building One in the morning, and you can request an audience. Hopefully, they will accept you within a few days, and then you can see the empress. I feel hesitant about trying to strong-arm my way through their system. It did not work well for me last time, but perhaps we can hope my position as high archivist will help speed up things for you."

Jo shakes his head. "I wish to perform my tale as soon as possible."

Viola pinches the bridge of her nose and exhales slowly. "Jo, we still have a long way to travel today; can we talk about this in the morning?" He shrugs, so she adds, hoping to appease him, "Well, let me hear your tale as you wish to perform it."

Crossing his arms, Jo shakes his head again. "I feel very strongly that the first time I share this tale as I envision it, I must do so to the empress herself."

"Oh, for the love of Haldria, then at least give me a rundown of the information you found. What facts are you basing your story on?"

"That I can do," Jo grins.

It's almost dark by the time Viola has finished cross-examining Jo's findings. She looks over at Eryk, worry twitching her brows together. "You have been at the helm for the best part of a day, Eryk. Should we not find an island to set down on and finish this journey in the morning?" A glance out of the window gives her pause. Down below, the ocean glitters in the sun's last light and on the horizon, dark clouds roll towards the land, the first signs of such she's ever seen on this planet.

Jo pipes up from behind before Eryk can answer. "I could help if you want. I can get us back in no time."

"How?" both Viola and Eryk ask.

"Not that again!" Jo chuckles.

Viola scowls at him. "What improbable possibility did you have in mind this time, Apprentice?"

The corners of Jo's lips quirk upwards. "I could call upon the wind to drive us faster towards our destination. It's moving that way already, just needs a little nudge. Or, what would be even faster, I could teleport us there, Master."

He's put on the same tone she used a moment ago, and Viola's insides sizzle. "What? You mean you think you can flit us from out here in the middle of the ocean to The Capital?"

"I don't think. I know." There's a hint of indignation in Jo's voice.

Viola tells herself to suspend her disbelief, but she simply can't do it. This is too impossible. She glances over at Eryk, who shrugs.

"If Jo can get us home sooner, without the need for a stopover, I'm all for it." He glances over at Viola and laughs. "You can pick up your jaw from the floor, Vi, my love."

She snaps her mouth shut while a warm glow pulses inside her. Eryk uses the endearment very seldomly, but when he does, it makes her feel fuzzy inside. She turns back to Jo and his impossible assertion. "Do it then." She winks.

A heartbeat later, the glider drifts onto the road a few steps from Viola's cottage. She blinks, glances at a grinning Jo, looks back at her home, and sighs. *He is never going to let me live this one down, is he?*

As if in answer to her thought, Jo hops out of the glider and rounds the side where Viola is sitting. He cranks open the hatch and holds out his hand for her. "Master, at your service," he says and bows deeply.

She laughs, accepting his assistance. Her back twinges, and she's forced to lean more heavily on Jo than she would have liked. The aches in her body and the glint in Jo's eyes guide her to a new conclusion. "You could have transported us this way from Vendale."

"But of course, Master." He grins.

Viola breathes through the agony of pins and needles assaulting her right leg from the knee down. She clenches her teeth as she stretches and bends the offending limb in an attempt to speed up the process. When the worst of it has subsided, she grits out, "Then why did you not do so? It would have saved me all this discomfort."

Jo's features turn serious. "You wouldn't have believed. You don't even believe me now with the much shorter distance." His eyes take on a faraway look, which he shrugs off quickly. "Besides, we needed the time to talk."

Remembering everything he's shared with her, Viola accepts his reasons. For it's true. She wouldn't have believed it possible for him to flit them all the way from Vendale, and she'd have strongly opposed any attempt with everything she had.

"Does that mean you can flit people great distances only if they're mentally prepared to do it? Is that what it takes?"

Jo cracks a smile. "Yes. I'm limited by others' beliefs if I'm to take them with me. What they believe is possible is what I can achieve. Earlier today, Eryk might have believed it possible from Vendale, but I felt you were not ready for such things, Master. When night was falling, and we travelled over the ocean, we had need as well as desire, which helped your belief. And you also healed a planet today. I'm certain that boosted your belief too. Yours and Eryk's."

Another thought tickles Viola's mind, and she focuses on it. Jo is bouncing on the balls of his feet, filled with energy, as he now supports her on the walk into the house. His boundless stamina is almost as astounding as the feat he's just produced. If she'd used magic to the extent he has over the course of the day, she'd be collapsing with fatigue. Yet here he is, bubbling with energy.

When she thinks back, he's never shown any signs of exhaustion from using magic. It's almost as if it gives him more energy.

As she navigates her way up the step, Viola broaches the subject. "How are you never tired after you use magic, Jo?"

He tilts his head while he helps her through to the settee, where she settles down to stretch her legs to counteract the cramped sitting she's done all day.

"I don't use my inherent magic," he says at last. Jo turns and fetches water from the kitchen area. When he returns, he clarifies, "There's magic all around us, and of course, now that the balance is re-established, there's more, and it's stronger than it was yesterday. When I channel the magic around me, I don't deplete the reserves in my body." He settles on a chair and continues. "Magic is an energy. It can be multiplied or depleted. When you use it the right way, it grows—expands. If used the wrong way, it depletes and can even kill the living thing from which it is drawn."

Viola thinks about that. It's not how she was trained to do magic. That all drew on the magic within her, but now he mentions it, she can indeed sense the magic all around her. It tingles on the air and thrums through the ground beneath her feet. It surrounds her in a gentle hum of energies, and intuitively, Viola knows she can reach out and nudge the different energies to respond to her will.

"Can you teach me?" she asks.

A smile dances on Jo's lips when he replies, "But of course, Master."

Chapter Twenty-Two

After breakfast the next morning, Viola prepares herself to request an audience with the empress. Perhaps if she does it in her position as the high archivist of the Imperial Grand Library, they'll have a better chance of success. Considering Viola has kept her distance over the years since she moved to The Capital, she doesn't know how this request will be taken. *Probably Mother will want to twist this to her benefit and get me under her thumb once more. I must be careful.*

She comes downstairs to see Jo sitting on a chair, one leg bouncing while he waits. As soon as her feet reach the bottom stair, Jo bounds to his feet. "Right, can we go see the empress then?"

Viola sighs. "Jo, it does not work this way. We have to go to Building One and request an audience. The empress has specific days and times when she accepts visitors. We have the additional difficulty that there is no record of you, or me for that matter. Neither of us has an identity tag, which is the currency of the bureaucrats in Building One. We also cut some corners, like that day when the Red Guard showed up at the bar in the White District. I created a fake report that was never actually sent to the empress. What I mean to say is that incident never happened from the perspective of the empire. No one knows you exist. And that makes an official meeting with the empress really difficult."

"Oh, you people enjoy jumping through hoops for the simplest things." He picks up his staff from where it leans against the table.

Taking a deep breath, he closes his eyes. Viola is ready to snap at him when she hears a soft hum and feels a magical arrow slicing through the air. She senses the projectile as it cleaves through the landscape, and in her mind's eye, she can see it hurtle over the tall white buildings of the city and zero in on the imperial palace. In the next blink of her eyelids, it's dived through the wall and seeks out Jo's purpose: the empress, sitting in the palace's solarium, listening to reports on her device. In a flash, Viola is jerked back into her body, miles away, at her home on the outskirts of The Capital.

"Right, I'll be back in a moment," Jo declares and knocks his staff on the ground.

"Wait—"

But he's already dissolved. *What is that boy doing?* Her heart clenches at the thought that he's putting himself in danger. There's a ward on the palace to stop magic users from doing what he's just done. *But I flitted into the palace without any trouble.* The thought gives Viola pause. She'd done it on the spur of the moment without even thinking, but now she wonders what might have happened to her. *Or is the ward a simple lie never tested?*

Thinking back on the moment she passed into the palace three years ago, she remembers a tingling sensation prickle over her skin as she moved from Building 1 into the palace gardens. *That did not happen when I flitted into the audience hall, did it?*

What might befall Jo if there's a functional ward around the palace grounds? Would he combust? Or become trapped? It's possible the barrier could even absorb his magic. Viola racks her brain for any concrete information she might have learned in her youth about the magical fortifications around the palace.

When she comes up with nothing, she begins pacing. *How can it be possible I do not know for certain what the magical protections are around the imperial palace? That ought to be something every member of the imperial family knows.*

Back and forth she goes, but Viola can't find any concrete proof that she needs to be worrying about Jo. *Calm down,* she instructs herself. After several deep breaths, she reasons, *Nothing happened to me. I must be patient and give him time.*

The door to the garden slides open and cool morning air blasts Viola. It smells fresh; there was rain in the night. She turns to find Eryk coming in with Motoko lolloping behind him. The sound of a bird trilling is cut off when the door closes behind them. Eryk is shirtless and drenched in sweat from his morning exercises, but for once, the sight doesn't bring delight because the stench of wet dog slams into her. Motoko's paws are also covered in mud.

Viola grabs a towel and squats down to clean his paws before he drags the dirt all over the house. By the time brown-streaked fur emerges from beneath the mud, Eryk has wiped himself and pulled on a shirt.

"Here." Eryk brings another towel and rubs it over the dog's coat.

Viola rises with ease. She stops short and looks down at herself. Her knee didn't hurt. *How can that be?*

"You had no trouble getting up," Eryk observes.

"How?"

Eryk wraps his arms around her. "Perhaps healing the planet also healed you?"

"That is a beautiful idea, Eryk. I like it." She pauses and muses, "But then why did it not manifest until today? Would my leg not have been better yesterday evening?"

"I don't know, Vi. Maybe it took time for the joint to respond to the healing energies." He holds her tighter.

Viola returns his hug before she turns around. Her eyes fall on the place where Jo was sitting. The thought of him trapped in some ward at the palace squeezes in her chest, and she wrings her hands as more thoughts flood her mind. She stands rooted to the spot, staring at the empty chair. *Will all truly be well?*

"Isperia, what is it?" Eryk's voice is tight with concern.

She twists her head back towards him. "Jo— He, um, well, he—" Frustrated, Viola throws her hands in the air before pointing at the place where Jo stood earlier. "Jo was there." She jabs her finger at the place next to the dining table. "And then he upped and left." Her hands gesticulate wildly about her head. "Without so much as a goodbye!" Her voice rises as she continues. "He just flitted himself to the palace without a care for protocol—no consideration of the *wards*—and—and—"

Viola's hands drop to her sides. *And what?* Jo could be trapped for all she knows, taken into custody by the Red Guard. Or frazzled by the magic barrier on the palace.

Or he could be fine, sitting drinking kopi in the solarium without a care in the world, a voice pops into her head.

Eryk steps over, towel in hand. While he dries sweat from his face and neck, he asks, "So he went to see the empress?"

"Yes!" Viola's heartbeat of calm is swept up in panic once more. "And I do not know what the ward could do to him. It is said to protect the palace from magical incursions."

"Did you tell him this?"

"He did not give me a chance to do so!" Her feet start pacing again but ram her right into Eryk's solid frame.

The impact slams the breath out of her, and Eryk catches her before she stumbles backwards. "Isperia." He looks at her, his eyes solemn. At the same time, his lips quirk slightly at the corners. "You're panicking."

"I am not." She yanks her arm from his grasp and steps back.

From behind her, a light voice pipes up, "Sorry to interrupt —whatever *this* is."

Viola whirls around once more. In the exact place from whence he departed stands Jo, a twinkle in his eyes.

"You are unhurt?" Viola rushes over, examining him carefully. "The ward did not do you any harm? Addle your brain? Zap you?"

Jo laughs. The sound stops Viola in her tracks, and she looks up into his eyes. It's the first time she's ever heard him laugh exactly like that—so full and boisterous. There's something magical about it. Beautiful, lighthearted, carefree. She breathes in the levity, and all her fear washes away on the wind of his high spirits.

Before Viola's bewilderment has quite let go of her, Jo steps forwards and flings his arms around her.

"I'm sorry I caused you distress," he whispers in her ear, and she can't help but return the hug. When Jo breaks away, his serious demeanour is back. "Thank you for your concern, Master, but it was entirely misplaced." Jo's eyes twinkle with mischief when he adds, "That miserable little barrier was no match for the magic of a Guardian."

Viola looks at him. "What?"

A grin grows on Jo's face. "The Forest Father gave me what remained of his Guardian powers before dissipating. It proved really useful. And I'm learning all the nuances of the powers. It's fun practising."

"What do you mean? How? When?"

Jo gives her another squeeze, and as he disengages, he replies, "Just before he passed on, the Forest Father pulled me into a sacred place and gave me some parting advice and a few added gifts. He didn't want me to be a Guardian on Haldria, but he was happy to give me some of the other powers he had to help me in my work for the Great Parent."

Viola stares at him for a moment. She wants to speak, to ask more questions, but her voice has abandoned her. After opening and closing her mouth several times, she throws her hands up and embraces the silence.

Eryk steps up beside her and slips one arm around her waist. Turning his attention to Jo, he asks, "And what about the empress? How did she take your sudden, unannounced appearance."

Jo shrugs. "She wasn't too pleased, but she eventually saw things my way and then we had a lovely chat."

Viola can't stop her eyes from growing wide. "A lovely *chat*. With *my* mother?"

"But of course." His voice is utterly serious. "She's a lonely old lady. Misguided, certainly, but quite sweet under all the trappings of her station."

Eryk pipes up, "So, did you perform your story? Or has she granted you an audience to do so?"

Jo's eyes crinkle, and the dimple in his left cheek deepens. "I'm to present myself this afternoon at the strike of fifth circ, and I'm to arrive in the *usual* way." His voice changes with this last, and Viola can't help but chuckle at his imitation of the empress' tone.

"Very good, Jo," she shakes her head. "We could have done

it all the *usual way* if only you had let me. But I suppose you have got what you wanted."

His grin deepens, and he says, "Yes. Now I need to get dressed for the occasion."

Viola follows Jo into the empress' grand audience hall. The place is packed. Voices tumble over each other in an ever-increasing swell. While she heads towards the seating, she scans the room, and there are several faces she recognises. As expected, the attending members of her extended family look down their noses at the other courtiers and whisper to each other from behind fans or glasses of sparkling drinks. Many have aged since she last saw them at the ball her mother organised in her honour a few years ago.

How did mother gather everyone here so quickly? Where has she been keeping them all, for that matter? It seems she tucks them away in a box to call upon whenever there is an event and hides them away for the rest of the time. Viola hasn't seen or heard anything about any of her uncles and cousins apart from Natesari, who was all over the news in the aftermath of the Kliavi sickness fiasco.

Dressed for the occasion in a yellow outfit and green cloak, Jo strides down the central aisle of the imperial audience hall ignoring everything around him while Viola slips into the back row of seating with Eryk beside her. It is Jo's turn to shine, and she wants to stay out of sight to let him.

It's unusual to find chairs in the audience hall. More often than not, the assembled courtiers are expected to stand; sitting is the empress' prerogative. *How did Jo pull off all of this? It is almost a miracle.*

Upon her raised platform, the empress sits on her gilded throne. Her silver hair is wound in an intricate style, making a mountain within the circle of her glittering crown. Her gown is diaphanous and transitions from white at the rounded neckline through several shades of pink until ending in salmon at the train and on the ends of the flared sleeves. She reclines on the throne, her hands trailing over the armrests and a look of boredom on her face as she scans the assemblage.

Viola notices the cane peeking out from behind the armrest. *So that is why Mother arrived early today. She did not wish for anyone to see her frailty.* Viola shakes her head. *Age should not be something to be ashamed of.*

Jo stops at the golden line running the length of the audience chamber nearest the empress' dais—a glittering division marking off a circular segment on the white marble. The young man takes a bow, billowing his green cloak out around him in a move Viola recognises as one of her own. A lute hangs behind him from a strap over his shoulder, and as she studies his back, she wonders how many of the spectators can see the lemon-yellow suit under his forest green cloak. There's a hint of the sleeves visible from her vantage at the back of the room. *Would anyone here understand the symbolic meaning of that particular combination of green and yellow?*

She considers the empress might grasp the subtle allusion to knowledge and wisdom combined. Ignoring the voice of a herald who announces Jo to the empress, Viola shifts in her seat, preoccupied with trying to work out how he manifested the clothes he's wearing. She knows Jo didn't have anything like that among the small offerings he carried with him when he arrived. Most of his clothes are grey or brown, but here he stands in colour, almost dazzling her with it, and he didn't go to a store to get these clothes. They're strange, unlike the current style of The Capital.

The empress' sharp voice cuts through Viola's thoughts. "And what is it you want, boy?"

Viola's attention shifts to the empress, and she bristles. She does not like that tone. And Jo is a young man now. *I call him boy all the time*, she reminds herself. *That will have to change. Jo deserves better from me; he is not thirteen anymore.*

She glances back at Jo and, out of the corner of her eye, catches sight of him standing before the empress in the same outfit he'd been wearing that morning. When she looks at him directly, Viola can see the dazzling green cloak again.

Jo holds silent, and she chuckles to herself. *He has mastered the art of illusion. And I never even had to teach it to him.* She notices several of the spectators twitch when the stillness drags out longer than it ought to. *He has definitely learned the skills,* she thinks. Here he is, using to greatest effect every trick of the trade.

When he does open his mouth, Jo's voice is clear, and although he speaks softly, Viola can hear him all the way at the back of the hall.

"I'm here to entertain, Your Imperial Majesty. I wish to tell a story." Even over the distance separating them, Viola senses her mother's ire. *How could he think her sweet? She is about to burst a valve.* But before the empress can voice her displeasure, Jo adds, "When I was apprenticed to Viola Alerion—" There's muttering in the crowd and several turn to look at Viola. "—I became curious about the tale, *The Last Warrior*. Oruna has always played a key part in Haldrian imperial politics, and the story made me wonder if there were any historical accuracies."

The audience is rapt now. Viola notices the rustling and whispering have stopped entirely.

"What I found through my research was not only confirmation that the key events are factual but also that the story doesn't end where the tale does. From the records in the archives, I've pieced together the rest of the tale, and I wish to perform my first official interpretation of it to you, oh Empress."

The sovereign gives a sharp nod and flicks her finger in Jo's direction. In one fluid motion, he pulls the lute forwards and sinks into a cross-legged position on the floor. He also sets his staff down by his side.

A purple-clad imperial servant rushes forwards with a little cushioned seat, but Jo waves the man away. His fingers dance over the strings, and Viola sucks in a deep breath. She didn't even realise how tense she's become. Inhaling a second lungful of air, she lets it out slowly and allows the music to fill her soul and Jo's story to replenish her heart.

Time drifts on Jo's words until, at last, he falls silent, and Viola snaps out of the trance his tale created. It's as though she's been floating in a dream. His story absorbed her so completely she didn't notice his magic at work. She's also impressed at the emotion he's built around the facts under-lying his story. *Silvana's Trial*, a good title for it—all about trials and tribulations.

Viola looks over at her mother. The empress looks ready to explode or possibly transform into a fire-breathing dragon, if that's possible. Even from the distance separating them, Viola can sense the staring contest taking place between Jo and the empress. She knows what Jo has told is based completely in fact—embellished a little, certainly—but factual nonetheless. Can the empress accept those facts when the story diverges so much from the myths built around the imperial family's origins?

The empress rises to her feet, eyes flashing with barely-contained lightning, and points a wrinkled finger at him. "How dare you!"

Apparently not. There's pure outrage. *Ah, Mother. Accept the truth*. Viola inhales and exhales with focused attention as if doing so might help the empress calm down.

Instead, the storm grows stronger. "How dare you diminish my ancestor so! Empress Silvana was the daughter of a high lord and the greatest healer ever to live! She was *not* the offspring of some wayward Shanti dog. How dare you!"

Viola is on her feet and striding forwards before she even knows what she's doing. As loudly and authoritatively as she can, she says, "The boy speaks the truth. I can confirm it." She stares her mother down. "I, High Archivist of the Imperial Grand Library, have seen the records this young man unearthed and attest to the veracity of his story. Even the pardon of Flynn, High Lord and Defender of Oruna, is accessible not only in the digital records, but a physical copy, signed by none other than Emperor Huneddzach of Haldria, is stored among the ledgers. The boy speaks the truth."

Viola reaches the centre of the hall before the empress shouts, her eyes ablaze, "Get out of my sight, Archivist!"

Viola's jaw tenses because, more than anything, she wants to shout at her mother, but this isn't the time or place to do so. It is also a matter of principle. Jo shared the truth. With her work in the archives, and everything she experienced as a result of lies, Viola wants to stand on the side of truth. She must. The disaster she averted but yesterday was built on lies and could have been avoided centuries ago if the early empire had been built on truth.

She glares at the empress and holds her hand out to her apprentice. "Come, Jo. Your talents are wasted here."

Jo pushes himself to his feet, slings the lute back over his shoulder and lifts the staff with his other hand.

He bows towards the empress, who shouts, "Seize him!"

For the second time in her life, Viola experiences the audience hall of the Haldrian Empire in chaos. The spectators from the court stampede towards the door at the back of the hall, and she's jostled by the panicked people, her voice drowned under a wave of screams. Through the hubbub, Viola makes out the members of the imperial family, who climb over chairs to reach a side door on the left. The sight of red uniforms snags on Viola's peripheral vision, and she tries to push against the crowd to get to Jo's side.

Instinctively, her hand goes to her belt, where her trusty bamboo staff rests. If she can get to Jo, together they can take on the Red Guard; she's sure of it. Eryk is beside her. How he reached her through half the chamber, she can't imagine. He jerks his head towards the row of chairs a few steps to Viola's right. Some of the seats have been knocked over; however, it's away from the crushing weight of the people fighting to get out of the room. Viola nods, and together they push their way to calmer waters.

Meanwhile, Jo's voice echoes through the hall. It slices the hysteria with the cool blade of serenity. "I speak only the truth as I know it, for I've been sent by the Mother-Father to bring peace and harmony to this universe." He pauses before adding softly, "Something you've neglected, oh Empress of Haldria."

A shiver goes up Viola's spine. No one speaks to the empress like that, and yet, Jo is right. Their journey to the Old Continent, the meeting with the Forest Father and the wolf clan who protect the true history of Haldria—everything she's learned in the past few days is staggering proof of the imperial family's failures over generations. *Mother is the product of those failures. She has been trained to see the world a certain way, but it is all based on lies.*

With a hoard of Red Guards converging on him from all sides, Jo lifts his staff. Viola watches it descend towards the ground, and she sees with clarity what he'll do. In her mind, she can see a mischievous glint in his eyes and a smile playing on his lips.

"We shall meet again." His words hang suspended for a fraction of a heartbeat before he's swallowed up into nothing.

Viola sags into Eryk's arms. *At least he can take care of himself. Why did I forget he can do that?* She looks at the stunned people around her. The Red Guards are bewildered; some even shout in dismay. The people bunched around the golden doors at the back of the hall turn with their eyes wide. The flood of screams and crashes of furniture subside. Viola sees several of her aunts and uncles, as well as some cousins, who stare from the sidelines, their mouths open.

"You!" The empress takes an unsteady step forwards, her finger raised to Viola. "You encouraged this heresy, Isperia! You embolden this slander!"

Viola's hands seek out the bamboo staff at her hip and the crystal in her pocket. She can feel the threat in her mother's eyes, sense the command about to spring from her lips, but Viola also knows she can't fight—not alone. She also has no wish to clash with her mother's guards again.

Is fighting the only way?

The voice is soft and opens a floodgate of thoughts. Out of all her options, Viola considers one to be the right one. *Speak the truth as you know it*, echoes in her mind.

The nearest Red Guards turn towards her in response to the empress' accusation. Viola's hand clenches around the cool stone in her pocket, and she pulls it forth. Energy tingles in her palm, but it's answered by a roaring symphony of power coursing through the ground and charging into her. More magic than she's ever believed possible dances at her fingertips, yearning to do her bidding.

In the instant the empress screams, "Seize her!" Viola

meets her mother's gaze and calls upon a shield to protect herself.

Light snaps into a bubble around Viola and Eryk. It is unlike any protective barrier she's created before. This one will not harm those who touch it, but they cannot pass through it, and she is delighted at this new ability. At last, she can protect herself without harming others. Even the magical batons of the Red Guard can't batter through this force field she's created around her.

Speak the truth as you know it.

Calm infuses Viola, and she realises she doesn't need to raise her voice to be heard. Words well up from a reservoir within her and freely flow as she holds her mother's gaze and speaks.

"Through no fault of your own, you have ruled this empire with fear and lies. This is not the way. All it does is bring harm and disunity. The Haldrian Empire has many evils to atone for, and I stand with Jo, who is my apprentice. He is doing that which is most difficult. He seeks to restore what was lost and make anew the worlds we live in. He strives to do good in every way."

Viola holds up her hands and turns slightly to encompass all who still stand in the audience hall. "Who can say they have such lofty ambitions? Who here uses every breath to do what they know to be right? I have spent a third of this century running from the lies—the manipulations." She snaps her attention back to her mother. "More than thirty annums ago, we stood in this palace, you and I, Mother. And you disowned me."

Anger flashes in the empress' eyes, but the old woman seems unable to speak, so Viola keeps the river of her words going. "In your misguided hubris, you believed doing so would bring me back to you—would make me follow your dreams and desires for a strong bloodline—for descendants to pass your legacy on to."

Viola can't help but shake her head, and her hands sink into each other, cupping the crystal against her stomach. "Instead, I forged my own path, and you hounded me like prey. But your need for control did not end there. You did not learn your lesson. You did not pay attention. Things do not work that way." Her gaze turns to Eryk, who stands beside her before she meets her mother's belligerent glare once more.

"You manipulated Eryk. You destroyed his father. You lied to the people and claimed I was infirm when in actual fact, I was out exploring the empire in all its sordid monstrosity."

Viola sweeps an arm to encompass the building around her. "You and the rest of the people who live here have slept in your little bubble of complacency, safe, with water extractors and plant incubators keeping you sheltered from the realities of the havoc wreaked on the natural world around you. You have sought to control everything from this speck of what you call modernity while sucking all else dry. The suffering on the thirteen spheres is immeasurable. The deaths caused by the Haldrian Empire's system—uncountable. Wherever our gazes have been turned, we have caused destruction. The indigenous peoples of all the planets have been obliterated. I once likened the human race to a parasite, and certainly, within the scope of the Haldrian Empire, it behaves that way, but I have also learned so much more about our potential."

She takes a deep breath, amazed at the silence around her. The hall holds its breath while she speaks, and her mind turns to what she experienced over the past few days. "Just yesterday, I met one of the ancient Guardians, those mythical beings we have heard about in folktales. They were once real creatures filled with magic and the power of possibility. Yesterday, I watched the last of them die to restore the balance and renew magic in the land." Viola holds out her rose quartz crystal on the flat of her hand for all to see. "Have you seen the ocean returned? Have you sensed the swelling of life all around us? Did you smell the rain last night? Have you heard the birds sing today?"

Viola meets the gazes of those nearest to her when she emphasises, "It rained last night for the first time in living memory! Wake up, people of Haldria!"

The empress takes a step forwards and raises an accusing finger. "And it is your fault the population of this city risks starvation with the plant incubators flooded on the ocean floor!"

"The rains have returned. The earth is fertile once more. There is no need for plant incubators. If we stop extracting water from the air, everything will go to what it ought to be, and the planet will support all those who live on it. The lies of the Haldrian Empire have made us believe we are better than the natural world, but we are part of it. We must change our ways to live in harmony with our planet."

The empress staggers back and sinks into her throne. Viola takes in the whole room with people huddled behind her, the crimson-clad guards between her and the empress, and her extended family staring wide-eyed and confused. Some of the faces in the hall display interest, and it is on these she focuses.

"For too long have we drifted without a purpose. For centuries we have gone with the rapacious current, seeking destruction, but the time has come for change." The injunctions of Jo's people flash into her mind, and they feel so right she lets them pour from her. "Be your truest selves and be kind to yourselves." Viola meets the gazes of many in the assembly. "Speak the truth as you know it and listen to the truth of others. Do not think only of yourselves, but care for all living things and do what you know to be right. Live in harmony with the earth instead of at odds with it. Do your very best to coexist with other beings who also call Haldria home."

She turns her eyes to her mother. The empress sits crumpled in on herself, but despite the wind having left her sails, her eyes glitter with malice, and Viola directs her words to her mother. *Please listen*, she pleads as she continues, "Acknowledge your failings, for when you do, you can strive to do better. It is how you learn from life."

Viola pauses, taking the time to acknowledge the people in the room once more before she says, speaking to each one. "Pursue the highest meaning in your life and be open to new experiences, people, and things. While doing all of this, you will find life rejoices. What was once hard flows in a torrent of possibilities that can transform lives—and the universe itself. Trust in these truths, for they will set you free, and be grateful for the beauty that surrounds you and the perfection with which everything can coexist."

The flood of words slows, and Viola relaxes into the knowledge that she's done what she knows to be right and has indeed spoken the truth as she knows it. The sands of these new thoughts drift into the people around her, and she can see that for some, it is settling into the sediment of new bedrock —a foundation to strengthen the work begun the day before with the renewal of the land. *Time for rejuvenation among the people too.*

From her slumped position on the throne, the empress screeches, "Seize her! Arrest the heretic!"

Viola sees hesitation in many eyes, but she also knows training and years of indoctrination won't allow the new ideas to take root just yet. She has much work to do, but, to bring it about, she must remain free. Although the shield protecting her still crackles with its charge, Viola realises there's no need to test the strength of her magical defence. Addressing the guards closest to her, she says, "A battle between the head and the heart will always lead to suffering. The heart knows what is right. Embrace the truth and break the shackles brought on by lies."

She takes Eryk's hand in hers, dips an ostentatious bow to the assembly and imagines her home—her old dream fulfilled —a little cottage nestled among trees, away from the cares and frenzy of the city. She pictures the arbour beside the fish pond with Motoko lazing in the sun, and in the next heartbeat, she's there—flitted further than she's ever before been able to. The magical energy of the entire Haldrian planet courses through her. Motoko picks up his head and looks over but makes no move to come to her.

Eryk pulls her close, and Viola sinks into the comfort of his arms around her and his frame supporting her. "You were magnificent," he murmurs into her ear. She squeezes, and he returns the hug. "Yesterday, I came to believe at a deeper level than ever before, and today you strengthened my conviction tenfold." He relaxes his arms, and they step apart. "There never is a dull moment with Jo around, is there?" Eryk chuckles.

Viola laughs. "No. No, there is not."

His eyes turn serious. "You can't stay. She'll have an army out to get you and drag you back to make an example of you."

Viola chuckles and shakes her head. "She never learns, does she?"

He sighs. A sad smile plays on his lips. "Where do you want to go? What are we going to do?"

She leans into him and looks at the green around her. *I will miss my little slice of paradise*, she thinks. Her memory takes her to the sweeping beauty of the mountains and the intense colours of the autumn forest. *The wolf clan has lived unhindered for thousands of annums, forgotten, neglected.* Her mind fills with possibilities, and a new dream takes shape.

Viola smiles. "We could go to the Old Continent, find the peoples who have been left to rot there." She remembers everything Jo told her about his experiences over the past years since she left him on Téarman. "And I need to write. Jo's story must be told, and I think I am the only one who knows all of it."

Eryk's returning smile is broad and fills Viola with light. He nods, and she can see thoughts flitting behind his eyes. He takes a moment to consider before he speaks. "We still have the glider. I didn't take it back, so we can go directly. Pack what you need. We can be on our way within moments."

"Good. I shall fetch some clothes and a few other things." Viola looks around her again. *I will miss this*, she thinks as she heads into the house. *Here I am, running away again.* The thought gives her pause, but her heart replies with conviction. *This time, everything is different. I must leave because I cannot stand by and be party to the harm being done in the empire's name. Leaving now is also making a stand for what is right.*

She pulls her old backpack from the darkened recess of her cupboard and begins packing. Her eyes dart to Eryk, who pulls out his case weapons, stashed there since he arrived on her doorstep in the middle of the night. *I am not alone. I never was. Even when Eryk was not physically present, he was with me in spirit. Now he is here, and together we are strong. We can face anything.*

Viola scans the room, and a decorative box on her night-stand captures her attention. It's where she stored Maitri's travelling stone. She flicks the lid open. The red gem glints—almost a wink. She plucks it from the velvet cushion it has been sleeping on and remembers she never had an opportunity to charge its magical energy. Maitri only shared the location in the palace grounds where the ley lines meet, but now Viola knows another, better place. She smiles. For all the years she's had it, she didn't need the ring, and now, when she has a use for it, she also knows where to go. Her mind fills with a vision of the grotto where she performed the Sacred Challenge—was it just yesterday? Viola knows it will be the perfect place to allow the travelling stone time to re-absorb the magic it needs, and after that, it will be able to serve her in her newfound purpose. She tucks it into a pocket of her backpack.

"Ready?" she asks Eryk.

He's at the top of the stairs and looks back. "I'm ready. Let's go."

He ripples down the stairs with fluid grace and Viola follows with a smile on her face. Her hands trail the length of the bannister. The weight of the backpack pulls at her shoulders. Walking through the room with her desk by the stairs and the sofa where she's spent many animated evenings talking to Eryk and Jo, or calmer ones petting Motoko, brings a wave of sadness. She collects the device on which all her work is stored. It's bigger than her pocketpiece but lightweight and also connected to the Imperial Grand Library's archives. Perhaps it will serve her in the months to come.

Eryk is already by the door, and he holds out a hand towards her. The look in his eyes makes it easy to brush away the sadness. Together, they step through the doorway into the afternoon's warmth. Eryk turns to the dog lying in the grass a few paces away. "Come, Motoko. Adventures await."

It's all Viola needs. She knows with the deepest of convictions that no matter where she goes or what happens, with her family beside her, she'll always find a way.

Epilogue

Dear reader,

From my exile and remaining hidden as the empire's minions seek to find and destroy me, I write to you in these uncertain times. The fate of many hangs in the balance, and the imperial structure teeters on the brink of collapse. I am certain you are curious to know of the young man who lies behind all this unrest. Many have heard or read about the Wordmage, the mysterious storyteller who appears unexpectedly in the most uncanny of places to tell a profound and deeply moving—and, more often than not, unsettling—tale before vanishing into thin air. Some of you may know of my association with him in his youth. Due to the curious twists of fate, that young man was my apprentice, in what feels like a lifetime ago.

Our paths crossed in the barren wasteland of Mshrali's Dust Bowl—a place of death and hardship beyond anything I have encountered anywhere else. Even at the tender age of thirteen, he burned with a passion I have never seen before or since. A passion for life and a curiosity to learn about the universe. At the same time, he was immovable in his belief. It radiated off him and strengthened his words with the steel of conviction.

Although his belief system and impassioned way of talking irritated me when I first met him, the depth of understanding and tolerance he showed for everything around him and his deep-seated love of life opened my eyes to the power of possibility we are all capable of accessing. However, few make use of this inherent potential we are all gifted with simply by virtue of existing.

If you had told me twenty annums ago that I would become the high archivist of the Haldrian Empire with access to every story collected throughout the history of this pinnacle of human civilization, I would have laughed bitterly at such an impossibility. The boy—whom I came to know by the name of Jo—showed me otherwise. Life is filled with improbable yet miraculously possible events, and doing the right thing, believing in one's own capacity for good, is all it takes to tap into that power.

I can attest it has worked for me, and over the course of this telling, I hope to show you that it will certainly work for you, too. But to do so, I must introduce you to Jo, whom I first met when he was a thirteen-year-old youth, and who crossed my path once more as a man filled with magical tales and the most awe-inspiring capacity to move hearts.

As his former instructor and the only person he has opened up to in his adult life, I find myself in the curious position of wanting to share his story. I, who have spent a lifetime sharing the already-written or at the least 'told' stories of our empire, find myself at the juncture of penning a first-hand account for the very first time. I will share with you, dear reader, everything I remember of my time together with the boy who has become the Wordmage, and then I shall share with you the tale he revealed to me more recently about what happened after the Bloodbath in Baile and the outbreak of Kliavi sickness.

Come with me now. Let us journey to the farthest reaches of the empire, to a small planet on the fringes of civilization where hovercars and drones are the province of the rich. The resources of this place are sucked into the engine of empire, leaving its inhabitants to face blight and death. Join me in the heat, among the shrubs clinging to life in the harsh wilderness of Mshrali's Dust Bowl, a place where the taste of sand is more familiar than food and a trickle of water more valuable than the empress' crown. There, some days' trudge from the town of Fásach, exists a cluster of buildings in the middle of nowhere. An oasis. A wayside inn—the place where it all began.

Thank you for reading! I hope you enjoyed this story. You can join Viola and Jo as their journeys continue in:

Becoming Spellwright
and
Master Wordmage

COMING SOON.

Want to stay up to date with the Wishmaster Series and the accompanying series of novellas, The Wordmage's Tales? Subscribe to my newsletter to get all pertinent updates about my new releases and get a free ebook of The Sewing Princess, one of the Wordmage's Tales. The Sewing Princess novella is available exclusively to my newsletter subscribers and street team.

The next release in The Wordmage's Tales series is *Dragons' Daughter* and you are welcome to sign up for a review copy by joining my street team linked through my website. If you are already a member of the street team, you will automatically receive advance review copies of my upcoming books as long as you leave reviews within a reasonable time. Thank you for your support.

Sign up for my newsletter and street team on my website: www.elisabethandedvard.com

Acknowledgments

This book owes its existence to many incredible people. First, I would like to thank my husband, Renato for supporting me in achieving my dreams. You are my bedrock. Thank you for everything.

Anne and Erica, thank you for tearing this story apart and helping me make it even better. I could not have done this without you.

Danke, liebe Oma. Thank you, for showing me that we are never too old to do the things we are meant to do and for giving me the courage, by your example, to take life by the horns. Thank you for being my inspiration and my guiding light. I know you joined me on this journey—coming back from wherever it is your path has taken you—and helped me when I got stuck. You are sorely missed and deeply loved.

Kyra, thank you for inspiring me to get out there and publish my books. Sharing this journey with you has been incredible. May you also publish many more books and share your fantastic stories with many more booklovers.

Tuomas Holopainen, thank you for your inspirational words that brought the spark of an idea into my life, halfway across the globe. And Tarja Turunen, thank you for your voice, which drew me out of my darkness and gave me glimpses of light. To the remaining band members of Nightwish, thank you for the music!

To those who contributed towards my crowdfund, thank you for making this dream a reality and for believing in Viola and me. Your support and engagement mean the world to me. Claire Stewart, Mahogany Silverrain, Caroline Bengtson, Astrid Provence, Alessandra Bosch, Samantha Graham, Douglas Pierce, Marie Hoping, Moira Floresta, Judith Korward, I cannot thank you enough! Extra special thanks go to Daphne Moore, Alice Gent and Amanda Marin. Thank you for believing in me and for raising me up and showing me what is possible. Of course, my family which has ever encouraged me, I thank you from the depths of my heart: Stella, Elena, Monika, Aliosha. Thank you for lightening the load and sharing your expertise to make this journey even more magical.

Special thanks go to my fabulous street team, Wishmaster's Book Angels: Ellen Fuller, Hinata Critchlow, Lisa Able, Pamela Forbes Fries, Stefanie Rls, Chelsea Nicole Warren, Νάντια Βαβάση, Kara Stogsdill, Brett Tourscher, Angela Hughes, Sarah Elyse Rodriguez, Jenny Bradbeer, Jessica Gwynn, Michelle Menezes, Brandy Van Den Broek, Lynda Simmons, Paula Neesam, Hannetjie Ae, Ingunn Helgemo, Jasmijn Van Beusekom, Marie Reed, Oksana Klindukhova, Sherry Hrozenszky, Samantha Seidel, Silke Van der Stockt, Miriam Dagestad Løvdahl, Julie Soper, Monika Vogel, thank you for being my most loyal supporters. You are the best!

My amazing beta readers, J.C. Seal and Jasmijn, thank you for your feedback and help. I am grateful for all the time you spent nurturing this seed so it could flourish and grow. Joy Sephton, my fabulous editor, thank you. You have been invaluable to this project. Emily, my cover designer, thank you for bringing Viola to life, visually. You are amazing and so incredibly talented.

I would also like to take this opportunity to thank the people who fostered my love of the English language and my desire to tell stories. Particular thanks go to Alan Northover, Mrs Van Loggerenberg, Mrs Erasmus and Mrs Bezuidenhoudt.

Thank you for inspiring me and giving me the bedrock I needed to achieve my dreams.

Mary Morrissey, Jennifer Jimenez, Matt Boggs, John Boggs and Rich Boggs, thank you for leading the way and showing me what is possible. Jordan Peterson and Natalie Ledwell, I am grateful for all the work you do in inspiring others to make their lives better, and in doing so, helping me draw the veil from Viola's journey. This book required me to grow so much, and I couldn't have done it without your enlightenment.

To Julie Soper I'd like to say: thank you for your words of encouragement and your enthusiasm. Your friendship means the world to me. Julie, I honestly couldn't have done this without your constant support. You are the world's best accountability partner and the most amazing friend. You are a light in my life, and you've helped guide my way.

About the Author

Astrid V.J. is a USA Today Best-selling and multiple award-winning South African author, social anthropologist and trans-formational life coach currently residing in Sweden. In early child-hood, she showed an interest in reading and languages—interests which her family encouraged. Astrid started writing her first novel aged 12 and now writes fantasy in multiple sub-genres, exploring her passion for cultures, languages and the human capacity to achieve success in the face of adversity. She is fluent in 5 European languages, is happily married and has two adorable children. When she isn't writing, Astrid likes to read, take walks in nature, play silly games with her children, do embroidery and play music.

Also by Astrid V.J.

Elisabeth and Edvard's World

Retellings of lesser-known fairytales

Gisela's Passion

Aspiring, Part 1 of the Siblings' Tale

Becoming, Part 2 of the Siblings' Tale

Naiya's Wish

Johara's Choice

<u>Forthcoming</u>

The Lion, the Lark and the Lady

Firmament

Down the Well

The Adventures of Tyrina Tursam

Pixie Tricks (A novella in the Ytherynia: Gifted Blood Academy
Freshman anthology)

Blood Island

Pixie Unity (a novella in the Ytherynia: Gifted Blood Academy
Sophomore anthology)

The Wishmaster Series

The Apprentice Storyteller, Book 1

Finding the Way, Book 1.5

Becoming Spellwright, Book 2

Master Wordmage, Book 3

The Wordmage's Tales

This is a series of novellas

The Companion's Tale

The Sewing Princess

The Artist and His Muse

The Last Warrior

Warring Lions

The Destitute Countess

Silvana's Trial

Dragons' Daughter

Divine Choice

The Showgirl

The Last Vasa Series

An urban fantasy adventure set in Sweden

It's a Bear's Life: That's no Picnic

Milena's Gift

Milena's Knights

Milena's Crown

Short stories

included in the following charity anthologies

The Naiad's Curse in Enchanted Waters

Willow Daughter in Enchanted Forests

Golden Apples in Enchanted Flames

Child of Destruction in Children of War:

a charity anthology to support the children in Ukraine

Star Dancer in Twice Upon a Name

Made in the USA
Middletown, DE
14 January 2023